Dixon pulled Aubrey into his arms

"There's no point in beating yourself up about the past." He held her in the dimly lit hallway, wanting to press comfort into her bones. Maybe somehow they could comfort each other enough to wipe away the grief.

She let him hold her for a few seconds, but she didn't relax a muscle. "I dread leaving here, having to say goodbye."

"I know." He dreaded seeing her go—for himself as well as the girls. They wouldn't accept Aubrey's absence easily...and he wasn't sure he would, either.

She leaned back to look at him, her eyes piercing even through her tears. "There's no way to make this easy, is there?"

"Not that I can see, no." Words gathered in his throat. *Don't go. Stay here. Help me with the girls, especially Sienna. Be with us. Be with me.*

He couldn't say that. She had a life far from here. They'd made a solid plan. They'd both be better off sticking with it. Even though letting her go now might be the hardest thing he'd done in a long time.

Dear Reader,

Before I had my son, I wasn't sure I would make a good mother. Like Aubrey, I didn't think I was that maternal. I was focused on my career, for one thing, but, really, kids seemed so fragile to me. There seemed to be so many things I could screw up. I figured motherhood was better left to those more naturally inclined...or at least more intrepid than I.

But Aubrey's sister Briana had it right: *Maternal is as maternal does... You learn together.*

That was certainly true in my case. That didn't make parenthood any less difficult or scary. When we had our son, my husband said the words that Howard says in this book about his baby daughters: *Why would we bring into the world someone whose pain we'll feel more strongly than our own?* Why indeed?

Out of love and hope. And that was how Aubrey decides to take on parenthood in her ready-made family. Dixon's already made that decision, but there are things he can learn from Aubrey about handling emotions and trusting his own heart.

The pair of them have quite a journey to their happily ever after. It involves climbing mountains, kayaking rapids, zip-lining canyons and running obstacle courses. They make it, but not without troubles. From their adventure, they learn that beauty can come from tragedy and grief can bring a greater love for those we've lost. As Aubrey tells her nieces, the person who died lives on in our hearts and in our minds and that is a tremendous comfort, I've found.

This story moved me as I wrote it. It touches on so many issues and feelings that I hold dear. I hope it touches your life, too, and offers you insights, a smile and makes you hug your loved ones just a little closer afterward.

All my best,

Dawn Atkins

DAWN
ATKINS

—

Adventures In Parenthood

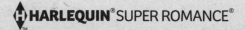

Recycling programs
for this product may
not exist in your area.

ISBN-13: 978-0-373-71885-6

ADVENTURES IN PARENTHOOD

Copyright © 2013 by Daphne Atkeson

Printed in U.S.A.

ABOUT THE AUTHOR

Award-winning author Dawn Atkins has written more than twenty-five romances for Harlequin. Known for her funny, sexy, poignant stories, she's won a Golden Quill Award for hot romance and has been a several-times RT Reviewers' Choice Award finalist. Dawn lives in Arizona with her husband and son, who taught her all about the adventure of parenthood. Contact her through her website at www.dawnatkins.com.

Books by Dawn Atkins

HARLEQUIN SUPERROMANCE

1671—A LOT LIKE CHRISTMAS
1683—HOME TO HARMONY
1729—THE BABY CONNECTION
1753—HIS BROTHER'S KEEPER
1809—THE NEW HOPE CAFÉ
1841—BACK WHERE SHE BELONGS

HARLEQUIN BLAZE

253—DON'T TEMPT ME...
294—WITH HIS TOUCH
306—AT HER BECK AND CALL
318—AT HIS FINGERTIPS
348—SWEPT AWAY
391—NO STOPPING NOW
432—HER SEXIEST SURPRISE
456—STILL IRRESISTIBLE

Other titles by this author available in ebook format.

To the *Now and Then Book Group*

You teach me more about what makes a book good every time we meet

CHAPTER ONE

"You saved my family." The grateful client grabbed Dixon Carter into a bear hug. Rattled, Dixon managed a back pat or two, hoping that did the trick. Emotional stuff threw him.

"We just gave you some advice, Eric. You earned the job." A laid-off auto tech, with an ill wife and two young boys, Eric had recently secured a job with the city, thanks to the help he'd gotten at Bootstrap Academy.

"You gave me the guts to apply," Eric insisted. "You taught me how to interview, what to say on my résumé. You got me the leads."

The man had tears in his eyes. *Tears.*

Dixon blinked back the moisture in his own eyes, pride making his chest burn. *We do good work.* "That's why we're here."

Dixon sometimes got so caught up in the business side of the agency he forgot the rewards. Bootstrap Academy was a last-chance job-training and placement agency in Phoenix. The place was his brother Howard's dream, and Dixon had been privileged to help bring it to life a year ago.

"All I know is that if it weren't for this place, my boys wouldn't be stepping off the bus next fall with new backpacks, new sneaks and snack money burning holes in their pockets," Eric said. "I don't know how to thank you."

"Tell them your story." He nodded toward the new clients in a meeting room down the hall. "That's all the thanks we need." Ideally, Eric would give hope to the men and women who'd been beaten down by economic hard knocks or their own mistakes.

"Thank your brother and his wife for me, too."

"Absolutely. They get back tonight." Howard and Brianna had taken a vacation to celebrate their fifth anniversary—their first trip away from their girls. Dixon was watching the four-year-old twins—and counting down the hours until their parents returned.

Not that he didn't love the girls. He adored them. But adding them to his own work, plus what couldn't be put off of Howard's, had been tough. Single parents deserved medals. Dixon would like a family one day, but not until he stopped putting in sixty-hour weeks here.

Oh, and found a woman to have one with.

Howard and Brianna were due back before the girls' bedtime, thank God. Dixon hadn't yet performed the elaborate night rituals to Sienna's satisfaction. Ginger was more tenderhearted, but a challenge in her own way.

Eric headed for the workshop, and Dixon saw his assistant barreling down the hall toward him. "What's up, Maggie?" he asked.

She nodded across the lobby to the small shop where they sold donated business clothes. "Tonya's about to lose her nerve with the interview."

Dixon backed up so Maggie could beeline for the young woman dressed in cutoffs and a tank top, who was glancing from a rack of blazers toward the exit door, ready to bolt. When Maggie reached her, she said something that made the girl smile, then led her deeper into the shop toward the manager.

Maggie had uncanny people instincts. She gave pep talks without being condescending, help without pity, support without being pushy. Tonya would walk out today with more confidence, a business suit and bus fare, if that's what she needed.

The smallest gesture could change everything for their clients. A smile, a word of praise, a phone call—all could be a lifeline for someone about to go down for good.

Maggie had been one of their first clients. Howard had wanted to hire a social worker, but Dixon had had a feeling about Magdalena Ortiz. And he'd been right. Dixon wasn't used to trusting his feelings. Facts and figures were predictable. People not so much. People were the whole show around here, though, so Dixon often found himself at sea.

Checking his watch, Dixon sprinted for his office. He had twenty minutes to finish and send the email to the foundation before he had to get his nieces from gymnastics. Late pickups were not tolerated, according to Brianna. *What are they going to do? Put me in time-out?*

Dropping into his chair, Dixon pulled up his draft of the intent-to-apply email due by five today. It looked good. Complete. He clicked Send, hoping he wasn't too bleary to judge. They had to win this grant if the agency was going to survive another year.

He'd been up half the night finishing the app. He'd laid out a convincing argument, based on Bootstrap's high success rate, efficient operation and range of services. Today he'd tried to bring it to life by weaving in the client stories Howard and Brianna had given him. Howard had been a social worker for seventeen years before starting Bootstrap. His wife Brianna had been a high school teacher. Now she ran their workshops and basic skills program.

The stories were heart-wrenching. They fired Dixon up, kept him awake nights hunting down grants, looking for more ways to help. Dixon had found the building and negotiated a killer lease, but money was always tight. Coming from business, Dixon had been shocked at what non-profits went through for modest bucks. Banks were stingy, grant entities required endless paperwork and sources dried up all the time.

A shriek of laughter rose from down the hall, where they provided child care for clients and staff—including his nieces—reminding Dixon he had to run and fetch them at gymnastics.

He was about to get up when the intercom clicked, and the receptionist spoke. "I'm sorry, Dixon, but there's an urgent call." Something in her voice put him on alert, every muscle tense. "It's a doctor. Calling from Reno."

Reno? Reno was near Tahoe, where Brianna and Howard had been staying. Except, they should be on the road by now. Electricity shot through Dixon like the zing of a sudden cavity.

Don't panic. It might be nothing. "Send it through."

Let it be minor. Let it be a mistake.

He picked up the line the instant it rang. "This is Dixon Carter." He held his breath, reined in his alarm.

"You're related to Howard Carter?"

Something's wrong.

"He's my brother, yes. Did something happen?" He kept his voice level and steady. Whatever it was, he'd need to stay calm.

"This is Dr. Finson, Reno Regional Hospital. I'm sorry to tell you that your brother and his wife were involved in a highway accident."

"Are they okay?" *No, they're not.* He heard it in the man's hesitation, his grave tone.

The doctor inhaled sharply before answering. "I'm afraid their injuries were too massive. They died on the scene."

"No!" The word exploded from him. *No, no, no. It can't be. It's a mistake. Howard can't be dead. Or Brianna. No.*

Not possible. He fell against the headrest and his chair rolled back, as if to escape the news. *This can't be true. They can't be dead. It's their anniversary. There's a party Saturday.*

"I'm sorry for your loss, Mr. Carter," the doctor said. His voice was hard to hear over Dixon's muddled thoughts. "They suffered fractured cervical vertebrae, so death was likely instantaneous. I'm going to transfer you to a liaison who'll talk over transportation arrangements."

"Transportation arrangements?" *The hospital had a travel agent? They'd get him a flight, a rental car?*

"For the bodies," the doctor said. He sounded young. A resident likely. Maybe he'd gotten the patient names wrong. They made mistakes at busy hospitals, right?

Dixon opened his mouth to ask for proof, for a second opinion, anything, but he was put on hold. His brain was moving through sludge. Howard was dead. Brianna, too. Killed on the highway. They lay in a hospital morgue, their bodies broken. *Oh, God.*

Waiting, he fumbled in his desk drawer for a pen, finally seeing the one on top of the yellow pad where he kept a running list of to-do items, some checked, some not. Insanely, he mentally added a task: *bury your brother and his wife.*

The social worker who came on the line was kind. She spoke slowly, waited for his questions after each piece of information. His mouth felt rubbery as he talked, and her voice came to him as if from underwater. She told him to contact a Phoenix mortuary, which would make arrangements with one in Reno to prepare the bodies and fly them home. *Prepare the bodies...fly them home.* The words were tiny bombs exploding in his brain.

She gave him her number if he had more questions. "Will you be all right? Do you have family nearby?"

"I'm fine. No one nearby. My mother's away." He'd have to reach her on the cruise ship in Europe. She would know how to reach his father, who'd skipped out when Dixon was ten. But Dixon wasn't close to his mother. His family consisted of Howard and Brianna and Sienna and Ginger. *Sienna and Ginger!*

He had to pick them up. His gaze shot to the clock on his desk. He'd be fifteen minutes late if he left right now. "I need to go. I'll call if I have questions." He jumped up, sending his chair crashing to the wall behind him and lunged for the door, patting his pocket for the keys to Howard's SUV. They'd asked him to drive the girls in it instead of Dixon's Subaru WRX since the SUV was built like a tank. Howard and Brianna had taken their sedan to Tahoe. Maybe if they'd had the SUV they would have survived the crash…

Too late. Too late. They're gone. He ran for the door. Maggie, two of the social workers, and Ben, a Bootstrap graduate they'd hired as a handyman, huddled around the reception desk. "What happened?" Maggie asked Dixon.

"Brianna and Howard were in a car wreck. Killed. They're gone." The words hit his ears like blows. He noticed he was trembling. The women gasped, faces shocked. Maggie covered her mouth with her hands.

"I have to get the girls. Cancel the United Way lunch, Maggie. Hold down the fort as best you can. I'll call when I'm able to. Ben, finish the shelves in the career center, then wire the computers."

He jumped in the SUV, squealed out of the lot and gunned the engine, wishing for his WRX with its turbo boosters. He leaned over the steering wheel as if that would get him there faster.

Sienna and Ginger, those two sweet girls, were orphans. Bile rose in his throat and his vision grayed. He twisted the steering wheel, swallowed hard. He didn't have time to get upset.

The girls were probably freaked enough that he hadn't arrived. How would he tell them what had happened? When? Not right off. Not until he figured out the right way.

Grief tugged at him, dragging him down, breaking him in two. He fought to stay clear, to keep going, to do what had to be done. Get the girls, feed them, find a funeral home, reach his mother—would her cell phone work at sea or would he have to ask the cruise line to contact her?

He had to call Brianna's twin sister, Aubrey, too. Aubrey was Brianna's only family, as far as Dixon knew. Their mother had died when they'd barely graduated high school. Breast cancer, he thought. He didn't know the story on their father, who wasn't in the picture. Where would he get Aubrey's number?

Probably from the stapled pages of instructions Brianna had left with details about the girls' food preferences, their schedule, what they needed in their backpacks for Bootstrap, the babysitter next door, plus a list of emergency contact numbers—a plumber, an electrician, several neighbors, the pediatrician. At the time the list seemed to be overkill. Who would ever need any of that?

He did. It was all he had.

How would Aubrey take the news? Would she even be in the country?

Supposedly, she was coming to the anniversary party in three days. He'd figured she would breeze in at the last minute with some extravagant, impractical gift like she'd done for the twins' birthdays. She'd brought her ski-bum boyfriend to the last one. Dixon and Aubrey had had a *moment* five years before at Howard and Brianna's wedding. Since then, she'd been prickly around him, and they'd hardly spoken to each other.

Now they'd be forced to work together. They had a funeral to plan.

He shoved that idea into the swirl of his thoughts and snagged a new worry. What would happen to the girls? They would need a guardian.

It had to be him. Dixon was the only option. His mother loved the girls, but only in small doses. And parenthood had to be the furthest thing from Aubrey's mind. She had some kind of travel blog about outdoor sports.

Of course, it was far from his mind, too.

You're it, Dix. You'll have to raise the girls. His gut churned, and he noticed that his jaw ached like crazy. He'd locked his back teeth, as if that would help him keep it together. He looked up, saw the red light and slammed on the brakes. Damn. It wouldn't do for him to get in a wreck on the way to get the girls. He was all they had now.

How would the twins react? Ginger would dissolve into tears. Would Sienna? He imagined screams and wails and howls of grief and wild questions he wouldn't know the answers to.

They'd be upset that he was late, and hungry, so he'd stop for fast food—always a hit—take them home and somehow find a way to tell them their parents would not be coming home tonight...or ever.

Call Constance. The answer popped into his head. The Bootstrap career counselor used to work as a school psychologist. She would talk him through this. He couldn't blow it. The girls were counting on him.

As he waited for the green, the icy fact of Howard's death trickled past his defenses.

Howard is gone. Your brother. The one person who loved you no matter what, your best friend, your family.

It can't be. It's not fair.

Howard deserved more time with his kids, more time

with the agency he'd only begun to build. Dixon wanted more time with him, too. He owed him so much.

He's gone. Forever. You'll never see that grin of his, never get to harass him about the Phoenix Suns, kick his butt on the court, eat his smoked ribs, watch him work wonders with people in need.

The light turned green and he stomped the accelerator to the floor, shutting down his pain. He had a job to do. Two minutes later, he whipped into the strip mall that held the girls' gym. He spotted them doing cartwheels on the sidewalk, watched by one of the trainers, who looked pissed. He parked, jumped out of the car and hurried over. The instructor looked pointedly at her watch.

"There was an emergency. I'm sorry."

Her face didn't change. She'd probably heard a million excuses. *I bet you haven't heard this one.*

"Where were you, Uncle Dixon? We've been waiting and waiting." Sienna's piercing blue eyes locked on his, more accusatory than her words.

"Uncle Dixon!" Ginger ran and leaped into his arms, wrapping her legs around his waist.

His chest tightened and his lungs seemed to shut down. He loved these girls so much. They had giant hearts, boundless energy and huge spirits. How would this tragedy harm them?

He would not let them suffer. He would keep them safe and secure, and make certain they knew they were loved. He loved them more than words could say already, but he would love them more. He would love them the way his brother had, the way their mother had.

Was that even possible? How could he possibly replace their parents?

He felt like he was running on air. He didn't dare look down.

The girls clambered into their booster seats.

"Are you hungry?" he asked. "How about Bernie's Burgers?"

"Yes! Yay! Bernie's, Uncle Dixon. Bernie's, Bernie's, Bernie's!" Ginger bounced up and down.

"Mom said only once a week because of the salt and the bad fat," Sienna said. "We already went."

"It'll be our little secret," he said, sick inside.

Soon the car filled with the comforting smell of fries and hamburgers. He bought milkshakes, too, which was too much, especially for Ginger, whose eyes were bigger than her tiny stomach.

He didn't care. And when they started a French fry fight, he didn't try to stop them. *Go for it. Enjoy every last second of carefree fun.* He listened hard to the light music of their sweet voices, the cheerful shriek when a fry hit its mark. How long before they would laugh like this again?

He blinked against the blur before his eyes.

At the house, Dixon set the girls up at the kitchen table to eat, leaving his own food untouched. Why had he even ordered? His stomach was in turmoil, and a bitter taste clogged his throat.

Once the girls were occupied, he grabbed Brianna's emergency notes and the phone book, and ducked into the guest room to make the necessary calls. He left a message on his mother's cell phone and alerted the cruise line, which would make contact with her.

Now Aubrey. Holding his breath, jaw clenched, he braced for her reaction, but the call went straight to voice mail.

"This is Dixon Carter. Call me. It's urgent," he said. He wasn't about to leave the terrible news on a recording.

Next he called the mortuary with the largest ad, figuring they'd be busy and efficient. The funeral director would contact the mortuary in Reno, then call back to schedule a time to arrange the funeral.

The *funeral.*

The word rang in his head. Images poured in: flowers, caskets, gravestones, hymns, everyone in black and sobbing. Meanwhile, the girls chattered happily in the kitchen, oblivious to what he was doing.

Dixon was finishing with the funeral director when he heard the landline ringing from the kitchen. By the time he reached it, the caller was leaving a message: *Hi, guys. Rachel here, checking to see if you need anything for the party Saturday. Should I bring ice? An appetizer? Watch the girls? Is there any way I can help?*

Rachel was Brianna's best friend. He picked up. "Hello, Rachel. It's Dixon." Glancing at the girls, he carried the handset down the hall. "There is something I need you to do…."

She could call everyone and tell them that instead of attending the couple's anniversary party, they'd be attending their funeral.

HER SPEEDOMETER HOVERING at ninety-five, Aubrey Hanson scanned the interstate for highway patrol cars lurking on the shoulders. She didn't have time for a ticket. Not today. Not with the good news she had to share with her sister.

Every time she thought about it, an electric thrill ran through her, making her forget altogether the scrapes and bruises she'd gotten in Norway.

She was *this* close to being sponsored by ALT Outdoors, the top recreation outfitter in the U.S., possibly the world.

The timing was crucial, since her inheritance was almost gone, and the ads on her blog and podcast barely paid her rent, let alone her travel costs.

She'd been *saved.* She could keep doing what she loved

and get paid for it. She couldn't wait to see the sunburst of pride in Brianna's brown eyes when she heard. She couldn't wait to hug her sister, jump around with her, shrieking their joy to the sky. Why did Phoenix have to be almost four hundred freaking miles from L.A.?

It wouldn't quite be real until she'd told her sister. Brianna alone knew how much this meant. With the sponsorship, Aubrey's blog—*Extreme Adventure Girl: Ordinary Girl on an Extraordinary Journey*—would reach thousands more women—hell, millions—and change more lives.

Calm down. It's not official. The test run would be at the adventure race in Utah next month. Still, she was so close she could taste the triumph.

She was especially glad to tell Brianna because of the odd talk they'd had on their mother's birthday—they always called each other then—right before Brianna left for Tahoe and Aubrey for Norway.

Brianna's question had come out of the blue:

You're sure this is what you want—the blog and the travel and all?

Aubrey had sucked in a shocked breath. *Of course. This is what I've worked for. You know that.*

Aubrey's blog and her podcast shared her trips and challenges, mostly outdoors. Her purpose was to prove women didn't have to be amazons or athletes—or even that coordinated—to achieve difficult challenges. The secrets were training, tenacity and guts.

The women who followed her lead became empowered. They found the courage to break up with bad boyfriends, demand raises, go to graduate school, snatch stars they'd thought out of reach. Aubrey was proud to have had an impact on their lives.

I'm saying you don't have to push so hard, Brianna continued. *If you wanted to quit, have a family, go to school, whatever, you can. You've done more than Mom could ever have wanted.*

Their mother's bedtime stories had been tales of all the places she'd biked, hiked, climbed and kayaked before she'd had them. They'd lost her to breast cancer the summer after they graduated high school.

Where is this coming from? Aubrey had asked, her stomach bottoming out at her sister's abrupt doubts about Aubrey's chosen path. Brianna was her number one fan. *I feel like you're out there for Mom and for me,* she'd always said. Now she wanted Aubrey to quit?

Then it hit her. *Wait, it's the money, huh? You know I'm running short. You don't want me to feel bad if I have to quit and get a regular job, right?*

I just want you to be happy.

Relieved, Aubrey had rushed on. *You don't need to worry. I might have big news when I see you. I have a meeting about a possible sponsorship.*

Brianna had been excited, but after they got off the phone, Aubrey still felt a shiver of unease. That wasn't the whole story. Her sister had sounded melancholy. She'd mentioned wanting to find their grandparents, who'd been estranged from their father, who'd been killed in a ski accident before Aubrey and Brianna were born. *The girls need more family.*

Brianna did have a point. Their other grandparents were gone—their grandfather at forty due to diabetes, their grandmother two years later from pneumonia.

The conversation had gnawed at Aubrey until she finally figured out what was going on with Brianna. *She misses you. She's lonely. The family the girls need more of is you.*

Once she'd figured it out, Aubrey burned with the need

to fix this, to make it right, to be there for her sister…and for her nieces.

How had she been so blind? Shame flared hot on her face. She'd fooled herself that the Skype chats and occasional visits had been enough.

They grow up so fast, Brianna always said. She'd been gently warning Aubrey, and Aubrey had missed it completely.

Brianna always filled Aubrey in on the cute things the twins said and did, sent Aubrey videos of them at gymnastics and martial arts—classes Aubrey had paid for. They didn't need more classes from their aunt. They needed more time with her. It made her ache to think that Brianna had held back her feelings for so long.

Aubrey knew why. Brianna understood the pressure Aubrey was under to keep her blog fresh and interesting. To keep her advertisers, Aubrey needed thousands of people glued to her blog and downloading her podcasts. That meant constant travel, research and training. *Stay fresh or die* was a fact of life in the blogosphere, where it was rare to make a living wage.

Brianna had been *too* understanding. Aubrey would visit more, starting with this trip.

"Meow." Her cat, Scout, offered up an opinion from her spot on the passenger seat, where she sprawled to catch the sun that shone on her spotted fur. She was a Belgian leopard cat—a blend of domestic cat and Asian leopard. Scout was brilliant and bold, and could practically read Aubrey's mind. Because she went with Aubrey on her adventures, usually tucked into a special pocket in Aubrey's backpack, her fans had dubbed her Scout the Adventure Cat.

"I know it won't be easy," she said to her doubtful cat. The ALT sponsorship would escalate her travel schedule, add promotional appearances and other obligations, but it had to be done.

Scout gave a disdainful blink of her topaz eyes.

"I'll make it work," she insisted. *Family matters most.*

Determination caused her to sit taller, drive faster. She'd set off for Phoenix right from the ALT corporate offices, stopping only to grab gifts for the girls, along with flowers, champagne and an anniversary card for Howard and Brianna, as well as a new burner phone. She'd lost hers somewhere in the snow-packed fields of northern Norway. Aubrey went through phones like tissues.

Scout didn't look convinced. Aubrey projected far too many human emotions onto the cat, but in her mind, a good cat was worth three bad boyfriends any day.

Scout was worth double that.

Not that Aubrey had had all that many boyfriends, bad or otherwise. She had fallen in love only once. Rafael Simón was a freelance travel writer heavy into extreme sports. They'd seen each other for nearly a year. Aubrey had broken it off once it was clear they wouldn't work out.

Aubrey rubbed her grainy, sandpapery eyes. She was bone-tired and jet-lagged from the flight from Norway.

She finished off the last of her third energy drink, tossed the empty can onto the floor of the backseat, where it rattled against the ice chest containing the champagne.

Maybe they sold caffeinated date shakes at the Date Ranch Market—the halfway mark to Phoenix. She had to stop to get the girls' favorite treat—the special red licorice only available there—and to use the huge, sparkling restrooms. When they traveled, Scout usually did her business hidden by trees, but Scout liked the Date Ranch facilities, even though people gawked and exclaimed over a cat using the toilet.

Aubrey sat up straighter, widened her eyes and blew out a breath. *Stay awake. Think about the girls.*

She'd love to bring Brianna and the twins on her adventures. In a couple of years, they could handle a whitewater raft trip on the Colorado. Howard would likely have to be talked into it.

He was cautious and overprotective anyway, but the plain painful truth was he didn't trust Aubrey with his girls. It had started when she made the mistake of buying sparkler birthday candles for their second birthday, excited to see the girls' surprise and delight. Instead, the sparks had stung their cheeks. Sienna had shrieked and Ginger cried. The next day, Aubrey had offered to watch the girls while Howard and Brianna went out to dinner and she'd overheard Howard tell Brianna he wasn't comfortable leaving the girls with her.

He hadn't liked the bikes and helmets she'd bought last year, either. She'd confirmed on her blog that four-year-olds could ride bikes, and she'd gotten the proper sizes and everything.

It hurt that he thought she would endanger the girls, but he would come around over time. She hoped he'd like her anniversary gift as much as she knew Brianna would. Through one of her advertisers, Aubrey had gotten a great deal on an adventure trip for two in New Zealand, a haven for outdoor recreation, with breathtaking scenery. Aubrey would watch the girls while they were gone. The only hitch had been that Brianna and Howard would have had to buy the plane tickets, and she knew they saved every extra dime for their agency.

But now, with the sponsorship, Aubrey could buy their tickets, too! She smiled, thinking how delighted Brianna would be. She'd give them the gift right off, not wait for the party.

If her timing was right, she'd reach Phoenix not long after Brianna and Howard returned from Tahoe.

She couldn't wait to make it up to her sister and her nieces for the time she'd lost with them. She was as determined and driven as she was when she faced a new adventure. She couldn't wait to see her sister's face when she opened the door and saw Aubrey on the porch, gifts in hand.

CHAPTER TWO

SIX HOURS LATER, Aubrey parked in front of the Craftsman bungalow where her sister lived. Thank God she hadn't fallen asleep at the wheel. Scout had sensed her drifting a couple of times and meowed in warning.

Whew! Made it. Cheated death again.

She smiled at the thought. She always said that to herself when she'd met a difficult physical challenge. It meant she'd pushed past fear and doubt, taken the risk, the leap and made it out alive. She always felt amazing afterward. Her nerves tingled, her skin hummed. Colors were brighter, the air fresher, smells so much sweeter.

Her adventures weren't always death-defying. More often, they were mental risks. Each win was a step up the ladder, a notch on her belt, a memory added to the stack. If she died tomorrow, she'd have enjoyed every minute to the fullest.

Shake every thrill from life. That had been her mother's advice to her and Brianna. She'd made them both promise to do it.

Aubrey had absorbed the advice to her bones.

Because her mom had died of breast cancer, Aubrey had always feared that the disease ticked away inside her, marking off the months, weeks, minutes she had left. It was part of what drove her so hard. *Do it now. Don't waste a second. Do it before cancer blooms in you like a toxic flower.* Brianna worried about cancer, too, but more quietly.

Scout meowed, eager to go. Aubrey unzipped the hard-sided carrier so her cat could jump in, closed it, put the strap over her shoulder and got out of the car, wincing as her new scabs protested the change in position. She had a bruise the shape of Scandinavia on her hip, along with scrapes from falling on the ice during the race. Reindeer were unbelievably fast, and the hairpin turns had scared the crap out of her. She'd squealed and yelped the whole way, but she refused to be embarrassed.

The whole idea of her blog was to be real—to share her worries and fears, her mistakes and pains. If Aubrey could do it, her readers would see that they could, too, shrieking all the way.

She slipped the gift-bag loops over her wrist, lifted her well-scuffed roller bag out of the cargo hold, tucked the flowers under one arm, grabbed the handle of the small ice chest in her other hand and trundled up the walk, Scout hanging at her hip.

The gift bag held in-line skates for the girls, who were just old enough to have the required balance. She'd bought boy skates—dark blue and much cooler than the babyish pink ones for girls. Why did manufacturers infantilize girls? She'd done a blog rant on the topic around Christmas time that three major news outlets had picked up.

She had her mountain bike with her, so she'd ride bikes with the girls while she was here. She'd bet money Howard had installed training wheels she'd have to take off.

Her sister's neighborhood was modest, the house small, but so well cared for it practically glowed. With its sunny yellow paint, friendly porch swing, and crowd of bright flowers in brass pots, the place matched Brianna's personality. Her sister made a house a home, for sure.

Aubrey glanced back at her car—an XTerra she'd chosen for its rugged versatility. Her tough, mud-spattered vehicle and her sister's cozy, flower-bedecked house reflected their different styles. Aubrey was the restless soul, Brianna the settled heart.

At the door, she saw someone had left a foil-covered cake pan on the mat. Maybe Aubrey had beat them home. That was fine. The babysitter—Jessica, who lived next door—was probably there with the girls. If not, Aubrey had a spare key.

She knocked, smiling in anticipation, expecting her nieces.

But it wasn't the twins who stood in the doorway. It wasn't Brianna or Howard, either. It wasn't even the babysitter.

It was Dixon. Howard's brother. Her heart lurched like it did each time she'd seen him since the humiliating incident at the wedding.

He was good-looking, for sure, with strong features—a straight nose, square jaw, generous mouth and serious eyes so dark they seemed black. He was built like a tennis player—tall and lanky with broad shoulders and long, strong arms—and he moved with an athlete's grace.

In a flash, she remembered him carrying her down the hall to her hotel room. He'd slapped in the key card, then kicked the door open so hard it slammed into the wall. It was as if he wouldn't let any barrier keep them apart. She'd felt a thrill that totally erased the pain of her ankle.

Except instead of throwing her on the bed and making love to her, he'd put ice on her ankle and left, shutting the door he'd so hotly kicked in moments before with a soft click. Damn. Just thinking about it pissed her off again.

"Aubrey?" He sounded surprised and not happy to see her.

Ouch. "I'm early," she said, though she had every right to visit her sister whenever she wanted. "They're not back?"

"No. They're not." The words seemed to desolate him. She noticed his eyes were bloodshot, his jaw rigid, his mouth grim. *Something's wrong.*

He glanced behind him, then pulled the door closed, joining her on the porch. "The girls are eating," he said as if that were a legitimate reason to keep her outside. What the hell was going on? He seemed shaken, as if he'd heard terrible news. Terrible news he was about to share.

A chill washed over her. Scout gave a mournful yowl, either picking up Aubrey's tension or wanting out of the carrier. Aubrey set it down, along with the gift bag and the ice chest, taking the flowers from under her arm. Three daisy petals drifted to the porch, white on white, snow-flakes landing on a drift.

"What's the matter?" she asked faintly.

"I tried to reach you, but I got voice mail. I left a message."

"I lost my phone. For God's sake, tell me what it is." Goose bumps moved in a wave down her body. She felt colder than when she'd tumbled over the crusted snow pack on that final turn in Norway.

"You should sit." He motioned at the porch swing. "It's bad."

"Just say it." Her legs wobbled, so she stiffened them, refusing to give in to weakness.

"Brianna and Howard were in an accident coming back from Tahoe."

She gasped.

Dixon swallowed, as if it would take effort to say more.

"And...?" she prompted him. *Get it out. Tell me.* Her heartbeat echoed in her ears.

"They were killed."

"No. No." Her insides froze. Her brain locked down. That couldn't be right. Was this a joke? Had her ears tricked her? They were buzzing now. "What? They...what? No."

"The doctor said they didn't suffer. Their necks... It was quick." He snapped his fingers. She saw he was blinking a lot. He was going to cry? Stable, solid Dixon Carter? Oh, God. It was true. This was no joke.

"They're dead? Brianna's dead? No. No. No. No." She shook her head violently. Her wobbly legs went liquid and she staggered, one foot landing in the middle of the foil-covered pan. Gooey liquid leaked over the sides. She smelled tuna fish and Lipton soup. *Tuna casserole? Who even made that anymore, let alone gave it to someone?* was her stunned thought.

Focus. Think. What did he say again? I can't breathe. I feel sick. I can't throw up in front of Dixon. I can't move. It was like someone had shoved a pillow onto her face, punched her in the stomach and tried to electrocute her all at once.

Dixon caught her arm to keep her upright. She gasped for air.

Don't faint. Don't puke. Don't lose it.

But she seemed to be dissolving from the inside out. The terrible sound of a human in agony filled the air. As Dixon pulled her into his arms, she realized it was coming from her.

Her heart was shredding, her lungs bursting, her brain going blank. Brianna was gone...lost...forever. Aubrey would never see her sunburst smile, feel her hug against her heart, know she was there, sharing their twin souls.

When she finally realized she was bellowing in the man's ear, she made herself stop and backed out of his arms.

She had the wild urge to run, to escape, to do something big and physical. She'd felt this way when their mother died. She'd run to the park, taken the obstacle exercise track through the trees for endless hours until her legs had given out and she'd collapsed on the grass, fighting for oxygen.

It hadn't helped. The heartbreak had followed her. She knew there was no use running now, so she sank onto the swing. It rocked forward, toppling the ice chest, so the lid fell off. Ice spilled and the gold foil on top of the champagne emerged. She saw she'd dropped the flowers, too. Red roses and white daisies. Fresh and romantic. She'd been so happy when she'd bought them, so eager to celebrate her own news and Brianna's anniversary. Now the flowers seemed fragile, damaged, ruined.

"There must be a mistake. It can't be," she said. Maybe she couldn't run, but there had to be some escape from this horror.

"I'm sorry." He crouched in front of her, steadying the swing with his hand, as if he sensed her dizziness.

"When?"

"A couple of hours ago. The hospital called me at work. I arranged to have them flown here for the funeral."

"The funeral. I can't... I don't... *A funeral?*" She squeezed her eyes shut. "The girls!" Her eyes flew open. "Do they know?" Ginger and Sienna had lost their parents. Another wave of horror washed over her.

"Not yet." He cleared his throat. "I wanted to explain it properly. I called a counselor at Bootstrap for advice, but she hasn't picked up the message. They're eating now and—"

The door burst open. "Uncle Dixon—" Sienna stopped short when she saw Aubrey on the bench. "Aunt Aubrey?" Sienna surveyed her with the same blue eyes Aubrey herself had. Her hair was the same strawberry-blond, straight and shiny, though not as sun-bleached as Aubrey's.

"It's me."

"You came already!" Ginger's eyes went wide. They were dark like her father's and mother's, and her wheat-colored hair curled like Brianna's.

"I did," she said shakily. *Get it together. Calm down. The girls don't know. Don't scare them. Be strong for them.* A band of ice water—as if she'd stepped into a mountain stream—gripped her rib cage and there seemed to be a golf ball stuck in her throat.

Sienna spotted the casserole with Aubrey's footprint in the foil. "Eww. Someone stepped in it."

"I did." Aubrey lifted her foot as proof, glad of the distraction. "Sorry."

Sienna bent to study the blob that had squirted out. "It's good you wrecked it. It's got peas." Sienna made a face. "Everything Ms. Wilder makes has peas. Yuck. Jessica hates it, too, but we can't agree with her because it's not polite."

"You dropped your flowers." Ginger picked them up, then noticed Scout's carrier and got down to look through the mesh window. "Hi, Scout."

The cat meowed a greeting. Scout loved the girls, tolerating their aggressive attention, even as toddlers, when they would haul her around like a stuffed animal. Most cats would have hidden under a bed, but Scout was made of tougher stuff.

"Can I take her out, Auntie Aubba?" *Auntie Aubba* had been Ginger's toddler name for Aubrey. Aubrey loved that she still called her that.

"In the house...sure." Aubrey pretended to cough to hide her shaky voice. Ginger's innocent eagerness was painful to hear.

"I get to do it, too," Sienna said, grabbing the handle while Ginger put the strap over her shoulder. "You have the flowers."

"You take the flowers. I thought of Scout first."

The two girls had a tug-of-war, but managed to get the carrier and the flowers into the house, only losing a few more petals. They were so excited, so lighthearted, unaware of the dark train roaring from the tunnel to plow into their tender lives.

"Guess we should go in," Aubrey said, putting the lid on the ice chest, picking it up, along with the gift bag and her roller bag handle.

Dixon stopped her with a warm hand on her arm. "You need a minute out here?"

She shook her head. "Let's get this over with." She preferred to remove bandages with a quick rip, not a slow, agonizing tug.

"I don't want to tell them yet," Dixon said. "I'll try Constance again."

She didn't see the sense in that, but she didn't want to argue with the man. She'd hardly absorbed the news herself. Dixon grabbed the ruined casserole and held the door for Aubrey, who walked into the house on legs gone numb. At least she no longer felt her Norway scrapes.

In a glance, she surveyed the living room, with its overstuffed sofa and love seat in a floral pattern, the jewel-toned area rug on the polished oak floor, the play corner with toys in bright buckets. Such a happy place. Such a happy family.

Gone now. A gloom seemed to fall over the room, dimming the colors, making the toys shabby, the furniture cold.

She turned to Dixon, and their eyes met. He looked sad and lost. Exactly like her. She turned to the girls and dropped to her knees. "I need hugs." She held out her arms, hoping she could keep from crying. Sienna gave her a quick, hard squeeze. Gymnastics and martial arts had turned the girl into solid muscle.

Ginger wrapped her thin arms around Aubrey's neck and clung to her, giving Aubrey time to breathe in her feather-fine hair, which smelled of bubblegum shampoo, French fries and the sweet salt of little-girl sweat.

When Ginger let go, Aubrey wanted to say, *I love you, I missed you, I'm so glad to see you,* but her throat was too tight.

"Why are you crying?" Sienna asked, staring at her with her sharp blue eyes.

"I'm just happy to be here."

"Happy doesn't make you cry," Sienna insisted.

She wears me out, Brianna had said about Sienna. *She won't let any question go unanswered. She probes and pokes and demands. Just like you used to.*

"Better let Scout out," Aubrey said to shift Sienna's attention.

Ginger was already at the zipper.

"No fair," Sienna said. "You carried her. I get to unzip." Sienna was clearly the take-charge twin.

The carrier open, Scout jumped out and shook herself indignantly, wiggling each paw, then her tail.

"She prefers to come to you," she reminded them.

"We know," Sienna said. The girls sat poised, hands out, eyes so eager Aubrey had to smile. Scout obliged them by delicately sniffing their fingertips, then rubbing her cheek against them.

"She remembers us," Ginger said. "She's showing us she loves us."

"She's putting her smell on us," Sienna said. "It's animal in-stink. That's what Jessica says. Cats and dogs are *animals*. They don't do people things like cuddle and kiss and love."

"Scout does," Ginger insisted. "Look in her eyes. That is l-o-v-e, love."

Aubrey remembered a similar disagreement with Brianna, who'd been convinced that the ducks at the park recognized them, while Aubrey was certain they only saw bread crumbs. Brianna had always had more heart than Aubrey.

The night their mother died, Brianna had held their mother's hand and whispered to her. Brianna had *been there,* brave and strong. Aubrey had run away. It still shamed her.

Scout jumped onto Aubrey's lap. The cat stayed close when Aubrey was upset, purring wildly as if to soothe whatever ailment Aubrey suffered.

"Will she do her tricks for us?" Ginger asked.

"She's got to get familiar with your house first." Scout could give a high-five, fetch things, drink from a glass and play dead.

Aubrey's thoughts began to buzz like angry bees. *It can't be true. Brianna can't be dead. The girls can't go through this. Please, no, Brianna. We can't go on without you.*

"You okay?" Dixon asked softly.

"I'm fine." She forced a smile, then turned to the girls. "How about you open your gifts?" She plopped the bag between them, delaying the bad news a little longer.

The girls reached in from opposite sides of the sack, orange hair against wheat, then lifted out the boxes, looking through the clear plastic at the contents.

"Rollerblades," Aubrey said. "What do you think?"

"Cool," Sienna said.

"It's too hard for us," Ginger said, scrunching her nose.

"Remember that big kid in the park with blood all down his arms?"

"We'll get pads for your elbows and knees," Aubrey said. "You'll wear your bike helmets, too. You'll be safe."

"Daddy took the helmets back. He didn't know what you were thinking," Sienna said. "The bikes are put away for when we're bigger."

"You're big enough," she said, irritated by Howard's attitude. "You girls are gymnasts. You have crazy balance. People on my blog told me a cool way to learn. Easy-breezy."

"Easy-breezy?" Ginger repeated eagerly.

"Easy-breezy. I brought my bike, so once you learn, we can ride together in the park. Won't that be fun?" Her voice cracked, but she had to give them something to look forward to, something to soften the coming blow.

She glanced at Dixon, who looked totally bereft. They had to get this over with. Her mouth was so dry she wasn't sure she could get out the words. "Listen, girls, we need to talk to you about—"

"First, ice cream," Dixon blurted, cutting her off. "Your aunt came early, so we should celebrate. Help me scoop, Aubrey." He grabbed Aubrey's arm and stood, pulling her up with him.

"Ice cream?" Sienna stopped tearing into the box and stared at Dixon. "But we already had milkshakes. Ginger will upchuck."

"We'll make it small, just a taste. Because your aunt surprised us." He headed for the kitchen, pulling Aubrey by the arm, Sienna's suspicious eyes burning holes in their backs.

"Ice cream? Really?" Aubrey whispered, once they reached the kitchen. "You want them to link ice cream with their parents' death?"

"I need to try Constance again. She'll know the best approach." He pushed buttons on his phone.

"We don't need an approach, Dixon. We should tell them flat out. Use simple words. They'll react, and we'll try to give them comfort." Dixon wanted magic words, but there were none. She'd learned that when her mother died.

At least you were eighteen. They're only four.

She clenched her fists, dug her nails into her palms to keep from crying.

"Bowls are to the left of the sink," Dixon said, the phone to his ear. "Chocolate chip for Ginger. Strawberry for Sienna."

She opened the freezer, the blast of cold air pleasant against her face, where nervous sweat had trickled down her temples. The freezer was jammed with plastic containers and big Baggies, each labeled with a dish—lasagna, chicken cacciatore, Chinese noodle casserole.... It looked like Jessica's mother had been helping out the bachelor babysitter.

Rummaging around, she found the ice cream and scooped out servings for the girls, sheepishly aware that he had known their favorite flavors, while she had no clue. Aubrey wasn't part of the girls' daily lives the way he was, and it was her own fault.

In the background, she heard the girls putting on their rollerblades. When she'd finished scooping, she stared at the family photos on the fridge—the girls with Mickey Mouse at Disneyland, the family playing miniature golf, the twins in leotards on the balance beam, doing a *kata* in martial arts gi.

She should have been here more, been part of all this. *Don't wallow. You'll spend more time. You'll pay more attention. You'll—*

She felt an icicle stab to the heart. *Who will raise the girls?*

Aubrey or Dixon. They were the only choices. Dixon's mother, Lorraine, was older and traveled a lot, according to Brianna. *Just like you,* Aubrey thought queasily.

How could Aubrey manage it? She couldn't move the girls to L.A. where she shared a tiny apartment with an actress-slash-cocktail waitress. She would have to move to Phoenix. And what about her travel, all the promotion she'd have to do if she got the sponsorship?

Anxiety sent an acid wash down her throat like a gulped shot of tequila, no lime or salt to ease the way.

"Voice mail," Dixon said with irritation. "I'll try again later." He slipped the phone into his pocket. Dixon lived here. He worked at Bootstrap, where the girls went for day care. He knew their ice cream preferences and a whole lot more about their lives.

Dixon would be the choice. No question.

What would Brianna want? *Wait. Was there a will?* Didn't people list guardians in wills? Aubrey sure hadn't seen a will. Had Dixon?

"All set?" Dixon picked up the bowls.

Aubrey felt woozy, like the stormy drift dive in the Bahamas before they'd sunk below the waves. Dixon looked just as green, as if he stood on the same rolling deck.

"Hang on." She stopped him with a hand on his arm. "We need something more." She ducked into the refrigerator for a can of whipped cream and a jar of maraschino cherries. As she squirted the cream and dropped the cherries, her hands shook. So did Dixon's holding the bowls. The resulting mounds were lopsided, the cherries sadly off center. "Good enough."

In the family room, the girls were holding on to each

other trying to balance on their skates, sliding forward and back, waving their free arms wildly.

"Ta-da!" Aubrey said. "Ice cream sundaes!"

Dixon set them on the table. "Have at it, girls."

"But we're not allowed to eat in here," Sienna declared, staring at the heaping, messy bowls. "And you said just a taste." She paused. "Where are Mommy and Daddy? They promised they'd be here by supper." Her voice was sharply alert.

Aubrey looked at Dixon, who closed his eyes briefly, then gave her a slow, resigned nod. It was time to tell them. "Sit down, girls," he said dully.

Still holding each other up, the girls clumped to the sofa, and sat, skates dangling from their skinny legs like moon boots. Already scared, they stared at Dixon and Aubrey with wide eyes. Dixon pushed the table to the side, making room for him and Aubrey to kneel in front of the girls.

"You asked about your parents…" Dixon started. "We… your aunt and I…need to talk to you about…them."

Looking into their still, wan faces, so vulnerable, so terrified, Aubrey couldn't stand it another second. "They were in a car accident."

Both girls gasped.

"They didn't make it," Dixon added quickly.

"What didn't they make?" Sienna asked in a tremulous voice.

"He means they died. The accident killed them."

"But it didn't hurt," Dixon said. "They didn't have any pain."

"What? No! You're lying!" Sienna's shrill cry, echoing Aubrey's first reaction, pierced like a hot spike to her heart.

"It's true," Aubrey said. "I wish it weren't, but it is."

"They're in a hospital in Nevada," Dixon said, "but they'll be flown down to Phoenix for the funeral." He paused. "That's a church service where people get together and talk about the dead person and—"

"Everybody knows what a fun'ral is," Sienna said. "We had one for our gecko that died."

"Are they getting fixed up at the hospital?" Ginger asked, clearly not grasping what Dixon meant. This was so hard. Aubrey wanted to pull the girl into her arms and erase her pain, but there were no magic hugs any more than there were magic words.

"No. It's just their bodies," Dixon said. He had to clear his throat to continue.

Aubrey put a hand on his arm to support him. "Their spirits are gone. In Heaven."

"With Grandma Hanson and Grandpa Carter?" Ginger asked tremulously.

"And Grandpa Metzger," Aubrey threw in, though she had no idea how Heaven worked or if her father would be there to greet the daughter he never knew he'd had.

"I don't believe you!" Sienna's voice broke, her anguish ringing in Aubrey's ears.

Oh, sweetie, I know, I know. It hurts so much, so very much. She was too young for so much suffering.

"I'm calling Mommy." She lunged off the couch and tromped, headlong in her skates, to the kitchen, where she grabbed the phone.

"I want my mommy and daddy," Ginger said, big tears rolling down her cheeks.

"I know you do." Aubrey held out her arms, but Ginger pushed off the couch onto Dixon's lap, her knees bent, skates behind, and sobbed into his shoulder with all her might. Dixon was more familiar to her, so it made sense she'd go to him over Aubrey.

It's done. They know. The worst's over.

But that wasn't true. Aubrey's mother's death had been

a boulder dropped in a pond, but grief had rippled outward for months and months, each wave a fresh blow. She'd feared it would kill her, then wished it would. Instead, she had had to endure the pain, day and night, on and on, as had Brianna. Would it be easier because the girls were so young, or harder? She had no idea.

Sienna stood by the phone, wobbling in her skates, so Aubrey went to help, steeling herself the way she did when she faced an impossible-looking rock climb.

"Mommy, call me back...*please*," Sierra said into the handset, her voice frantic, her eyes jumping here and there, like a trapped bird desperate to escape a cage. "It's an emergency." She put the handset in its dock, then stared at it, willing it to ring.

"I know it's hard to accept, Sienna." Aubrey racked her brain for soothing words. "I can hardly believe it and I'm way older than you. It's a terrible shock. It takes time to get used to, but we'll do it."

Sienna's lip trembled, her face slowly crumpled.

"We'll help each other." Aubrey held out her arms.

"Leave me alone!" Sienna turned and hop-tromped down the hall, slamming the bedroom door so loudly the living room windows rattled.

Now what? Go to her or leave her be?

In a flash, she remembered holding Sienna the day she was born. Brianna had thrust the tiny bundle of a baby at her. Aubrey had cupped her hand around Sienna's delicate skull, examined her tiny fingers, fragile as twigs, looked into those clear trusting eyes and panicked. *Here.* She'd tried to hand the baby back to Brianna. *I'm scared I'll break her.*

But Brianna refused to take the bundle. She looked at Aubrey, her eyes glowing with a new fire. *Everyone feels like that. You learn together.*

That flash of memory, hearing Brianna's voice again, felt like a gift to Aubrey and calmness washed through her. *Go to her. Shared pain is less pain.* Brianna and Aubrey had gotten each other through the terrible times, after all.

At first, Aubrey hadn't understood that. When the minister's wife had said, *You're so lucky. You have each other,* it had been all Aubrey could do not to smack her. They'd lost their *mother,* their only parent. *Lucky* was the last thing they were.

Soon enough, she saw the truth in those words. They'd comforted each other like no one else could have. She would do her best to comfort Sienna. *You'll learn together.*

CHAPTER THREE

GINGER'S LITTLE BODY trembled in Dixon's arms, and he had to tighten every muscle to keep from breaking down. He was no good with feelings in general, and his niece's heartbreak was more than he could grasp, let alone figure out how to fix. Aubrey had gone after Sienna. He hoped she knew what to say.

Ginger raised her tear-drenched face and looked at him. "Will you take care of us, Uncle Dixon?"

"Of course I will," he said, fighting the urge to squeeze her tight—too tight—as if that would somehow help. His insides seemed to be churning and melting at once.

"Forever?" she added.

"Forever." *I will watch over you and protect you from all harm, no matter what, or die trying.* The experts would probably frown on such a grandiose promise. Right now he didn't give a damn. To help Ginger feel better, he would say *anything.* He would move in with them—at least at first— so as not to disrupt the girls any more than necessary.

They knew him and loved him. As ill-equipped as he felt, he was the best they had. He wanted to make this right, but how did you make something right that is more wrong than anything that could happen to a child? The girls needed each other most of all, he assumed. Aubrey would know about that, since she and her sister had lost their mother, too. *Not this young.*

"Shall we go talk to Sienna?" he asked.

Ginger nodded against his shoulder.

He stood, still holding her. As he walked, the skates bumped his legs. What the hell had possessed Aubrey to buy rollerblades? For their third birthday, she'd given them an indoor trapeze and tightrope set. One of the few quarrels Dixon had ever heard between Howard and Brianna had started when Howard bitched that Aubrey was clueless about the girls—buying them classes and toys they were too young for. Brianna had defended her sister with a surprising ferocity.

Aubrey meant well. He knew that. She clearly adored the girls. He felt kind of sorry for her. She seemed to think she had to prove her love with gifts and activities, as if she thought the girls wouldn't remember her or, hell, love her back.

In the bedroom, Sienna lay facedown on the bottom bunk and Aubrey was pulling the skates from her dangling legs.

"That's my bed!" Ginger shrieked. "Get off my bed!" The girls were up in each other's grills about private areas—beds being a flash point. "Daddy said you can't be on my bed without my permission."

Sienna raised her face, her cheeks wet with tears, her nose running. "Who cares what Daddy says? Daddy's dead. So is Mommy. They're never coming home. They left us all alone."

Her raw pain hit like a punch in Dixon's chest. Aubrey dropped a skate with a clunk and hunched over, as if she'd been hit by the same cruel fist. Her eyes met his, their usual crystal-blue gone cloudy.

"We're not alone," Ginger said. "Uncle Dixon promised to take care of us forever."

Aubrey's eyebrows shot up in surprise. He wished they'd had a chance to discuss him being the girls' guardian first, but it couldn't be helped. Besides, she would likely be relieved to know he was willing to take over.

The leopard-spotted cat appeared out of nowhere and leaped onto the bed to lick Sienna's cheek, purring wildly. "Her tongue's rough," Sienna said.

"She wants you to feel better," Aubrey said.

"She just likes the salt," Sienna said, but a smile flickered on-off.

"I'm sad, too, Scout," Ginger said, holding out a cheek. "I've got tears. See?"

"She wants to be with me," Sienna said.

"You have to share," Ginger whined. "It's not fair."

"She'll be with you, too, Ginger," Aubrey said. "We have plenty of time for Scout to make you both feel better."

"Will you stay forever, too?" Ginger asked, swiping at her nose.

Aubrey blinked, opened and closed her mouth, clearly not knowing what to say.

"Your aunt lives in L.A., so she can't," Dixon said to help her out.

"I'll stay as long as I can." She shot him a look, but he could tell she'd been caught off guard.

Ginger sighed sadly.

"How about that ice cream?" he said. "It's out there melting." *Like that will help, you idiot.*

"My stomach hurts too much," Ginger said.

"It's gross when it melts," Sienna said.

"Then let's run your baths, huh?" He figured keeping to the routine was the smartest way to go.

"I don't want a bath," Sienna said, her arms buried in Scout's fur, her cheek resting on the cat's back.

"You had gymnastics. Your mom's rule is baths before bed after activities."

"Maybe tonight we can skip baths," Aubrey said

brightly. "Rules are made to be broken. Right, girls?" She winked at Sienna, who managed a crooked smile.

"A bath will relax them, and they'll sleep better," he said, trying to catch her eye, get her to present a united front.

"Auntie Aubba said we can skip," Ginger said.

"Your parents put me in charge and I say you're taking baths."

"You can't make us. You're not our dad. Our dad is gone. This is our house. We own it. Now we make the rules." Sienna was getting wound up, scaring herself, testing the limits.

He opened his mouth to say something firm, but Aubrey spoke up. "Have you girls ever seen a cat dive?"

The twins' eyes zipped to Aubrey.

"If you take your baths, I bet I can get her to dive for you."

"Really?" Sienna asked.

"Really. Scout loves water. We have lots of adventures in lakes and rivers."

"You're kidding," Dixon said.

"I never kid about Scout the Adventure Cat, do I, girls?"

"Never," Sienna chimed in. He noticed the little girl's eyes were the same shade of blue as her aunt's. They had the same noses and straight, red-blond hair, shiny as spun bronze. "Come on, Ginger." Sienna bounded off the bed and headed out the door.

"Great diversion," Dixon said to Aubrey. She'd shifted the girls' attention away from the impasse. "Would you mind managing the bath? I should check messages. I turned off the sound so the girls wouldn't hear anything upsetting before they knew. I likely got a call from the funeral director."

"No problem."

Aubrey headed after the girls, and Dixon tackled the machine, which had a message from the mortician, as well as tons from friends offering condolences, food and help, their voices full of shock. Rachel had done her job.

He'd torn off the note with the appointment time at the mortuary, when shrieks drew him down the hall to the bathroom. Were the girls fighting?

As soon as he walked in the door, he got hit in the crotch with a cup of warm water.

"Whoops, accident," Aubrey said, but she'd clearly done it on purpose. The girls burst out laughing, which, no doubt, had been the point.

"It's a water fight, Uncle Dixon," Sienna explained.

"I can see that," he said. There was an inch of water on the floor and the bath mat was soaked.

"Get her back," Ginger said, holding out a plastic measuring cup brimming with soapy water.

"Hit me with your best shot," Aubrey said, giving him the same grin she'd delivered on the cliff in Mexico when she'd dared him to jump.

"You look pretty wet already." Her hair dripped appealingly, her shirt clung to her breasts.

Don't stare. There are children here. Despite himself, he flashed on a memory of that night, carrying her back to her room, dripping wet, her silk dress all but transparent.

Forget that. Don't think about that.

"You look like you peed your pants, Uncle Dixon." Sienna pointed gleefully.

"Splash his legs so it looks like he was wading," Aubrey said, clearly working to stay cheerful for the girls' sake.

Sienna tossed a bowl of water at his slacks. Both girls squealed with delight at the results.

The bath was supposed to relax the girls, not hype them

up, but he was glad to see smiles and hear laughter, even if it had a hysterical edge.

Giving in, Dixon sat on the wet floor, drenching his backside, too. The steamy air smelled like the cherry of the girls' soap mixed with the spice of Aubrey's perfume.

He found himself studying Aubrey. She was as strikingly pretty as when he'd met her at the wedding, with an expressive face, full mouth and remarkable eyes. *Arresting.* That was the old-fashioned word for her brilliant blue gaze, which stopped you in your tracks, made you want to raise your hands in surrender.

Arresting? Jesus.

His gaze shifted to her body, shapely and athletic. Her deep tan and sun-streaked hair were evidence of hours spent outdoors. Damn. A sigh escaped his lips.

The sound made Aubrey look his way, catching him still staring.

Luckily, Ginger broke the spell. "Scout picked up a block from the bottom of the tub, Uncle Dixon. Can we show him?" The question was for Aubrey.

"I think Scout's done for the night," Aubrey said. The cat sat on the padded toilet seat wrapped in a towel, fur fluffy, eyes closed in an expression of serenity. "So are we, right?"

Dixon held out a towel for each girl, then took two more from the shelf, handing one to Aubrey before he kneeled to sop up water from the floor. She did the same and their hands met in the middle of the room.

Dixon met her gaze, and received a sexual jolt.

Aubrey's eyes lit up, as if she'd gotten the same charge. "We crashed, girls," she said, clearly covering for the high-voltage moment.

He remembered her as a very physical person. She touched you when she talked, as if to ground herself, fingers brushing your hand, squeezing your upper arm, patting your back. That was how they'd ended up dancing at the wedding. She'd kept touching him, coaxing him, until the next thing he knew he was on the dance floor. And he hated dancing.

Earlier tonight, when she'd stopped him with a hand so she could glop goo on the girls' ice cream, her touch had somehow steadied him for the task of telling the girls the terrible news. At least that was non-sexual. There was no place for sex here. Not in their situation, and certainly not around the girls.

Now Aubrey launched into a camp song about a frog that required her to bug out her eyes, stick out her tongue and make a gulping gargling sound during the chorus.

The girls were transfixed. The woman knew how to have fun, for sure. He'd seen that in Mexico.

Eventually, they herded the girls to their room, and Aubrey challenged them to see who could get into their pajamas first.

Afterward, tops mis-buttoned, bottoms inside out, the girls argued about who'd won.

"I'd say it was a tie, wouldn't you, Dixon?" Aubrey said.

"I won," Sienna insisted. "You just don't want Ginger to cry."

"It was a tie," Ginger said, tears the size of jelly beans shivering in her brown eyes.

"You're such a baby," Sienna said.

"No, I'm not. Daddy says you can't be mean to me."

"Daddy's gone."

"Stop saying that!" Ginger burst into serious tears this time and Dixon felt his own eyes burn.

"Please don't cry," Aubrey said. "We were having fun and laughing, remember?" She shot Dixon a look. *What do we do now?*

He had no idea.

"I can't help it," Ginger sobbed. "I forgot what happened. I think they'll be here soon to kiss us good-night."

"But they won't be," Sienna said angrily. "Stop thinking that." She climbed up the ladder, got under the covers and turned her face to the wall.

Ginger cried quietly.

Dixon racked his brain for something to talk about.

"Is this your bedtime book?" Aubrey picked up *Ramona the Pest* from the nightstand.

How had he forgotten? "Yeah," he said, taking the book. "Time to read."

"Can Auntie Aubba do it?" Ginger asked.

"If she wants to." He looked at her.

"I'd love to." She smiled hesitantly.

"That's the reading chair right there." Dixon motioned at the tiny chair a foot from the bunk beds.

"You're kidding."

"Trust me. It's the rule."

She sat in the low chair, set the book on her knees, which jutted up to her chin, and opened it to the marked page.

She'd barely finished a paragraph before Sienna gave a strangled cry. "You have to stop. Make her stop, Uncle Dixon."

"What's wrong?" Aubrey closed the book on her thumb, bright red blotches on her cheeks.

"That's not nice, Sienna," Dixon said. She was upset, but that was no excuse to be mean.

"She's trying to sound like our mommy," Sienna said. "You're not her," she said to Aubrey. "Don't pretend you are."

"Your mom's my sister. We sound alike, I guess."

"Now my stomach feels sicker," Ginger said.

"That's probably all the junk food I let you eat," Dixon said to ease the moment.

"I'll let you finish." Aubrey handed him the book, ducking his gaze, clearly mortified. "Night, girls," she muttered, almost running out the door. She pulled it shut.

"No! Leave it open!" Ginger called. "We need the line of light!"

The door cracked. "Sorry," Aubrey called from the hallway.

"You girls need to be kinder to your aunt," Dixon said. "She lost her sister, and she's sad, too. In the morning, I want you to say you're sorry."

Sienna didn't respond, and he didn't feel like pushing it.

"Now get some sleep," he said. Sleep would help. But from the doorway, he saw both sets of eyes staring at him, wide-awake.

Please let them sleep, he silently prayed. *It's their only escape.*

Their wide eyes still haunting him, Dixon headed for the living room to talk to Aubrey, uncertain how emotional she would be. He'd been startled when she'd fallen against him on the porch. She'd always had such a sexy swagger. She was more fragile than she let on.

They all were. He felt raw, like the skin beneath a blister, sensitive to the air. And the girls were on the brink of hysteria every minute. They would all have to be careful with each other. That was all there was to it.

HER VOICE HAD made the girls cry. The sting of that shame threatened to level Aubrey, but she forced herself to forget it, to stay busy. She wasn't ready to sink into the sorrow that awaited her. She grabbed her roller bag to get settled in the guest room.

Except there she saw Dixon's suitcase open on the floor

beside the computer desk, and smelled his cologne. Of course he'd be here. He'd been staying with the girls.

"You can have this room." His voice floated from the doorway, and she turned to find him leaning against the doorjamb.

"No, no. I'll use the other bedroom." She started to pass him, but he stopped her with a gentle hand on her arm. "But that's Howard and Brianna's room. It might be difficult for you." He held her gaze. She'd forgotten how intense his dark eyes were, how they pulled you in, turned everything else into a blur. At the wedding, it had been the way he'd looked at her that had convinced her to drag him onto the dance floor, then out to the beach, to get more of those eyes on her.

"I'll be fine," she said. She had to be.

"You sure?"

She blew out a breath. "Truthfully? I'm not sure about anything. For now, let's go with *fine*."

"I'm sorry about that nonsense over your voice. I asked Sienna to apologize."

"There's no need for that." She threw back her shoulders, hating that Dixon had noticed her hurt. "I understand completely. Brianna and I went through that after Mom died. One of us would use one of her expressions and it felt like a sucker punch."

"Still, Sienna was harsh." He frowned. "They usually don't pick on each other so much, either."

"That's normal. Brianna and I had a terrible fight when we got back from the funeral over a borrowed sweater. We were taking out our anger about Mom dying on each other. That's what the girls are doing, I'm sure."

"That makes sense." His gaze gentled.

"It won't last long. It didn't with me and Brianna. In

fact, we got a lot closer, leaned on each other more. We were all we had."

"It must have been hell to lose your mother so young."

"At least we were nearly adults. The twins are so little." Her eyes stung, but she refused to crumble like she had on the porch. It was strange. They hardly knew each other, but they'd been forced into an intense intimacy.

"I hope Ginger and Sienna will get closer, too," Dixon said.

"I'm sure they will. And they have you and me, too. And your mother."

"She doesn't visit much."

Brianna had told her as much. "Actually, the last time I talked to her, Brianna said she wanted to look for our father's relatives. He was estranged from his family."

"Do you want that?"

"If the girls have more relatives, it would be good for them."

"It would," Dixon said.

"Maybe I'll see what I can find. Later on...after we get past all this."

"Sure."

Standing so close, she couldn't help but respond to how male he was—broad and strong, with straight, square features. He'd rolled up the sleeves of his chambray shirt, revealing muscular forearms. There was something sexy about that look.

Dixon was sexy, period.

For one second, she wanted to reach for him, go to bed with him, stop fighting so hard to keep her head above the waves of grief that threatened to engulf her. He would be her life raft. She would be his.

A soft sound escaped her lips. Dixon's breath hitched

and twin candle flames lit in his dark eyes, just as they had that night in Mexico.

When the band had quit playing, she'd kicked off her heels, grabbed Dixon's hand and snatched a nearly full bottle of good champagne on the way to the beach, running, laughing, feeling lighter than air....

Now Dixon's breathing shifted, he tilted his mouth closer.

Why not?

They could open up a sliver of time to escape, to hide out in each other's arms.

"We have things to discuss," Dixon said, flipping the switch, making them both blink in the sudden harsh light of reality.

It took her a second to adjust, but she knew he was right. This was no time to escape. "Let me put away my things, and I'll meet you in the living room."

She rolled her bag down the hall. Stepping into the room was almost too much for her. The space was full of Brianna's happy energy, and it smelled of her perfume— *Joyful,* a perfect word for her sister. Every surface held framed photos of the couple and their girls.

She remembered Brianna showing her the room, gleefully dancing from item to item—the curtains and pillows she'd made, the antique bureau she'd refinished to match the headboard. She'd been so proud, so happy.

How can you sleep here, with Brianna's lost happiness swirling like smoke, burning your eyes and searing your throat?

Aubrey braced herself against the bureau, closed her eyes and silently recited her mantra: *you are stronger than you know. Trust your training. Trust your will. Trust your courage. The only obstacles are your own doubt and fear. Conquer yourself and you conquer all.*

After a beat and a breath, strength poured through her. *It worked.* It always worked, and it always surprised her.

Fix this. First, the pictures. One by one, she turned them facedown. Next, the sheets. She got fresh ones from the hall linen closet and remade the bed. Finally, she misted the air with her own spicy cologne, overriding her sister's airier scent.

Whew. Better. It's just a room now, not Brianna's cozy nest.

She gave the bathroom the same treatment, placing Brianna's hair stuff under the sink and claiming the space with her own toiletries.

After that, she splashed water on her face and pulled her hair into the ponytail she wore for physical challenges. That seemed right. This was the biggest challenge of her life—coping with Brianna's death and deciding what was best for the girls. With a last calming breath, she went to meet Dixon.

He was on the couch working on his laptop. When he saw her, he set the computer on the table and stood. "You all right?" he asked, searching her face so closely she felt... *exposed.*

"I'm fine." She ducked his gaze and went to sit on the sofa. Rafe had given her space, at least. Of course, they'd rarely spent quiet time together. They were always doing something outdoors—kayaking, hiking, skiing or diving.

Dixon sat beside her, legs angled toward her, watching her face. She guessed you could get used to so much attention. It was like he really cared about her. It was probably just his way. He likely read the backs of cereal boxes, too.

"It's all set with the Reno funeral people," he said. "They'll fly them to Phoenix tomorrow."

"That's good. How did you even know what to do?"

"A social worker at the hospital explained the procedure. It was mostly a blur. We're due at the mortuary at nine to choose flowers and the casket and all. Just now, I called our minister and we'll meet him at the church after that to plan the funeral."

Flowers...casket...funeral. The words echoed in her head.

"We're supposed to post the obituaries on the mortuary website so people can write their condolences. We'll need to choose photos."

"Photos...right." She had to write her sister's *obituary.* Obituaries were for old people, not young mothers.

"I figure we'll have the funeral on Saturday."

"Saturday...? Wait... What about the anniversary party? We have to tell people!" She started to get up.

"It's done. I had Brianna's friend Rachel call everyone. We already had caterers coming. It seemed smart to use them. We'll take the words off the cake—" He stopped abruptly, his jaw muscle twitching, clearly struggling against sadness.

"That's very...practical." What else could she say? "Plus everyone was already planning to come." She gulped. "I don't know what I'm saying."

"Me, neither. Believe me. My mother should be able to get here by Saturday. She's on a cruise. I had to leave word for her."

"Will she want to stay here?"

"She prefers hotels, which is better for all of us. I love her, but there's always drama and it's always about her." Aubrey had enjoyed Lorraine at the wedding. She was lively and funny and full of stories.

"Is there anyone else we should notify?"

"She'll get the word to our father. If we're lucky, he'll send a card. We don't know any of his relatives." Anger and hurt flared in his eyes. "Mom's mother died three

years ago. Grandpa's in an assisted living place with de-
mentia. There are cousins we don't know." He shrugged.
"Everyone who needs to know knows. The rest can read
it in the paper."

"You've done a lot." She'd barely accepted the news,
and Dixon had been making arrangements. "I feel bad this
has been on your shoulders."

"I had a couple hours' head start. You're here now. We'll
do the rest together."

"Right. So we have to pick photos and write the
obituaries…" she repeated, trying to get up to speed, to
contribute to the process. "What else?"

"Decide the music and who should speak and in what
order." He studied her face. "You look dead-tired. We can
go over all the funeral stuff tomorrow."

"Sounds good. It's mostly jet lag," she said. "I flew in
from Norway early this morning for a meeting in L.A.,
then drove straight here."

"No wonder you're wiped out. Go get some sleep."

"I'm too wired for that." She smiled sadly. "But I could
use a drink." Her gaze snagged on the ice chest on the floor
beside the table. She opened it and took out the champagne,
melted ice dripping from the bottle. "Might as well drink
this, right?"

"Why not? Sounds practical," he said with a weary
smile. "I'll get glasses."

She picked up the flowers. "I should put these in something."

In the kitchen, Aubrey opened cupboards until she spotted a crystal vase on the top shelf. She was too short to
reach it, but Dixon was plenty tall.

She turned to ask for his help, but he was looking at
the fridge photos. "This was before they got married." He
tapped a shot of Brianna and Howard at a picnic table.

Brianna grinned at the photographer. Howard stared at Brianna with pure adoration. "They thought they had a lifetime together," Dixon added gruffly.

Aubrey remembered the margarita-stoked conversation she'd had with Brianna when the girls were babies. *I just want to get them through college, you know?* she'd said. *High school was too soon. I wasn't ready. My core wasn't solid yet.*

You won't get cancer, Aubrey had insisted. *You live a seatbelt life, totally strapped in.* Of all the words she could have chosen. Seatbelts hadn't saved Brianna this time.

"I can't believe she's gone," Aubrey said, unable to hide her sadness. "It's like I lost half of myself. There was so much I should have told her." *I'll be here more. I miss you, too. I'm sorry I let you down.*

"I know what you mean," Dixon said, his voice husky with emotion. "The last time I talked to Howard I bitched about a report he forgot to finish before the trip." His eyes were watering now.

"You didn't know it would be the last time."

"Howard was the one who raised me after Dad left. I was ten. He was fifteen. I was wild as a kid."

"*You* were wild?" He'd seemed like a straight arrow to her.

"Mom blamed me for Dad leaving. I'd been screwing up in school, getting in trouble, but after he left, I ran off the rails. Mom worked days and went out nights, but Howard stayed on me, kept me out of jail and in school. I owe him so much…" His jaw muscle worked. "Working at Bootstrap was a way to pay him back."

"I'm sure he knew how grateful you were." Her words seemed so hollow in the face of the pain Dixon was feeling.

"I can't remember his voice." Dixon forced the words out. "Or see his face. That's what's killing me."

"I know what you mean. You feel so...*alone*."

"Yeah. Alone."

Then she remembered something from back when her mother died. "The voices and memories come back," she said. "A grief counselor told us that the shock blanks out your brain for a while. Over time, it all comes back."

"It does?"

"It happened for me in dreams first. After a while, the happy memories covered over how sick Mom was at the end, and that's how I remember her now."

"That's good," he said. "I'll look forward to that."

She could tell he was about to break down. So was she. "This is so hard." Dixon must have sensed that she was crumbling, and pulled her into his arms, tucking her against his chest. They held each other tightly, as if for dear life, against the storm lashing them both.

Dixon smelled like citrus and starch, and his heart thudded steadily beneath her cheek, saying, *I'm here, I'm here, I'm here.*

She rested against him, calming herself, breathing in time with Dixon, sharing the same sorrow, the same pain. They stood, swaying slightly, for a long time. Gradually, another feeling took over—this one more primal.

Desire.

She *wanted* him. Of all the wrong times to react like that. All the turmoil had her riled up, of course. Her emotions flitted like fireflies lighting her up here and there.

Dixon jerked, so she knew he'd been struck, as well. He let her go as if she'd scalded him. "We were getting glasses and a vase." He cleared his throat.

She reined herself in, a little irked at how easily Dixon had backed off. He never let physical needs rule him. She admired that...and resented it, too.

"Could you reach that?" She pointed up at the vase.

Dixon retrieved it and filled it with water. She put the flowers inside, feeling his gaze on her as she worked. When she looked up and caught him staring, he colored, then moved to the cupboards. "I think the champagne glasses were...here."

They were. When Aubrey reached in to help, she startled Dixon, who pulled back, knocking three glasses off the shelf. Aubrey nabbed two in the air. Dixon caught the third.

"Not bad," she said, holding out her hand for his glass. When he gave it to her, she started an easy juggle, careful to compensate for the uneven weight of the flutes. A rush of pleasure hit her. She loved demonstrating a skill. *Careful...watch it...easy...easy.* She shifted her body to even the arc. *Concentrate. Don't get cocky.* She juggled a few more seconds, then quit while she was ahead, catching the glasses one by one.

"Wow," Dixon said.

She bowed, a faint surge of hope rushing through her. Life would go on. She would smile again, go on new adventures, learn new skills. Grief wouldn't take her down for good. "I took juggling during my circus adventure last year."

"You ran off with the circus?"

"I ran *to* the circus. Off-season. For training. I took juggling, trapeze, unicycle and lion taming."

"In a cage, with a chair and a whip?"

"That's the idea. The trainer was there, but it was still terrifying."

"Is that your criteria for an adventure? Terror?"

"That's part of the challenge, yeah."

"Feel the fear and do it anyway?"

"In the end, yes. The secret is going in prepared. I read,

talk to experts, take classes, and practice what I can. After that, it's mostly self-doubt you have to conquer."

He didn't seem convinced.

"The trapeze scared me more than the lion. Trusting a stranger to catch you?" She shivered at the memory. "It was so worth it. The thrill of flying. I gave the girls an indoor trapeze set for their birthday."

"I remember."

"Did they ever set it up?"

"Not that I saw." He seemed to be fighting a smile.

"What? You thought it was a bad idea, too? Howard's a worrywart. The girls are gymnasts, for God's sake. They know balance cold. I asked people on my blog about the right age for various skills."

"You trust anonymous posters?" His lip quirked again.

"They're not anonymous to me. They're very knowledgeable. One of them told me about a quick way to teach kids to ride a bike. You put them on a slight slope so the momentum keeps them from wobbling, and, boom, they're cycling. I'll teach the girls while I'm here."

Dixon didn't react to her words, and she suspected he didn't think her plan would work. She didn't want to argue about it, so she was happy when he peeled away the foil from the champagne and popped the cork. A mist of bubbles drifted out.

"It's weird to hear that pop and feel sad instead of happy," she said. "It's like when someone tells you a joke when you're crying. It hurts."

"Colorful way to put it." Dixon filled their glasses and handed her one.

The champagne glowed golden, looking almost magical. "What the hell, it's still champagne." She raised her glass. "Cheers."

"Cheers," he repeated, but he sounded sad, too.

Despite how bittersweet the moment was, Aubrey relished the bubbly sting and the warmth in her stomach.

"Shall we?" Dixon motioned toward the living room, and they returned to the sofa with their drinks and the bottle.

CHAPTER FOUR

"So, about the girls," Dixon said, getting right to the point.

Aubrey usually liked a direct approach to problems, but this was so important and so personal she wasn't ready. The room seemed to close around her. She needed air and space. "Could we talk outside? Look at the stars?"

"We should stay close in case the girls need us."

She blinked. "I didn't think of that." Her cheeks went hot at her thoughtlessness.

"No big thing. You're not used to dealing with kids. I've had to learn." He was trying to ease her embarrassment, but it didn't help. He seemed so far ahead of her. She decided to jump in. "Do you know if Howard and Brianna had wills?"

"I'm not sure." He thought for a few seconds. "We'll need to look through their papers. The funeral director mentioned that. We need to know what insurance they had, close out their bank accounts, deal with their bills, all of that."

"It's a lot to think about," she said, white noise starting up in her head.

"Tomorrow," he said, sounding daunted, too. "But I wanted to tell you that I'll raise the girls, so you don't need to worry. I live here. I work at Bootstrap. I'm familiar with their routines. It seems the most logical." He paused. "Do you agree?"

What he'd said made sense. Dixon had promised Ginger he'd stay forever, while the best Aubrey could offer was to stay as long as she could manage. Her plan before had been to leave Tuesday so she could do her Wednesday podcast, but if the ALT PR woman had set up a video podcast with a special guest, that could change.

Dixon was right, but some stubborn part of her wasn't ready to agree. She sipped at her drink to buy time. Now the champagne tasted flat, as if it had been left out open overnight.

Scout, ever her wing-cat, jumped onto the back of the sofa and curled around her neck to soothe her.

Why can't you take care of the girls?

There were practical reasons—she lived in a small apartment with a roommate, and she'd travel a lot more if she got the ALT sponsorship—but it was the deeper ones that bothered her more. *Because I'm not maternal. Because I don't have Brianna's heart. Because cancer lurks in my genes.*

She realized she'd let the silence hang too long. "That does seem sensible." But her voice sounded as heavy as her heart felt.

"Then we agree. I'll be the girls' guardian." Dixon sounded like he'd just saved a business deal he'd been afraid to lose. "This way there won't be any disruption in their lives."

"They lost their parents, Dixon. Their lives are totally disrupted." How would they cope? Would Dixon do the right thing? What if Aubrey would do better?

"Nothing says I couldn't work from Phoenix," she found herself blurting. "I understand there's an airport here." The joke came out flat. Why was she pushing this? Dixon had offered up his life for the girls, relieving her of any worry or obligation.

But that was the problem. She *should* be worried. The girls were her family, and she'd just handed them over. She didn't know everything Brianna wanted for the girls, but she wouldn't have wanted *that*.

"What are you saying?" Dixon looked as confused as Aubrey felt. "You travel a lot, don't you? How could you—?"

"Lots of parents travel. They hire nannies or bring the kids. They juggle their schedules." Her mouth was so dry her lips stuck together, and there was that blasted golf ball in her throat again. "And you're busy, too, Dixon. It's already crazy getting the agency going in the new place, and with Howard and Brianna gone, you'll be even busier."

"We'll adjust. The girls love the caregivers at Bootstrap. And if they have any problems, I'm right there."

Not racing reindeer in Norway. She got his point. Still…. "Have you thought about what a sacrifice this will be? You'll have no free time, no social life. You date, right?" There'd been the girlfriend at the girls' first birthday party, but he'd come alone to the last three.

"Not at the moment."

"Because you're too busy, right? Now it'll be worse."

Dixon sighed. "Like you said, people juggle their schedules."

"You shouldn't be the only one. That's my point. We have to be fair."

Everyone feels like that. You learn together. Brianna's voice in her head spurred her on. Scout began the tanklike rumble of her feline version of *you-go-girl*.

"What if we take turns?" she said. "You should start, since you know the girls better. I'll have time to get my schedule in order."

Her mind raced over what lay ahead. After the podcast, she had Primal Quest Camp the next weekend. It was a big deal to be chosen for the training for the premier adventure race in the West. ALT had been jazzed by how much visibility their products would get among elite outdoor sports people. Not long after that was Utah Adventure Fest, which would decide the ALT sponsorship once and for all. Sometime before that, she and her partner, Neil, had to schedule a trial run to shake down their equipment.

At the moment, all that effort seemed far away and totally beyond her. She felt like rabbits were jumping up and down on her diaphragm.

Dixon, meanwhile, filled his glass to the rim and topped hers, clearly preparing for a fight. He gulped half the glass—for courage?—then met her gaze. "I appreciate what you're trying to do. In theory, it sounds fair."

"But…?" She tightened every muscle, braced to defend her plan, herself, and the life she'd offered to share with the girls.

"But the girls are so young. They need people and places they can count on. They don't have the resilience to cope with musical-chairs parents."

"Musical chairs? Come on. Divorced parents work out shared custody and the kids do fine. They often thrive because they have the parent's full attention when they're with them."

"We're not their parents, Aubrey. They're not bonded to us. That builds over time as they learn we'll be there whenever they need us."

"And you don't think I can do that." Her mind jumped to the time Howard hadn't trusted her to babysit the girls.

"I didn't say that. Shared custody can also mean constant strife and confusion. I've seen it with friends, and hear about it with some of our clients."

"We won't be like that. We weren't married. We don't have built-up resentments. I live an active life. They need to see that, be part of it, learn to be open to new experiences."

"They're four, Aubrey. Give them a few years before they wrestle alligators or wing-walk a biplane."

"I'm not saying that. Don't exaggerate."

"You can be their role model without being their guardian. You'll visit a lot. Later on, you can take them on trips."

She stared at him, breathing hard, fighting to be sensible, to not make promises she might not be able to keep.

"Look, we're both upset," Dixon said, sounding suddenly exhausted. "We want to do all we can for the girls, but we can't get too ambitious, because if the plan flops, the girls will pay the price." His eyes searched hers for agreement. "My plan's easy. Yours is hard. How much of your schedule can you actually clear? Don't things change a lot?"

All the time. Even before the ALT endorsement was a possibility, she'd been swamped. When she wasn't on an adventure, she was planning one, or doing a podcast, booking guests, doing research, on and on. The simple promise she'd made to herself to visit more often would have been tough enough to manage without ALT in the picture.

And now she thought she could share custody?

The truth finally cut through her muddy thoughts. She was fighting Dixon out of guilt and ego, not in the best interests of the girls.

That was wrong.

The girls trusted Dixon. He knew them better than she did. He knew their routines. Aubrey could learn, but in the meantime, she would disappoint them, and they'd had more disappointment today than anyone should have in a lifetime.

"You're right. You should be their guardian," she said softly. "That's best for the girls. I'll stay as long as I can after the funeral." She'd see if she could slow down things with ALT. Maybe they could use an adventure race later in the year to test the sponsorship. "Like you said, I'll visit a lot. Take them on trips." *She would be a bright light, a shot of fun. She would open their eyes to the world.*

"I think it's the right thing to do," Dixon said, sympathy in his gaze.

So why does it feel so wrong? She felt like she was letting everyone down—the girls, her sister, herself. Embarrassed by her emotions, she jumped up from the sofa. "I need water. You?"

"No, thanks."

In the kitchen, she grabbed a water glass, then threw open the freezer door for ice. Spotting a bag, she tugged at it, which caused a casserole dish to fall out. Clumsy from exhaustion, she didn't get out of the way in time and the corner slammed onto her foot. Her instep and toes shared the brunt of the blow. She yelped as pain shot through her, grabbing her foot.

Dixon was there in a second. "What happened?"

"A casserole attacked me," she ground out.

"Let me take a look."

She started to hobble toward the kitchen table, but Dixon swung her into his arms like he had that night in Mexico. For an instant, she felt the same thrill, her pain erased.

Dixon carried her to the sofa and lowered her to the cushion. He sat and set her injured foot on his lap, then clicked on the high-intensity reading lamp on the side table. He touched her instep, which had puffed up and was turning purple.

"Ouch."

"Can you flex your foot?"

She did. "Ow. Damn. That hurts."

"Doesn't seem broken," Dixon said, then touched her big toe.

"Ouch. Stop. You have no bedside manner."

"It's hard to know with toes. I'll tape it and get ice for the swelling." He slid out from under her injured foot and went to the kitchen.

While she waited, their time in Mexico filled her mind.

It had been a cliché—the best man and maid of honor hooking up after the wedding, but he was hot and she was totally into it. He chased her along the beach until she turned for the water and ran in, gasping at the cold, totally exhilarated, high on the ocean, the moment, the man. They were both in their wedding clothes and she carried most of a bottle of good bubbly.

Once they were chest-deep in the water, she wrapped her legs around him and kissed him. He had generous lips that tasted of champagne and cold saltwater.

They kissed until she began to shake from excitement more than cold. "Let's warm up," he'd said in that sexy voice of his, but she had a better idea. She ran toward the cliff, taking the steep stone path to the rocky ledge where they'd watched skin divers perform the night before.

It was scary as hell up there. The water seemed miles away, but she refused to be intimidated. She dared him to jump with her, never expecting him to do it. He was a serious guy, totally responsible, like his brother, except better-looking and with some sense of fun. She'd managed to captivate him, and that was a total rush.

"We're drunk and we don't know the bottom," he'd said. He didn't even sound like a wimp saying that. He had guts, but wouldn't be goaded into proving it. That was very, very sexy.

When he winked at her, then jumped, she'd been so surprised, it took her a second to leap off, too. She pushed hard, running in the air to catch him, which was why she'd landed wrong, jamming her foot between two boulders near the bottom. She surfaced in agony, but hid it, proud she'd kept her thumb over the champagne bottle and hadn't spilled a drop.

Dixon saw through her smile to her pain, and carried her in his arms to her room, as effortlessly as if she weighed nothing.

DIXON RETURNED WITH scissors, tape, a stretch bandage and a Baggie of ice. He taped her big toe to the one beside it and wrapped the bandage around the ice bag on her instep. "Feel okay?"

"It's fine."

"It's the same foot, isn't it?"

"Yeah." The ankle had been weaker ever since Mexico, but she wasn't about to tell him that.

"I warned you it was too rocky."

"Come on. You didn't say *I told you so* then. Don't ruin it now."

"It was my fault you got hurt."

"It was all me. I was trying to catch up with you."

"Again, my fault." She liked his teasing tone. It reminded her of how he'd been that night. "Though hanging on to that bottle probably didn't help you."

"I wasn't about to waste expensive champagne."

"How did you manage that anyway?"

"Sorry. That's a trade secret."

He laughed.

She grinned, happy she'd amused him.

He examined her leg, which gave her a thrill, until she realized he was studying the scabs showing below her shorts. "What happened here?"

"I was in a reindeer race."

"You rode a reindeer?" His eyebrows shot up. It was fun to surprise him.

"You don't *ride* reindeer. Well, maybe Norwegian cowboys do, but in a reindeer race you wear short skis and the reindeer yank you down an iced-over trail. It's like a standing bobsled ride. Very intense. I've got the ice rash and bruises to prove it." She shifted to one hip, unzipped her shorts and showed him the spot.

"Ouch." A complicated look came into his eyes—sympathy, amusement and a wisp of sexual interest.

"The footage is on my blog if you want to see."

"Sounds dangerous."

"Scout would agree. She bailed on me a hundred yards in."

"Your *cat* was with you?"

"We don't call her Adventure Cat for nothing. She loves to move."

"And swim, right? Unusual for a cat."

"Scout is totally intrepid. I found her on a hike in Yosemite, not far from the highway. She was sick. Someone had dumped her. She was terrified, hissing at this goofy retriever who'd cornered her."

Dixon smiled.

"I nursed her back to health, and she's been glued to my side ever since. My readers love Scout stories."

"So what's your blog like?" The amusement in his eyes made her wonder if Howard had mocked her career to him. Not that it mattered. She knew the value of her work.

"There are tons of outdoor recreation blogs. My niche is women. My tag line is *ordinary girl on an extraordinary journey.* The idea is to show women they don't need to limit themselves. I talk about the scary parts and the mistakes, as well as the thrills and triumphs."

"Yeah?"

"Take the reindeer race. I shrieked and fell, but I kept going anyway. That's important for fans to see. Another time, I got lost in a Marrakesh marketplace, which is a very hinky place for a woman to be alone at night. I kind of panicked."

"Who wouldn't?"

"Maybe, but the point is that I shared that with my readers. If an ordinary girl like me can do it, anyone can."

"You don't seem ordinary to me."

Pleasure sang in her veins at his praise. "Your brother thinks I'm crazy."

Dixon didn't react to that, making her surer she was right about Howard's opinion. "You've tapped into a market if you can make a living at it," he said.

"I make enough from web ads to live on, but travel costs have eaten up my savings. But I got great news today. My meeting in L.A. was with ALT Outdoors."

"That's a big outfit."

"I know. And they're close to offering me a sponsorship, which I really need."

"Yeah?"

"If I can't afford to travel, I might as well hang up my kayak. An old blog is a dead blog. I need ALT to stay in business." She crossed her fingers, her stomach churning over all that was at stake. "They're looking to reach my demographic—single females, 18–35—so it'll benefit them, too."

"When will you know?"

"ALT's sending a camera crew with me for an adventure race in Utah next month. I'll use their gear and talk about it on camera."

"Do you have to win the race to get the nod?"

"We have to at least place. Last year, Neil and I took sixth. It's a challenging race, but not brutal."

"So you dumped the boyfriend you brought to the party? Rafe?"

"What? Wait. Neil and I aren't together. Neil's gay." She stared at him. She could tell by his tone he hadn't thought much of Rafe. "What makes you think I dumped Rafe?"

"Did you?"

"We broke up, yes. And it was my idea." Not that it was his business. "Why do you ask?"

He colored. "I don't know. You were different around him."

"How?"

"Subdued. Preoccupied, I guess. You kept tracking him."

"Hmm." So her concern had been noticeable. That trip had showed her they wouldn't work as a couple. An hour into the visit, Aubrey was having a blast with the girls when Rafe sent her a text from across the room: How much longer? He'd endured the visit for her sake, but he had no interest in her family, not even after a year of being a couple.

Rafe had never said he wanted to get serious, but they'd been so good together, had so much in common, she'd assumed that was where they were headed. She'd spun a cotton-candy story in her head—a sweet and fluffy cloud that melted to nothing the instant her tongue touched it. She'd felt like a fool.

"How'd he take it?" Dixon asked.

"Fine. We're friends." Aubrey, on the other hand, had been *devastated*. She hadn't realized how attached to him she'd been. It took her months to recover, scaring her so much she'd vowed to think long and hard before she got involved with another man.

Dixon watched her, reading between lines she'd prefer to stay invisible.

"What about you?" she asked. "What happened to the girl you brought to that one birthday party. She was a reporter. Bobbi? No. Tommi. I liked her."

"Tommi. Yeah." His eyes went soft.

She'd been pretty—dramatic features, dark hair—and mouthy and lively and ambitious. She'd figured Dixon would go for someone more settled, mature, sedate. *Boring?*

That wasn't fair, but it was kinda what she'd thought.

"So what happened?" she asked him.

"She wanted to work for a bigger paper. She's in Chicago now." His eyes flicked away. He'd been hurt by the breakup.

"You wanted her to stay?"

"Yeah." He smiled sadly. "We'd settled into a groove and I thought she was as content as I was."

He'd made up his own cotton-candy story. "That's kind of what happened with Rafe. I thought we had more than we did."

Dixon nodded.

"So you were serious about her?"

"Sure. I was thirty-one. It was time to get married and have kids."

"And now?"

"Now I'm thirty-four." He shrugged, but he was smiling.

"And you'll be locked down with the girls." She suffered a jolt of guilt for hanging on to her own freedom, while he got trapped.

"It'll happen when it happens. What about you? You plan to settle down?"

"Maybe. I don't think that far ahead." She didn't know how much time she had, after all. The countdown to breast cancer ticked away in her brain.

"What about a family?"

"I'm not the type," she said. "When we were little, Brianna played house and I played Lara Croft."

Dixon smiled. "People change."

"Not that much. I'm not built for it. Mom said I was like our father, who was a total outdoors guy."

"Outdoor guys have kids."

He wanted more of an answer, so she gave him one. "It's too easy to screw up with children. So much can go wrong."

"Life is risk, Aubrey," he said softly. "There are no guarantees."

"You're right. There are car wrecks and cancer." The harsh words burned like a brand. "I'm not as brave as Brianna." Her sister had been scared of cancer, but she'd married and had children all the same. *And look what happened.*

She swallowed hard, suddenly overcome by her sister's tragedy.

"I'm sorry. I didn't mean to remind you."

"It's okay. Everything reminds me."

She remembered the last thing her mother had said to her before she died. Her mother had pushed herself out of her morphine fog to look straight at Aubrey, fire in her eyes: *make your mark, Aubrey. Carry on for me. Don't hold back.*

Her mother had always claimed not to regret having had Aubrey and Brianna, but she'd given up the life she'd loved for them.

"How's your foot? Need an aspirin?" Dixon asked.

"It's fine." She thought about Mexico again, relieved to change the subject. "It was fine that night, too." She tilted her head, challenging him. "I didn't need an X-ray." Citing stats about untreated foot breaks, he'd wanted to take her to a hospital.

"Your ankle was the size of a watermelon."

"More like a large peach. I wasn't in that much pain."

"Correction. You couldn't *feel* that much pain, thanks to Tylenol 3 and champagne. That was a crazy stunt. I don't know why I did it." There was fondness in his tone.

"I do," she said. They locked gazes and the air tightened, holding them, suspended, not breathing.

"Yeah. That."

As if a starting gun had gone off inside her, sexual desire shot through her, like the adrenaline surge she experienced before a new challenge.

What was it about Dixon? He was not her type. He was serious, steady, careful…*boring.* It had to be the glint in his eye that said he could be tempted, that *she* could tempt him. Aubrey alone.

At that moment, she was glad to feel something besides sadness and exhaustion. In the back of her mind, cold shadows loomed—her sister's death, her nieces' fear and loss—but in the golden light of this room, with the sizzle of champagne in her veins, and this man looking at her *that way,* she was free of all that.

Behind the burn of desire in Dixon's gaze, she caught flickers of the grief waiting to ambush him, too, but for now, he was drinking her in, wanting her, and that sent a flare from her belly to her brain, lighting her up inside. They were in this together—playing hooky from hell.

The seconds stretched, their breathing loud and uneven. She shifted her wrapped foot to the floor and leaned closer to him, fingers reaching across the back of the sofa to touch his. "Why did you leave me that night? Really?"

"It was late. You were hurt. I was drunk." He paused.

"By the way, did you throw something at the door after I left?"

"Yes. The ice bucket. I was mad." She paused. "It was more than that, the reason you left." She'd seen it in his face.

He didn't answer right away, then seemed to see she wouldn't back down, so he spoke. "Earlier that night, I'd made a decision and I wanted to stick with it."

"What was it? To go celibate?"

Dixon laughed. "No. Howard asked me if I was happy. I realized I wasn't even close. I made plenty of money, but I didn't love my job or my life."

"You managed property, right?"

"Yeah. I ran some major office complexes. But what I did didn't *matter.* I spent my evenings and weekends hunting down distractions—parties, clubs, sports, women. I wanted more."

"So having sex with me in a luxurious suite made you feel like your life had no meaning?" She'd joked, but she was still hurt. His rejection had stemmed from a lecture from his judgmental brother.

Dixon laughed, a big boisterous sound that made her smile. "That didn't come out right. You were injured. You were being a good sport about it, but you were suffering. You could have been killed. That sobered me. We were following a script—best man and maid of honor hooking up after the reception—and it didn't feel right. I knew if I was going to change my life it had to start then." He blew out a breath.

"I should be offended, but I'm not." He'd gotten to the heart of it all. She *had* been playing a part, following through on her dare, and her ankle had hurt like crazy. "At least I was tempting," she said. "Even though I reeked of seaweed and had an ankle the size of a watermelon?"

"Are you kidding? Of course I was tempted. I hit the lobby and started back up until I realized the codeine had probably knocked you out by then." He studied her, his gaze heating up again. "I wanted you, Aubrey. Badly." His eyes settled on her mouth. "I still want you."

He gripped the fingers she'd extended and pulled her close enough to feel his breath on her face. Her heart was beating so hard her ribs hurt. Electricity and desire poured through her, washing away everything else.

Their mouths met. His lips were warm and firm, and he tasted of champagne again. All they needed to complete the memory was cold saltwater.

He braced her head, guiding her onto her back, still kissing her. Once she lay flat, his lips moved more urgently, his tongue seeking hers. Her head began to spin.

He broke off, pressing his lips against her throat. "What are we doing?"

"I don't know, but it feels like that carnival ride—the centrifuge? The one where you're plastered to the side of a drum and they drop the bottom and you know if they stop the ride, you'll hit the ground like a stone."

"So we want to keep going?"

"We do."

This was exactly what she needed—to get lost in the arms of a man who would meet her intensity with his own.

She lifted her hips against his erection. His eyes closed in response, and when they opened, there was fire there. He seized her mouth with his own, covered her with his body. They moved against each other, slowly, but hungrily.

Aubrey was totally lost in the moment when Dixon froze. He raised his head to listen.

She listened, too, and heard crying. One of the girls was sobbing.

Dixon sprinted for the girls' room. Aubrey followed, limping on her bruised foot, which throbbed again.

When she arrived, Dixon was sitting beside Ginger on her bed. "I want my mommy," she wailed, her cheeks wet with tears.

"I know you do," Dixon said. "I know you do." He clearly didn't know what else to say.

"You're a baby." Sienna's voice came from overhead, wobbly with emotion.

"No, she's not," Aubrey said, forcing words past the lump in her throat. "Crying gets out some of the sadness, like when you pop a blister. It's a relief."

Sienna's eyes gleamed in the dim light from the hallway. She was listening closely, desperate for help.

Aubrey had to say the right thing. If she expressed sympathy, Sienna might break down, which would make her feel weak and exposed. That had been Aubrey's experience after her mother's death.

"What you need is sleep," Dixon said. "You'll feel better in the morning."

"I'm scared I'll have a nightmare," Ginger whispered.

"You're too tired for a nightmare," Dixon said. Totally lame. Plus wrong.

"Nightmares aren't so bad," Aubrey said. "They're how your mind works out what scares you so you're not afraid during the day."

"Really?" Ginger asked.

Dixon looked at Aubrey, the same question in his eyes.

"I read that somewhere. Does it help?"

Ginger nodded and settled into her bed. Sienna sighed out a breath, telling Aubrey it had helped her, too.

Dixon and Aubrey said good-night and backed out of the room. This time, Aubrey remembered to leave the door open for the *line of light*.

"Where'd you get that bit about crying?" Dixon asked.

"I just said what felt right."

"I need to talk to Constance." He seemed totally at sea.

"Forget Constance. Speak from your heart, Dixon."

"That's the whole problem," he said ruefully. "My heart's not that smart."

They stood close in the hallway, but now a canyon had dropped between them. The girls had reminded them of their responsibilities.

"I should apologize for earlier," he said.

She raised a hand. "Please don't. You get to want sex. You're human. So am I." Still, it shocked her that only minutes before they'd been totally lost in each other. He'd walked away in Mexico because of a vow to make a better life for himself. This time it was to make a better life for the girls, and Aubrey agreed with him.

"Tomorrow's a big day," he said wearily. "Let's give the girls as normal a day as possible. We'll drop them at Bootstrap while we meet with the funeral director and the minister. I get them up about seven for breakfast."

"I'll be up early. I have calls to make." She had to talk to the ALT PR person about pushing back the sponsorship so she could stay longer.

"Good night, then." Dixon lifted his arms as if to embrace her, then let them drop.

She had to agree. Better to leave well enough alone.

She should write a blog post, but she didn't have the energy. She shared the good and bad, but she wasn't ready to share her grief. She climbed into her sister's bed, and found that despite the clean sheets, the bed was still her sister's. Aubrey burst into tears.

CHAPTER FIVE

YOU GET TO want sex. Dixon shook his head at Aubrey's take on the lust he hadn't been able to contain. It was Mexico all over again, where the sight of her lying on the bed in that wet dress, so transparent she was as good as naked, with an expression of pure desire on her face, had burned through his alcohol fog and lit him up inside.

It had taken all his willpower to resist her. Tonight, he hadn't even tried. The shock, strain and sorrow of the day had worn him down. Ginger's cry had served as the cold shower he'd needed.

What was it about Aubrey that grabbed him so hard? Probably the constant challenge in her eyes, the unspoken demand that he prove himself to her. Why? He had no regrets about the life he'd chosen. His work meant more than just a paycheck now. He made a difference every day.

Yeah, he was lonely at times, but he'd fix that eventually.

In the meantime, he couldn't stop thinking about kissing her, how it had blanked out everything but a white-hot need to get her naked. She'd been right about that spinning carnival ride. They didn't dare stop.

There had been more to resisting her in Mexico than he'd told her. Carrying her over the threshold, drunk and barefoot—their shoes God knew where—wearing ruined wedding clothes, he'd seen they were mocking the event they'd come to celebrate. Howard's words had rolled across his mind like a billboard: *what Brianna and I have is big. It's forever. It's so good to have someone to count on, thick and thin, someone to take care of, who'll take care of you.*

Dixon wanted that, too, he'd realized. And a year later, when he'd met Tommi, he'd thought she was the one. He'd been wrong—he'd projected his own happiness onto her. He wouldn't make that mistake again.

Now he could smell Aubrey on his clothes. That perfume she wore stayed in his head—sexy without even trying. Like the woman who wore it.

He was glad to hear she'd booted the ski bum from her life. He'd been too wrapped up in himself, hadn't paid her enough attention. She deserved a guy who knew what he had with her, one who returned her love in full measure.

A guy like you?

Not in a million years.

They had chemistry, sure, but that didn't mean they were good together. Chemistry had nothing to do with compatibility.

Aubrey seemed to see life as a battle she had to be armed to the teeth to fight. He wouldn't want to live that way, constantly braced for trouble.

Tommi had a similar attitude. She constantly tested herself. It wasn't enough to *be* great, she had to *do* great.

His reaction to both women was the urge to hold them, reassure them, guard them from their own doubts—a favor neither wanted, by the way.

Now he had two little girls who did need his comfort and protection. He kept seeing Ginger's frightened eyes. And Sienna, an angry soldier, hurting but unable to ask for help. Sienna was nothing like Brianna, who was as gentle as Ginger. Howard wasn't particularly stoic, either. He realized it was Aubrey Sienna resembled—in behavior, as well as features.

That might have been why Aubrey seemed to reach the girl so easily.

He'd been surprised at how readily she'd written off having kids. She would jump off cliffs, get dragged by reindeer, wander a medina after dark, but the challenge of having a family was too much for her.

It wasn't like he was any more equipped to be a parent than she was. *Howard, what do I do?* His brother had been great with people in emotional turmoil. Dixon had seen it at Bootstrap every day.

He's gone. You're on your own.

He braced himself against the doorjamb of the guest room to keep from being sucked down by more sadness.

Abruptly, Aubrey's advice about lion taming came to him. *The secret is going in prepared.* Okay, so he could do some research. Find out what the experts said about helping kids who'd lost their parents. The family computer and printer were in his room, so he did his web search there, finding several worthy articles.

Printing them out, he noticed the pages of Brianna's babysitting instructions. Handwritten at the bottom of the last pages were the words: *vital papers in bottom drawer of computer desk.*

The funeral director had told him he'd need death certificates for all their major accounts, so he might as well start figuring how many they'd need.

The drawer held a folder labeled *Important.* Inside, the first thing he noticed were two legal sleeves labeled *Last Will and Testament.*

So Brianna and Howard *did* have wills. The date was a month back, so they'd drawn them up before their trip. It had been the first time they'd left the girls for more than an overnight. It would be just like his brother to get wills together just in case. No one was more cautious and careful than Howard.

The wills would say who would be the twins' guardian. Dixon pulled his brother's will from the envelope sleeve and began to read.

"I WAS THINKING the Colorado race in August might be a better venue for ALT," Aubrey said to Tabitha Styles, the ALT PR rep, her heart in her throat. "Or that rock climb in Nevada. They're both smaller and—"

"We don't want small," Tabitha said, cutting her off. "We want big. Utah Fest is perfect." The treadmill made Tabitha's voice vibrate like she was very upset. Aubrey had called at five, knowing Tabitha hit the gym early to beat L.A. traffic. "There's the festival, too. Tons of people. I'm sorry about your sister. I really am. But it's Utah Fest or nothing."

"Okay," Aubrey said, sinking into the mattress along with her heart. She'd been up since four after a restless night.

"I know this is hard for you," Tabitha said. "I don't want to pressure you, but it took a lot of convincing to get Percy on board."

"It did?" Percy Moore was the marketing VP who would make the decision on the endorsement. Tabitha was a fan of Aubrey's blog, so she'd pitched the idea to Percy.

"Plus, the promotion budget gets locked down right after that. If we delay, the money's gone."

"I get it," she said. If she wanted ALT, she had to stick with the plan. She exhaled loudly.

"Down the line you'll be glad you did this. Think how proud your nieces will be of their famous aunt."

"They're only four."

"They'll get older. Once we get your schedule nailed

down, you can plan a visit. Kids are flexible. They adjust.
You can talk to them on the phone."

"I guess."

"If it makes you feel any better, I booked a studio for a
video podcast, and I scored a great guest. You know him.
Rafael Simón. The wing-suit flyer."

"Rafe? Oh." That surprised her. She hadn't seen Rafe
in nearly a year.

"It's so cool. He's bringing video of a wing-suit flight."
Gliding from a cliff in a suit with winglike fabric exten-
sions was spectacularly dangerous, but the closest thing
to real flight a human could experience. Rafe was among
the handful of people who had.

"We're lucky to get him," Tabitha continued. "He's been
grounded after a snowboard accident in Denver. We caught
him before he got booked up again. When I told him it was
your podcast, he got excited. So you're friends…?" She
dangled the question, clearly wondering if they'd been a
couple.

"We are. Yes." Though she hadn't heard he'd been injured. He wasn't big on email or phone calls. He kept up
with friends when he saw them at events or on trips, but
their paths hadn't crossed much lately.

"Does that cheer you up a little?" Tabitha asked hopefully.

"Sure," she said, but she hardly had the energy to get
out of bed, let alone do a podcast or even think about a
race. Maybe she should forget ALT and stay here with the
girls. Maybe by leaving she was running away.

*You need ALT to survive. With ALT, you can live your
dream. You'll influence more women, do more good.*

But she had two little girls right here to influence.

Make your mark, Aubrey. Carry on for me. Don't hold

back. Her mother's words rang in her head, followed by Brianna's refrain: *I feel like you're out there for me.*

Aubrey's head throbbed.

"Aubrey? Did you get that?"

She'd zoned out on Tabitha's chatter. "Sorry. What?"

"We need to do the video podcast on Tuesday instead of Wednesday because of Rafe's schedule. Also, I booked an early photo shoot with you and Scout at our flagship store. We'll need you here by 6:00 a.m. on Tuesday."

"Wait. I can't." She couldn't leave Monday. That was too soon.

"We've got the studio booked. You're on the corporate clock now. Time is money. I've already placed some ads. That should spike your numbers, which we need if we're going to get Percy fully on board."

"I can't leave any sooner than Tuesday. I'm sorry."

There was a long silence. The treadmill stopped and she heard Tabitha breathing hard, then paper rustling.

Finally, Tabitha spoke. "I can give you the morning if I shift the photo shoot to 1:00 p.m. The podcast isn't until five. Can you get here by then?"

If she left at dawn Tuesday morning, yes. "I can. Thank you." She could return to Phoenix on Wednesday. Except Friday evening was the start of Primal Quest Camp. So she'd drive there Friday morning. She'd commute. So what if these were eight-hour trips? She'd just have to handle it.

"We'll go with that," Tabitha said. "I probably sound like a heartless bitch about your sister. I'm sorry. I get obsessed with work at times."

"I understand." She got that way, too.

"Just think ahead to the exciting parts," Tabitha said. "We'll announce the sponsorship at the closing ceremonies at Utah Fest...*after you win.*"

"We might not win."

"You'll at least place. But I have a good feeling about this. I think you'll win."

She was nowhere near as confident. Tabitha's voice seemed to come to her from far away. Nothing was real at the moment.

"One last thing," Tabitha said. "I wouldn't get into your sister's death on the blog. Let's stay upbeat, okay? Focus on your podcast and Primal Quest and Utah Fest, okay? Is that bad? Heartless? I don't mean to be."

"No. I get it." And she didn't want to bare this pain to her readers. Not yet anyway.

"I know this is tough, Aubrey, but you're the bravest woman I know.

"I don't know about that." She had to get off the phone. The pressure was making it hard to breathe. "We'll talk later."

She felt wiped out—exhausted, flat, as if she'd been run over by a truck. When was the last time she'd felt this way? *When Mom died.*

She knew what was going on now. She'd sunk into depression—grief's best friend. Depression made you dull-witted, bored and restless, robbed you of energy, and stole even the simple joys from your life.

Fight it. You have to. Be depressed on your own time.

It was close to six. Dixon woke the girls at seven for breakfast. She should get up, make coffee and do breakfast. It should be something special. *Face pancakes!*

On their birthdays, their mother used to make faces with banana slices for eyes, raisins for the mouth and coconut for hair and eyebrows.

Thinking of the girls' delight gave her the pop of energy she needed to get up and get dressed. She was heating the oil for a test batch when Dixon came into the kitchen. He glanced around. "What exploded?"

"Pancake batter. I forgot the blender lid. I'll clean it up."

"You've got some in your hair." He moved close and pinched a lock of hair between two fingers, sliding off the dough. Coffee steam filled the air between them, along with the scent of oranges and coconut; it was like a tiny tropical vacation right there in the kitchen. Desire tugged at her the way Dixon tugged on her hair. The instant it hit Dixon, he stepped back, breaking the connection so fast she thought she heard a pop.

He held up two fat packets with envelopes clipped to each. "They made wills, Aubrey. I found them in the desk drawer." He gave her Brianna's—her name was typed in fancy script on the sleeve. "Wow," she said. The attached envelope bore Aubrey's name in Brianna's handwriting.

"Do they list the guardian?" She was suddenly breathless, her heart in her throat. Had they chosen Dixon?

"Read it." He sounded calm, so she assumed they had.

Aubrey unfolded the pages, which crackled in her trembling fingers. She skimmed over the legalese, her gaze locking on the space where the guardian's name had been typed in. *Dixon J. Carter.*

Aubrey stared at the words, then looked up at Dixon. "It's you."

"Like we figured," Dixon said.

"Right." So why, deep down, did she feel disappointed? *So stupid.* Brianna would never have asked the impossible of her. Her sister would never set her up to fail.

"You okay?" Her expression seemed to puzzle him. "Maybe read the letter. Howard wrote me one, too."

Aubrey tore open the envelope, her fingers damp. The letter was on yellow legal paper in Brianna's even script.

Dear Aubrey,

Just a quick note about the "wills" since we're heading out the door to Tahoe in a jiff. Howard read in a magazine that couples should be sure their wills are up-to-date before they travel. Honestly. The odds against the two of us dying at the same time are huge, as I pointed out to him, but you know Howard "You-Can't-Be-Too-Careful" Carter. If I had a dollar for every time he said that, well, let's just say we'd be flying by private jet to Tahoe, ha, ha, ha.

If you're reading this, however, now that I think about it, it means the worst thing ever has happened. We're gone. Oh, my. That is sobering. In that case, I want to explain why we chose Dixon as the girls' guardian. I'm sure you already know, but I want to be absolutely clear about it.

First, let me apologize for how melancholy I sounded on the phone the other day. I'd gotten the official wills in the mail and it made me sad, thinking about how small our family was. I do want to get serious about finding our grandparents. We'll talk when you get here.

I hope you don't think when I asked if you were happy, that I didn't believe you were. I do. I'm totally proud of you and totally crossing my fingers about the sponsor.

And, obviously, you wouldn't be able to raise the girls. You have your exciting career to pursue! With all your travel, you could never juggle pediatrician visits and soccer practice and buying school clothes and packing lunches. Our life is full of routines and you are not a "routine" person.

Dixon lives here. He loves the girls. He's over here constantly. He sees them at Bootstrap every day. It would be an easy shift for him to take over for us. He's a good man. I know something weird happened between you two at the wedding, but I trust him and you should, too.

That doesn't mean I don't want you to spend more time with the girls. I do! They need to know their "Auntie Aubba" better. You know what it's like to not have a mother, so you'll know what to say and what the girls need.

And also…if I thought for *one* minute that you were ready to settle down and have a family, I would have written your name in that open space for guardian in a heartbeat.

Now here's a secret. My dearest hope for you is to one day experience the joy and wonder of being a mother. You'll be a great one. I don't care what you say. Maternal is as maternal does.

Maybe you're like our father in some ways, but you were a mother to me after Mom died, so never doubt yourself. I know I bitched about all the trips and the sports you dragged us into, but you saved me from sinking too low.

If it's about the cancer—that you might die young like Mom—if that's what's holding you back—stop that right now! I mean it. None of us knows how long we'll live. We have to have faith and hope and go after our dreams. I dream that one day your children will play with their cousins Sienna and Ginger.

Oops! Howard is calling me. Gotta run.

One last thing. I know you'll miss me, but remember how it was with Mom. She's always in our hearts. I'll always be in yours.

Love,

Your twinster, Brianna

P.S. There's some good stuff in this letter. I should always write on the fly. When we get back from Tahoe, I might let you read it anyway.

As Aubrey finished reading, the paper was shaking so hard in her hand that she could hardly see the words. She blinked back tears, fighting the sting in her nose and the ache in her throat. She would not cry. Not now. In private.

"What did she say?" Dixon said, looking worried. "Is it bad?"

"No. It's good. She explained about you being guardian and other personal things." Her sister had made it sound reasonable and right for Dixon to take over, as long as Aubrey spent more time with the girls.

"What did Howard write to you?"

"The same kind of stuff." But he was holding something back, she could tell. She didn't want to push for more. It was private, after all. "So now we know what they both wanted," he said.

"Right." And Brianna wanted Aubrey to have a family. Aubrey felt a little heartsick. The idea seemed so distant, so impossible. How could Brianna ask it of her?

"You sure you're okay?" Dixon seemed never to miss a mood change.

"It's just sad, that's all." *Enough wallowing. Stick to logistics.* "I should tell you that I'll be leaving early Tuesday. ALT booked a photo shoot and a video podcast that afternoon. I'll be back the next day. I'll need to be in Yosemite by Friday night for a training camp. But after that, I think I'll be free until a trial run for Utah Fest."

"You can't be driving back and forth like that, Aubrey. You have obligations. We'll be fine."

He almost sounded...*relieved.* Like he wanted her gone. That bothered her. A lot.

"The kitchen's all messed up."

Sienna's voice made Aubrey and Dixon turn. The little girl's hair was snarled, her face pillow-creased, her eyes sleep-soft.

"What do you mean mess? This is a face pancake extravaganza." She gestured toward the plates with decorative items.

"We have cereal for breakfast," Sienna said.

"Not today. Today you get to make faces in pancakes with bananas and raisins and coconut."

"I hate coconut," Sienna said. "And Ginger hates raisins."

"So orange slices and maraschino cherries. Or marshmallows and pretzel sticks. You choose." Sienna remained suspicious, but she watched as Aubrey poured batter into the pan. The smell brought back warm memories for her. She hoped it would become one for the girls.

Dixon strode off to get Ginger, returning with the sleepy girl braced against his hip. "Look at this. Your aunt wants you to make faces on pancakes."

That seemed to wake Ginger up, and soon they were all sitting down to heavily decorated pancakes.

Sienna took one bite of hers, announced the oranges were sour and pushed her plate away. Ginger had used too many cherries and spit out her bite. Aubrey and Dixon did their best to eat the cluttered, too-sweet cakes the girls had made for them.

Breakfast had taken too long, so they had to hustle to get the girls dressed, their teeth brushed and backpacks loaded with toys, snacks and extra clothes, while the girls whined and dragged their feet.

In the van, driving toward Bootstraps, Ginger said, "Tomorrow I'll put Cheerios and M&Ms on my pancakes."

"That was a one-time deal," Dixon said.

"No, it isn't," Aubrey said. "We can have them every day while I'm here."

"How many days?" Sienna asked.

"Four," Dixon said too quickly. He'd done the math. He was counting down the days until she left.

"Five if we count today," she corrected.

"Why do you have to go so soon?" Ginger asked.

The question was like a stomach punch.

Dixon glanced at Aubrey, concerned for her feelings it seemed. "You know why. Your aunt lives in L.A. She has a job there."

"She does 'ventures," Sienna added with a sigh.

Aubrey couldn't find words.

"That's right," Dixon said, filling in the silence. "She just got back from a reindeer race. Tell them about it, Aubrey."

"Was Santa there?" Ginger asked.

Relieved by the change of subject, Aubrey smiled at her in the rearview.

"They weren't Santa's reindeer, but Norway is pretty close to where he lives. The reindeer pulled me on skis and we went very fast."

"Wow," Sienna said

"Wow," Ginger echoed.

Dixon shot her an encouraging smile, so she kept talking. "I choose adventures that might seem scary or hard to girls, but after I try them and write about them, they want to try, too. They see that all it takes is practice and determination."

"I want to go on adventures, too," Sienna said.

"I'm glad to hear that, because we'll *definitely* have adventures together." Aubrey felt a surge of tenderness and hope.

"When you're older," Dixon threw in, reminding her of

Howard, putting away their bikes, taking back their helmets and hiding the trapeze set.

"Everything is when we're older." Sienna fell back against the seat.

"It depends on the adventure," Aubrey said, shooting Dixon a look. "One adventure could be trying your rollerblades on the playground at the elementary school or learning to ride your bikes."

"That's too scary," Ginger said. "We could be injured."

"Not if we get helmets and pads," Aubrey said, "and practice safely."

"Maybe another time," Dixon said. "We've got a lot going on. No sense frightening them."

"I'm not frightened," Sienna said.

Aubrey thought it through. They were pretty shaky already. Learning to skate, they'd definitely fall, and they'd want their mother to soothe their owies, for sure. Maybe it was too soon to learn a new skill.

How will they survive without you, Brianna? How can any of us?

On the other hand, exercise boosted serotonin, which was good for depression. Without knowing the science of it, Aubrey had instinctively kept herself and Brianna active with sports and trips after their mother died.

Physical activity would help the girls fight their sadness. "Taking a walk or a hike can be an adventure, too," she said. "We can go to your favorite place after that."

"Bucky's Pizza Palace?" Sienna said. "They have an arcade and you get tickets for prizes."

"Bucky's! Yay!" Ginger added. "It's our favorite, favorite place."

"So that's where we'll go after our walk," Aubrey said.

"Can we get pepperoni?" Sienna asked.

"Pepperoni makes me upchuck," Ginger said. "I want plain cheese."

"We'll do half and half," Aubrey said.

That seemed to satisfy both girls. Dixon stared straight ahead, not reacting to her plan either way.

Aubrey would make the most of the short time she'd be here with the girls. She would ask her fans for ideas about adventures appropriate for different ages. That would be a fun post.

She felt better after that, steady enough to face the funeral planning after they dropped the girls off at Bootstrap Academy.

Dixon pulled into a strip mall and parked in front of a two-level office building. It was older, but well maintained and freshly painted. The girls jumped out, backpacks on, and ran for the door.

Aubrey started to get out of the van, but Dixon touched her arm. "I know you're trying to help, but the girls need time to absorb what's happened. They don't need to be constantly entertained."

Hurt zinged through her. She was hypersensitive from lack of sleep and emotional overload, but she heard Howard's disdain ringing in Dixon's voice. "You mean they need time to mope and sulk, dwell on how sad they are? They're only four, as you reminded me. They're not going to go Zen over losing their parents. Distraction is useful."

"They also need to learn to cope with grief, so they're not afraid of it. Here." He reached under his seat and held out a folder. "I did some research last night and printed this out for us."

Inside the folder were pages and pages about kids and grief. "We know the girls better than any experts," she said.

"Didn't you say being prepared is the secret to your adventures?"

She couldn't even bristle. The guy was quoting her back to herself.

"You can read through it while I touch base with my assistant," he said.

"Okay." She tucked the folder under her arm. Dixon was ahead of her at every turn—with the funeral, with the wills, with the girls. He was clearly the right choice to be their guardian.

Dixon sighed, not reaching for the door.

"What's wrong?"

"I'm not looking forward to going in there."

"No?"

"They'll all be worried. So am I. Howard and Brianna were the heart of the place. How do you replace a heart? I'm just the business manager."

He climbed out of the van before she could respond. She had no idea what to say. She hadn't thought about how the deaths would affect Bootstrap. Poor Dixon. She hurried to catch up with him. "This seems like a good location," she said, trying to stay positive.

"It is. It's on major bus routes. I got a great deal on the lease. We're finishing up the build-out now."

Inside the office, the lobby held a roped-off clothes shop and a small library where a young guy wearing a work belt was setting up computers.

"Looks like Rex got the shelves done," Dixon said. "That's our career library. Clients can do job searches on the computers. We signed up with some databases. I keep the job bank going."

"Sounds helpful."

"That's the idea. Let's check on the girls."

He led her to a glass-walled area to the left of the hall, the rooms brightly painted, filled with tables and play areas. The girls were already playing. A petite black woman, fiftyish, noticed Dixon and stepped into the hall.

"I'm so sorry, Dixon," she said, her dark eyes full of compassion. She wore a batik dress and matching scarf, which held back short dreadlocks.

"Thanks, Grace," he said, accepting her hug. He turned to Aubrey. "This is the girls' Aunt Aubrey. Grace manages our day care."

"You're Brianna's sister. I see the resemblance," Grace said. "We're so sorry she's gone." She pulled Aubrey into a quick, reassuring embrace. "I'm sure the girls are happy to have you with them."

"I hope they are."

"How are they doing?" Grace asked Dixon.

"Ginger's clingy, Sienna's pissed. They didn't eat much breakfast, but we packed snacks. I hope they behave for you. You have my cell if anything comes up. I'll be back this afternoon."

"We'll keep them occupied, don't worry."

"Nice to meet you," Aubrey said.

They turned to go. Through the glass of a room down the hall, she saw a dozen people of various ages and ethnicities filling out papers. A tall woman with curly red hair stood at the head of the table.

"What's happening there?" Aubrey asked.

"Constance is giving skills assessments. We get people at all levels of education and experience. They come from rehab, bankruptcy, a long illness, sometimes prison."

"Brianna told me some stories." They'd been heartbreaking.

As they turned to go down the hall, the kid who'd been working on the computers approached. "I'm ready to start that mosaic, Mr. Carter."

"Right. Grab the broken tiles out back."

Rex's face lit up. "I'm on it." He set off at a run.

"I asked him to do a mosaic for the front wall. Now I've got to figure out how to pay him for the work. He's a good kid. He dropped out of college when his dad lost his job to be sole support for his family."

"That's hard."

"Yeah. I've been trying to keep him busy. Howard warned me not to live every client's troubles or I'd burn out. But you have to do what you can."

"Of course."

"Howard had so many plans." He swallowed, then cleared his throat. "My job was to handle the business details so he and Brianna could work their miracles. Now I've got to keep the place going."

A Latina headed toward them, eyes locked on Dixon, message slips fanned out in one hand. "The phone's been ringing off the hook," she said, but when she caught Dixon's expression, she closed her fingers around the slips. "I'll do some triage."

"That'd be great, Maggie."

Dixon introduced her to Aubrey as his "wonder of an assistant." Maggie blushed. She had a kind face and eyes that didn't miss much.

"Give me fifteen minutes to scope things out with Maggie," Dixon said.

"I've got reading material." Aubrey held up the folder Dixon had given her, then headed for the career center to read what the experts said about handling grief in young children.

CHAPTER SIX

IN THE CAREER CENTER, Aubrey noticed a woman in a wheelchair looking through a guidebook, a young girl at her side. Had she been injured on the job? Was she sole support for her daughter?

Bootstrap Academy was a lifeline to people in trouble. As much as Howard annoyed her, she respected what he and Briana had built. The tragedy of their deaths rippled outward, affecting so many people. Aubrey's stomach hurt thinking about the burden on Dixon. He had all this, plus the girls to care for. Guilt burned through her again. How could she help?

She wasn't a teacher or a social worker. She knew nothing about job placement or social service programs.

You know about fighting for a dream.

But her dream was a luxury. She hadn't had to struggle to survive like the people here. They humbled her.

You give women courage. You get emails from people who changed their lives, improved their futures because of your example.

Much of the battle, no matter what you strove for, was internal—self-image and self-confidence. To change, to move past fears and obstacles, you had to have guts, discipline and tenacity.

The difference Aubrey made was quieter, but it still mattered, and it meant everything to her.

She sighed, then reviewed the printouts Dixon had given

her. They were about how to talk about death, what to do about the funeral, reactions and behaviors based on the developmental level of the child.

Dixon had highlighted some lines: *be consistent, establish routine, reduce disruption as much as possible. Let them know life is predictable, not chaotic.*

Dixon probably thought her running back and forth from California would be upsetting to the girls. Would it be? She wasn't sure.

When Dixon finished, they headed out to the van. Tension rolled off him like heat from a summer sidewalk.

"Is it bad?" she asked tentatively.

"It's not great." He spared her a glance. He looked hunted. "We got most of our funding on the strength of Howard's reputation. I'm finishing up the renewal application of our main grant. If we don't get it, we're dead."

Bootstrap Academy was in trouble. Her heart jumped into her throat. "I didn't realize things were so dire."

"In a small agency, it's always dire." He gave her a quick smile, clearly trying to ease her mind, but the tendons in his neck twisted like cable filaments. "We'll figure it out." He squeezed the wheel like he was trying to stop the bleeding. "I'll hire two social workers and take on Howard's executive tasks. Constance can pick up some of Brianna's workshops in the meantime. Maybe we'll get counseling interns from ASU."

"If anyone can save the place, it's you, Dixon."

He shifted in his seat, clearly uncomfortable with her praise. "If we go down, we'll go down fighting. I promise you that."

She felt foolish, like a cheerleader waving ragged pompoms in the face of a battered team down six touchdowns. "If I can help in any way—make phone calls, run errands or—"

"There's noth... seemed to catch him...

She wasn't giving... dle things at home—m... that need to be filed. Th... instead of going to day ca...

"I'm sure you have thing... at her, dismissing her. *Just l...*

"You can't do it all, Dixon...

He waited until he'd braked... answer, turning in his seat to face her, his... s deeply shadowed. "There's no need to jump th ough hoops to make up for leaving. For all our sakes, I'd rather you didn't."

It was like he'd shoved her away, arms stiff as rebar, and the blow reverberated in her bones. *Keep your distance. You don't belong here.*

"You want me gone," she blurted. "You're counting down the days."

"No. But the more involved you get in the girls' lives, the harder it will be when you leave. They've already lost their parents. Losing you will likely be a setback. I don't look forward to dealing with that on top of everything else."

Aubrey sucked in a breath. She saw his point. "So the less I do, the less it will hurt when I leave. I get it." The idea set up a pulsing pain in her head. "Next week is kind of hectic, but after that I should be able to visit longer."

"Maybe give us a few weeks to settle into a routine. Two months? I want to reduce their misery as much as possible."

Are you nuts? How dare you? She wanted to smack him for thinking he could keep her away from her nieces. *He doesn't mean to hurt you.* He was as foggy, lost and sad as she was. He wanted what was best for the girls.

't sure what it was. Put her on a
ke trail and her instincts were golden.
rust herself. But she didn't trust Dixon,
as leaning on web experts, for God's sake.
me, Brianna. Tell me what to do.

They need to know their "Auntie Aubba" better. Her sister's words strengthened her resolve. "I intend to be a regular presence in the girls' lives, so don't think I'm going to disappear."

"Of course not. That's not what I'm saying."

"They need to know I'm there for them, even if it's only over the phone. I'll call every day while I'm gone. Before bedtime. We can use Skype so we can see each other, and they can see Scout."

He considered that. "That sounds okay. As long as it's predictable. That's what the experts say they need."

"What they need is people who love them and tell them so." That much she knew cold. *They needed family.* That's what Brianna wanted, too. Aubrey decided right then she would seek out her father's family as soon as she could. If she had to hire a private investigator to find them, she would.

THAT EVENING AFTER the girls were in bed, Aubrey opened her laptop to write a blog entry. She was so *tired.* Her mind was a blank white wall. *Strange.* Her blog always flowed, natural as talking, totally open. Not anymore.

Write something. Anything. Don't let people down. Write about the girls maybe.

That got her going:

> *Hey, Team Extreme, I'm visiting my nieces right now. They are darling. Adventure girls in the making, fo' sho'.*

Her false cheer made her cheeks burn. *Adventure girls?* Right now they were frightened orphans. But she made herself face forward, think of the future, after the grief had faded. She kept writing....

So, tell me, you brilliant adventurers, what age should my nieces be before I take them far and wide on outdoor adventures? They're four. My sister and I camped at that age. Started skiing at six, if I remember right. They live in Arizona, so they swim. What do you think? When can they kayak, rock-climb, scuba dive? Enquiring future adventure girls want to know....

This just in—exciting news about this week's podcast. It will be video—yippee—thanks to the good folks at ALT Outdoors. My guest will be the incredible Rafael Simón, wing-suit flyer extraordinaire....

She rattled on about Rafe, then signed off, promising to respond to comments later in the morning. She rubbed the back of her neck, which had tightened and twisted as she typed. She wasn't sure she'd ever fall asleep.

AUBREY SAT BOLT upright in bed, breathing hard, grasping for the wisps of the dream she'd been having. They'd been in a car. Brianna had been laughing. Aubrey had seen the semi bearing down on them and had been screaming through thick glass to warn her sister.

Air hit the sweat that drenched her skin, and she shivered. Squinting at the clock, she saw it was after midnight. Her mouth was dry, so she went to get water from the kitchen.

As she passed the laundry room, she caught movement. Sienna stood on a step stool shoving sheets into the washing machine and sniffling, her pajama bottoms different from her top. *She wet the bed.*

"Sienna?" she said, coming into the room.

The girl jerked and glanced at her, then continued pushing the cloth into the machine. "They need cleaning," she said, slamming the lid.

"Let's run the washer tomorrow. For now, can I help you put on fresh sheets?" She didn't want to embarrass Sienna by mentioning the reason. "It's faster with two people."

Sienna considered the offer solemnly, finally nodding assent. She led the way to the linen cupboard, where Aubrey found a set of daisy-covered twin sheets and a mattress cover she was glad was rubberized.

In the bedroom, the light from the hall showed Ginger lying on her stomach, thumb near her open mouth, breathing soft and slow.

Sienna climbed onto the top bunk and crawled over to tuck in the far side of the sheets. Aubrey handled the rest. When they'd finished, Aubrey whispered, "Want to pee before I tuck you in?"

"I don't have to pee." Her face crumpled. "Not anymore."

"It's no big deal, sweetie," she said, her heart clenched in sympathy. She pulled the covers up to Sienna's chin and smoothed them. "Sometimes you sleep so deeply you forget where you are. I once dreamed I was in the bathroom, but I was walking in my sleep and I peed in our mother's closet." She hadn't thought of that in a long time.

"You did?" Sienna's eyes were wide, her voice breathy with relief.

"I did. You've heard of a sleepwalker? I was a sleep pee-er."

Sienna's laugh was sharp with surprise.

"It wasn't funny when your mother told all our friends."

"My mommy did that? That was mean, huh?"

"It sure was. Sometimes sisters tease each other. You know that."

She nodded, blowing out a big breath as she turned on her side to face Aubrey instead of the wall. "I miss Mommy," she said in a bewildered voice.

Aubrey kept her voice level and calm. "I know you do." She ransacked her weary brain for a thought to loosen grief's grip on her sweet niece.

Find the right words. Ease her pain. Comfort her.

Mentally, she flipped through the lines Dixon had highlighted in all those articles. Nothing came to her.

Speak from your heart. Maybe she should take her own advice. "You remember that Grandma Hanson died a long time ago? She was your mom's mother and mine, right?"

Sienna nodded.

"We were older when it happened—eighteen—but it still was terrible to go through. We were both so sad we didn't think we could keep on living." Her voice clogged, but she cleared it, forcing herself to continue. Maybe this story was too adult for a four-year-old, but it was what her heart told her to share.

"The world seemed all wrong, everything was screwed up. I felt sick inside, like my bones were breaking, my muscles ripping. Noises seemed too loud. When Brianna crunched the ice in her lemonade, I wanted to scream. And I was so mad. All the time. At everyone."

"You were?" Sienna's gaze was glued to Aubrey's face.

"Furious. I was mad at people who felt sorry for me, at my friends who still had their mothers, at kids in grocery carts whining for candy instead of hugging their moms. Little things upset me—a mosquito bite, a stain on my dress, all the stupid food people brought because they felt sorry for us."

"Like Ms. Wilder does?"

"Exactly. Except we got Jell-O salads. We hated Jell-O with a purple passion."

"Mommy says it's too mushy-gushy."

"Exactly. We threw one bowl over the back fence and it broke into pieces. We just laughed, even though the lady who made it would want her bowl back. We didn't care."

"You didn't?" Sienna asked.

"Not one bit."

"Did she get mad? The lady?"

"We never told her. She never asked for the bowl. It was wrong, but we were so upset we weren't thinking right. When someone dies who is so close to you it's like they're part of you, you react in a bunch of ways—your feelings get tossed in the washing machine like those sheets— crying, laughing, getting mad, feeling like a baby again even."

"Like Ginger sucking her thumb?" Sienna asked.

"Like that. Yeah." *And you wetting the bed.*

"I keep forgetting Mommy won't come back."

Tentatively, Aubrey put her hand on Sienna's back and rubbed gently, the way Aubrey's mother used to do. The long hugs Brianna loved were smothering to Aubrey. She sensed Sienna felt that way, too.

"That's what grief does," she continued. "Grief grabs you where it hurts the most. I know it feels like it won't ever let go, but it will. I promise. I still miss my mom, but when I think of her, I don't feel empty or scared or lost anymore. I feel full and warm. Now I always have her with me right here." She tapped her chest. "And here." She tapped her temple. "You will, too. We both will. I miss your mom a lot."

"You do?"

"Oh, yeah. It's that old grief after me again."

"It will go away?"

"In a while. You have to wait it out."

Sienna nodded, staring at Aubrey, her eyes shining with gratitude.

Aubrey wanted to wrap her arms around the little girl, hold her tight, and swear, swear, swear she'd never let anyone or anything hurt her ever again. But she couldn't promise that. *Life is risk. There are no guarantees,* as Dixon had pointed out.

She kissed Sienna on the cheek, tucked her in and said good-night. In the doorway, she looked back at the girls—Ginger curled up on the bottom bunk, Sienna on her back, easing into sleep—and her heart squeezed so tight she put a hand to her chest.

Something Howard once said came to her. It was just after the twins were born and he was holding one, while Brianna held the other. In an anguished voice, he said, *what were we thinking, bringing two people into the world whose pain we'll feel more strongly than our own?*

His tender trepidation had endeared him to Aubrey.

In answer, Brianna had smiled, her face glowing, her voice as sure as sunrise. *Isn't it amazing?* Brianna had been intrepid in her own way.

That had to be partly why Howard loved her so much. She had enough faith for both of them. Aubrey's love for the girls was a pale shadow of her sister's, but she would give them all she had.

DIXON STOOD IN the hall listening to Aubrey and Sienna talking. He'd heard voices and come to check on the girls. It sounded like Sienna had wet the bed.

It had been a tough day for all of them. He and Aubrey had spent the morning going over funeral details, giving each other numb looks of horror as they chose casket upholstery, lead lining, flower sprays, stands, and toppers, what to engrave on the markers, on and on. The meeting with the minister was even more overwhelming.

When he'd collected the girls from day care, he found Sienna in time-out for hitting a boy and Ginger curled on a nap cot sucking her thumb.

When they'd gotten home, Aubrey had dragged energy from somewhere and entertained the girls with a game she called *Toxic Swamp,* which entailed crossing the house without touching the floor by jumping from chair to couch cushion to table.

Listening to her talk to Sienna now, he was awed by her wisdom. She'd voiced some of his own feelings, but in a way that Sienna could understand. For a moment, he wasn't so sure he was the right person to raise the girls. Here he was looking up advice on the web, leaving frantic messages for Constance, while Aubrey jumped in and said what was in her heart.

He was clearly clueless when it came to emotions. Take what he'd said to Aubrey in the van—basically *don't let the door hit you on the butt on the way out.* What the hell was wrong with him?

The truth was it wasn't just the girls who would suffer when Aubrey left. *He would miss her.* The house would be emptier than it already felt without Howard and Brianna.

It was ridiculous. She'd only been here two days. But she filled up the place. She had fire and life and personality. She'd juggled champagne glasses, for God's sake. He never knew what she'd do or say next.

At the wedding, he'd seen her as a party girl, but she had far more depth.

Worse, he felt close to her. The sexual connection was bad enough, but now he sensed an emotional bond, and that was no good.

He wanted to be with her. He knew it wasn't real. It couldn't be. It had to do with their situation, with the roles they found themselves in, like at the wedding, only this time it was a funeral. On top of that, they were the girls' only family, not counting his mother.

Whether they wanted it or not, when it came to the girls, they were acting like a couple—giving them baths, fixing their meals, putting them to bed, talking over how they were coping. It was hard not to start believing they were together.

He was so lost in thought, he missed when Aubrey told Sienna good-night. Before he could slip away, she appeared in the doorway. "Dixon?" she whispered, pulling the door nearly shut behind her.

"Yeah. I heard voices...." He was embarrassed that she'd caught him lurking in the hall.

"We woke you?"

"No. I was awake."

"How much did you hear?"

"Most of it. Sorry I eavesdropped." He hadn't meant to be a creep.

"Did I do okay?" She didn't seem to mind that he'd listened in.

"You did great."

"It seemed to help her." She smiled, relieved.

"I never know what to say to Sienna," Dixon said. "She puts on such a tough front."

"That's to protect herself from the hurt. You have to step back, put up a barrier or it's too much to take."

"That's what you do? She's like you?"

"Evidently." She shrugged.

"She looks like you, too, you know. You have the same hair, same blue eyes, same piercing stare."

"Piercing, huh?" A smile flickered.

"Like a pair of bright blue searchlights."

"That's Sienna, for sure. Brianna always said she was relentless. Maybe I am, too."

"That can be a good thing. Anyway, you handled her very well. Hell, you made *me* feel better."

"I'm glad. I mostly feel useless. You're so on top of everything. I'm tossing and turning all night, feeling sorry for myself, while you're looking up grief in children."

"I'm not even close to on top of things," he said. "Take what I said about you leaving. That was all wrong. I was rude. You should call every day like you said. The girls can tell you all the ways I screwed up and you can make it right." He forced a smile that seemed to snap rubber bands in his cheeks.

"I wish the girls knew me better. It's my fault, I know. I've been so wrapped up in my career, building my blog. I didn't visit enough. Brianna missed me, but she never said anything. She didn't want to slow me down." Tears swelled in her eyes and she blinked them back.

"I thought I had more time, you know?" She searched his face, as if he could somehow fix this. "My plan when I drove out here was to tell her I'd be visiting more. I had all these trips planned in my head—sister trips, trips with the girls. My anniversary gift was an adventure trip to New Zealand for her and Howard. I was going to watch the girls." She was wringing her hands, as if to twist off her fingers. He couldn't stand to see that, so he took her hands in his. They were ice-cold.

"Even if you were here every day, Aubrey, you'd want more time. I do with Howard." He rubbed his thumbs over the back of her hands.

She shook her head, which made tears spill down ace. She scrubbed her cheeks so hard she likely left bruises. "I dread leaving, having to say goodbye." Her voice broke.

"I know." He felt the same, and not just for the girls' sakes.

She gazed at him, tired and sad and hurting. "There's no way to make this easy, is there?"

"Not that I can see, no." Words gathered in his throat. *Don't go. Stay here. Help me with the girls, especially Sienna. Be with us. Be with me.*

He couldn't say that. She had a life far from here. They'd made a solid plan. They'd both be better off sticking with it.

"Good night, then," she said softly, staying right there.

"Good night," he answered, not moving, either.

Then, as if someone had shoved them, they crashed into each other. She was soft against his bare chest, warm, very warm, the fabric of the top she slept in thin as tissue, her arms strong around him, fingers digging into his back, palms hot.

He tightened his hold on her, fingers half on her skin, half on the cloth, assuring her that he had her, that he wouldn't let go. He pressed his face against the top of her head, breathing in her heady scent. Her heart thudded against his own, a greeting too long in coming.

His body reacted, wanting her beyond reason. His brain went fuzzy, good sense dropping away like the bottom of that carnival ride. She released a ragged breath, and they shifted positions, bodies a perfect fit. They were the calm center of a raging storm, clinging to each other, surrounded by tossed branches, bitter rain and whipping wind.

In a few days, they faced the funeral, saying goodbye to the two people they loved above all others. It would be terrible, soul-shredding, but for now, they held each other, safe in this moment.

He leaned back to look into her eyes. She met his gaze with fire and certainty. She wanted him, too.

He bent, swept her into his arms, and carried her to his room, trying not to think or doubt, trying to enjoy the moment for all it was worth.

Practical tasks slowed him down—pulling back the covers, laying Aubrey on the sheets, asking about protection. She was on birth control, so they didn't need a condom. That time gap allowed doubts to rise. *This is a bad idea. It will lead to pain. You'll want more and that won't happen.*

As if reading his mind, Aubrey lifted her face to kiss him, and desire roared back like a tidal wave, drowning every doubt.

You get to want sex, she'd said.

Yeah. We get tonight. We'll face tomorrow tomorrow.

He slid his hands beneath her sleep shirt, pushing it up, and she raised her arms to help him. Bared to the waist, she took his breath away. He wanted her with every pulse of blood in his veins, every harsh breath he drew into his lungs. He cupped her breasts. They were firm, but soft, too—impossibly soft—and their pink tips tightened at his touch. He had to taste. When his lips made contact, she gasped in pleasure, and when he ran his tongue over the surface, she shivered beneath him.

He wanted *inside.* He wanted to feel her move around him, he wanted to thrust into her, deep, to chase the relief she'd made him burn for, to give her what she craved, too.

He slid one hand down her belly to her shorts and inside the waistband, to find her swollen and wet and silken to his touch.

She lifted her hips, offering herself, inviting more. He slipped his finger inside her, then out, then again. She writhed against him, gasping for air. She reached inside his boxers and gripped him, sliding her fist slowly up and down.

He wanted to tell her how good that was, how good she felt to him, but his mouth couldn't shape the words. All he had was want and need. Her face was lit with desire, her eyes glowing like blue fire.

She shoved his boxers down and he did the same with her shorts. When she opened her legs for him, he slid into her in one hard thrust.

They both gasped with the shock of sudden pleasure. She locked her heels on his backside, digging in, as if to force him as deep as he could go.

He stayed still, wanting to feel it all, the heat, the softness, the way they held each other, connected below. He wanted it to build, and it did, until the urge to move was inescapable.

They rocked back and forth, holding each other's gaze, while their bodies worked, limbs and hips, each stroke, each touch of his shaft to her swollen spot bringing a cry from her lips, each squeeze of her inner muscles making him groan in sweet agony.

She tightened, went still, then gave a sharp cry as her eyelids closed and she shook wildly. Her climax sent him over the edge, and he emptied himself into her, getting lost in the weightless rush, the miracle of release.

When it was over, he felt like he'd traveled for miles to a place where he could finally rest. After a few seconds, he noticed that Aubrey's shoulders were gently shaking. *She was crying,* not making a sound. "Aubrey?" he said softly.

"I'm sorry," she gasped. "I don't know why I'm crying."

"Go ahead. Let it go. I'm right here."

She nodded, then dropped her cheek to his chest, allowing the tears to fall, while he ran his hand down her back in a way he hoped comforted her.

After a few seconds, she raised her face and wiped her cheeks. "Better," she breathed.

"Good."

"This was good for us."

He could only nod, hoping it was true, and drew her down to his chest. She released a happy sigh. He gave himself over to holding her, breathing in her sweet musk, tasting the salt of her skin, feeling the weight of her on his chest, her leg between his, letting his mind drift, his thoughts distant puffs of clouds. When she left a few moments later, disappearing like the dream she'd been, he buried his nose in her pillow, refusing to feel stupid about it, and let the sweet scent lull him to sleep.

AUBREY BRACED HERSELF against the hall wall outside Dixon's room, dizzy from the wonder of what they'd done. Had it been as good as it had seemed? Never before had she been so relaxed, so natural. She hadn't worried about the pace or if she was pleasing him or if he was about to stop doing something she liked. It had just *flowed*. It had been *right*.

And she'd had to force herself to leave. They'd given themselves this moment in time, not letting second thoughts interfere. *Quit while you're ahead.* She knew that was the proper ending.

She pushed off the wall and walked on jelly legs to her room. Despite her wise conclusion, her thoughts raced. *There's more here. You want more.*

Get a grip.

You're doing it again. Like with Rafe. You made up a fantasy that the two of you were more than good sex partners and travel companions.

This with Dixon was worse, of course, because of all

they shared—the girls and their sorrow. *If you were together, you could raise the girls, be a real family.*

It would never work. They lived too differently, they wanted different things. Dixon wanted a woman who would be there every day, not one who had her bags packed by the door for the next trip.

As unlikely as it was, she knew her blog could fizzle or she could lose interest in traveling or coming up with challenges for herself.

All she had to go on was her life now and it did not fit with Dixon's or the girls'.

Still, it had been so lovely lying in his arms. She'd felt complete, calm, at home, safe from harm.

Safe from grief. That's what was really going on.

In Dixon's arms, she'd forgotten her sadness, and so had he. As she well knew, grief followed you wherever you went, including bed.

They'd had their moment. If they tried for more, someone would get hurt. Possibly the girls. And they'd suffered too much already.

CHAPTER SEVEN

THE NEXT MORNING, Aubrey found Dixon at the coffee pot. When he turned to her, their gazes met so fiercely she swore she could hear electricity crackle in the air between them. The swoosh of lust nearly dropped her to the floor. *Let's go to bed. This is too good, too right, to give up.*

Golden flames flickered in Dixon's eyes, telling her he agreed. His lips parted and he tilted his head, as if ready to kiss her.

An alarm went off deep inside. *It won't work. Don't risk it. Be smart. Be safe.* This time, she was the one to back off. She said what had to be said. "That's over. We need to go on from here."

There was a breathless few seconds, when she thought he was going to disagree, say something important, a game changer. But all he said was, "Right."

She turned for coffee to hide the stupid disappointment inside her. Instead, she thought about the day ahead. She was taking the girls out for some fun followed by pizza. She was making happy memories, she hoped, that would help them through the funeral the next day.

The girls woke up cranky and quarrelsome, not a good sign, but Aubrey made face pancakes anyway. The girls picked at the food and each other. Dixon left for Bootstrap and Aubrey let the girls watch a little educational TV while she did some work.

First, she handled her blog. The responses to her question about adventuring for the girls were a little confusing:

They're never too young. I put skis on my nephew at three.... My sister backpacks with her two-year-old.... Let them try. They'll let you know what's too much.... Wait until they express an interest. Don't push them. I fell out of a raft when I was five and was afraid of water for years....

She thanked everyone for their ideas, then posted her news:

Scout and I are chomping at the bit to get to Utah Adventure Fest. Three weeks. Can't wait. Check here for video of each day's events. Cheer us on to victory—or at least to a top finish. Prep training will be tight this year. I've had some personal issues. Don't want to get into it now, but I'll do my best to be the ordinary-to-extraordinary girl you want to hear from. Exciting news coming up, gotta keep it on the DL for now.

She reminded everyone of the podcast, then logged off. After that, she touched base with Tabitha, scheduled a drop-in with Neil to plan their trial run, called three possible podcast guests, then did some online research. She had to stay on top of trends and was always on the lookout for activities that would be challenging, but doable, and interesting to her fans.

While she worked, flashes of the previous night popped into her head, distracting her. Dixon's mouth on hers, the look on his face when he came, his hand stroking her back as she cried, as if it were completely okay. The magic stayed with her. She wasn't sure if that was good or bad.

When she finished working, she searched online for an easy hiking trail for the girls, then came across an ad for an indoor trampoline park. Talk about a fun way to get exercise! The girls would love it.

Except they didn't.

Older kids dominated most of the net-separated trampolines, and the girls were intimidated by the size and noise.

"Come on, I'll jump with you," Aubrey said, grabbing them by the hand and leading them onto one of the height-restricted trampolines.

"You're too tall," Sienna protested. The ruler was clearly marked at four feet.

"Shh," she said, finger to her lips. The employee monitoring the tramps wasn't looking their way. She started with a low jump. Soon, the girls smiled, and jumped higher. A few seconds later, Ginger was squealing and Sienna giggling.

Aubrey grinned. *It's working. They're having fun.* Then the monitor spotted Aubrey and motioned her out, whistle at her lips. Aubrey nodded, released the girls' hands so the guard wouldn't blast the whistle and mortify the girls.

Unfortunately, her abrupt move off-balanced the twins and they crashed into each other. Ginger's mouth hit the top of Sienna's head. Ginger's hand came away from her lip with blood, and she shrieked. Sienna howled, clutching her hair.

So much for that.

Aubrey helped the girls out and they got Baggies of ice from the first-aid area. "You made us crash," Sienna said to Aubrey, tears in her eyes.

"I know. I'm sorry."

"You said it would be fun," Ginger said. "It was the

opposite of fun." They were overreacting, she knew, because they were so emotionally shaky. A tiny setback became the end of the world. She hated that she'd made them feel worse.

"You still up for pizza at Bucky's?" she asked.

Both girls nodded solemnly. Ice bags firmly in place, they trudged to the van and Aubrey put the kiddie playlist on the iPod, typed the address of the pizzeria into the GPS and headed off. The girls took turns rejecting songs, and Aubrey missed a road because she couldn't hear the GPS over the music. She swore under her breath.

"She's doing it again," Sienna said. "She's sucking her thumb."

"No, I'm not," Ginger said.

"Yes, you are. You're lying. Your thumb is all wet."

In the rearview, Aubrey saw Ginger kick her sister.

"Ow. She kicked me, Aunt Aubrey."

"You're a tattletale."

"Girls, please. Don't fight." The GPS voice said something, the girls were yelling, and she didn't notice the light was red until she was almost in the intersection. She slammed on the brakes, panic zinging through her. A horn blared. Her brain just about popped. "Stop fighting. We almost crashed!"

The girls gasped, eyes wide with terror.

Crashed...like their parents. What was wrong with her? She'd made them remember their parents' wreck. Nausea climbed her throat. "I didn't mean that. We won't crash. I'm driving very carefully. It was the noise. I'm sorry."

The girls sat stock-still the rest of the way, Sienna worriedly watching Aubrey's every move. Aubrey could only hope the delights of Whack-a-Mole and pizza would override the memory of their aunt threatening them with death.

DIXON LEFT WORK early to be home for supper with the girls. His mind spun with all he'd left undone, but the girls needed to know they could count on him to keep up the routines.

It felt like the roof was caving in on him at the agency. He'd missed two key appointments on Howard's calendar and a job fair on his own. He'd have to hit the ground running on Monday. The United Way director had to consult the board about giving him an exemption on the meeting required to qualify for a grant.

Even with Constance taking some of Brianna's workshops, they'd had to cancel several, which could send clients on a final downward spiral. Where did you go when your last chance failed you? His gut clenched.

At least he'd consulted with Constance about the girls. She'd agreed that they needed a predictable environment, and that it might be best if Aubrey didn't visit until they were more emotionally settled. Aubrey would be disappointed, but she'd do what was best for the girls.

And for you?

He pushed away that thought, along with the dreamy wash of happiness that poured over him whenever their night together slipped into his mind. Standing at the coffee pot that morning, he'd almost swept her into his arms and back to bed. Thank God she'd shut him down.

Constance had also offered to counsel the girls. Dixon felt guilty accepting the offer, considering the pressure on Constance to double her workshops, but he was grateful. Everyone at Bootstrap wanted to help. They were a family. That, too, worried him. Now his employees' faces would join the faces of the clients that kept him awake at night.

He would not let them down.

And if you do? And if you don't get that grant?

His clenched gut churned. He needed some heavy-duty

antacid when he could find time to hit a store. *What now, Howard?*

Dixon was the money guy, but his knee-jerk response to trouble was to go to Howard, who'd been there for him when his parents had brushed him off like cobwebs in an attic. Dixon's love had had no hold on them. He'd been devastated to realize that. Howard had saved him. Howard had loved him no matter what.

Now Howard was gone. The solid ground beneath Dixon's feet had cracked wide-open. *You're alone.*

That core-deep loneliness must explain why he'd made love to Aubrey. Maybe they deserved sex, but it hadn't helped him. Now he knew how it felt to be with her, inside her, feeling the warm silk of her, hearing her cries of pleasure.

He'd felt good…really alive…like he belonged with her.

An illusion, he knew.

It would be tough when she left, but better in the long run. He had all he could handle with Bootstrap and the girls. The last thing he needed was a useless longing for an impossible relationship.

Been there, done that with Tommi. Near the end of their relationship, at a party with reporter friends, he'd seen her eyes light up when she heard about openings at other papers, and he knew he would lose her. Not a month later, she'd said yes to the job in Chicago before he'd even known she'd had an offer. *If I could stay for anyone, it would be you, Dix.* She couldn't. His love wasn't enough to hold her. He'd wished her well, but he'd been torn up. Hell, he'd been tracking homes for sale near good schools, thinking ahead to the family they would have.

There were plenty of smart, interesting women who wanted the kind of life he did. He'd find one eventually. In the meantime, he'd steer clear of free spirits—though his heart was racing and he was smiling as he pulled into the garage, eager to see Aubrey again. She was a guilty pleasure.

He got out of the car and loped for the door, peace washing over him, warm as sun on his face. He was *home*. His family was inside. Fake, of course, but he was tired and worried enough to take any relief he could find.

Aubrey had spent the day having fun with the girls, so he knew he'd return to three happy females, who'd escaped sadness for the day.

He entered the kitchen, smiling in advance, to find the girls throwing Legos at each other, red-faced and irritable, cheeks streaked with what he first thought was blood, until he saw the pizza box. *Tomato sauce.* Aubrey sat at the table, her face gray with exhaustion. Scout crouched on the back of the sofa, braced to flee.

"Uncle Dixon!" Ginger threw herself at him. He lifted her into his arms. "Sienna's being a bully."

"Ginger upchucked all over Bucky's," Sienna proclaimed. "It was gross. Kids screamed. We had to leave, so I didn't get my prizes."

"The little merry-go-round upset her stomach, I guess," Aubrey explained sheepishly.

"I *said* no pepperoni," Ginger said.

"I ordered half cheese, but they screwed up. It was too crowded to reorder and the girls were starved." Aubrey seemed to need his forgiveness.

"Sienna cut my lip with her head. See." Ginger peeled down her lower lip to show Dixon teeth marks lined with blood.

"Ginger gave me a dent in my skull-bone," Sienna said. "It was cuz Aunt Aubrey broke the trampoline rule and made us bump heads."

"And we almost had a car wreck," Ginger said softly, her eyes wide.

"I explained that, remember?" Aubrey said quickly, her face now pink. "The girls were arguing, the music was too loud and I had to slam the brakes. We weren't in any danger, Dixon. I swear. I said the wrong thing." She looked totally bereft.

He had no idea what to say. Emotions zinged every which way, and he wanted to duck behind the sofa. "Did you thank your aunt for taking you out?" he finally asked, realizing too late how lame that was. Both girls hung their heads.

"Why should they? It was miserable," Aubrey said. She seemed to see how confused he was and took charge of the moment, forcing a smile for the girls. "We'll do better next time, won't we?"

"Can we go tomorrow to get my prizes?" Sienna asked.

"Tomorrow's the funeral," Dixon said.

"After the fun'ral."

"People will come to the house then. Also Grandma Carter will want to spend time with you." His mother would fly in late tonight.

"Grandma Carter squeezes too hard," Ginger said. "We want to have fun with Auntie Aubba."

"Then we'll have fun on Sunday," Aubrey said. "All of us and Grandma Carter."

"Church is on Sunday," Sienna said.

"After church," Aubrey said.

"That's too short," Sienna said, cranky panic taking over.

"We have Monday, the next day," Aubrey said hopefully.

"And the day after that?" Ginger asked.

Aubrey sucked in a breath, looking at Dixon.

"That's when Aubrey leaves," he said.

"But you've hardly been here any days," Ginger said.

"I'm sorry, but I have to be back in L.A. I'll call to say good-night every night. We'll use the computer camera so we can see each other and Scout and—"

"I don't want a computer camera. I hate computer cameras." Ginger burst into tears. Sienna ran down the hall, Ginger on her heels.

Aubrey looked at Dixon, desolate. "Maybe I should come back on Wednesday after all."

"Constance agrees that you should wait a couple months until the girls are more settled."

"Constance? She's not God, Dixon. We have a say here, too." Anger sparked in her eyes.

"I know that. You can see how upset they'll be when you leave. You want to put them through that twice in five days?"

Aubrey looked away, her hands in fists, her muscles taut. "I get what you're saying. I guess it's for the best."

What's for the best is for you to stay. Screw your blog, your adventures, your sponsor. The girls need you. I need you.

The thought made him feel weak and lost, which was not useful. "It is for the best," he repeated firmly, trying to convince himself, as well as her.

As HE LEFT the podium, Dixon glanced at the mourners who filled nearly every pew of the church. Brianna and Howard had been well loved.

He'd managed to talk about his brother without breaking down. Thank God for Aubrey, whose steady gaze had given him strength, even when he looked at the girls, so small and sad, their legs dangling inches from the floor on the front bench.

Now he pulled Ginger onto his lap and put his arm

around Sienna. It was only the girls, Aubrey and himself in the family pew, since his mother had missed her connecting flight out of Chicago last night. She'd been furious that Dixon wouldn't reschedule the service, but she would meet them at the house for the reception.

Now Aubrey made her way to the dais. As she stood at the microphone, light from the stained-glass window lit her face and turned her hair to copper.

She inhaled a shaky breath. He knew she was nervous. When she locked eyes with him, he made a pinching motion. She'd said if she started to cry, he should pinch her.

She smiled at the sight, and stood taller, calmer because of the reminder. He was glad he'd helped her. She'd done a lot for him.

She'd been a rock with the girls, getting them dressed, showing them how to play cat's cradle, tucking paper and pencils into her purse so they could draw if they wanted. She'd promised the girls that after the funeral they could cry or scream or yell or run around the block.

Can we throw a casserole over the fence? Sienna had asked.

Absolutely, Aubrey had declared.

She'd warned Dixon to brace himself for lame remarks. *I almost punched the minister when he said that God took Mom because he needed another angel.*

She began to read, the paper shaking in her hand. "My sister liked faces on her pancakes, bumblebees, baby quail, and fresh pack on a diamond slope." She swallowed, blinked, then continued. "She liked stained-glass windows, bath salts, thrillers with no blood, fairy tales, roller coasters and tapioca pudding, though she hated Jell-O because it was too wiggly."

Light laughter rose from the mourners.

"Brianna laughed hard, listened close and she hugged

you so tight you could hardly breathe. She never quit smiling, not even when our mother was dying of cancer."

Aubrey's eyes shone with love and tears and memory. Dixon teared up, too.

"She sat up with Mom when the pain kept her awake all night. She wasn't afraid of Mom's pain or our sadness. She wasn't afraid of anything. She was bigger than me, a stronger and better person than I will ever be." Her voice cracked, and she made herself stand taller, then looked at the girls.

"Girls, your mother was a wonder, and she loved you more than life itself. She's with us always. Here—" She touched her heart. "And here." She tapped her head. She lifted her gaze to look out at the full chapel. "Thank you all for coming to honor her."

She'd done a great job. Dixon had squeezed a few words about his brother over a knot the size of a tangerine in his throat, but nothing as poignant and personal as what Aubrey had said.

Dixon brushed a drop of water from the program on his lap, puckering the part that held the quotation Aubrey had chosen—her mom's favorite, she'd said: *boats are safe at harbor...but that's not what boats are for.*

That summed up Aubrey completely—challenging herself to push past fears, steer her brave boat through any storm. His heart swelled with pride and affection, and more that he didn't dare name.

"You up for this?" Dixon said.

Aubrey peered up at him, grateful for his sturdy presence at her side near the front door. "I'd better be. They're all on their way." Guests would be arriving for the reception any minute.

"It's almost over," he said, a hand to her back. "Soon we'll be tossing casseroles over the fence."

She smiled, grateful again. All through the funeral, their eyes had met in mutual support. When she'd written her speech, he'd listened to her talk about Brianna and held her while she succumbed to tears. It was bad enough she was attracted to him, but now she felt connected. He was a good guy. Solid. Warm. Kind. Any girl would be lucky to have him.

Any girl but her, and she didn't dare forget that.

"Brace yourself. Here comes Lorraine," Dixon murmured.

Through the window, Aubrey saw Dixon's mother pay the cabdriver, then head up the walk. She wore an elegant black suit and a short-brimmed hat.

When she reached them, she spread her arms and said dramatically, "I finally made it!" She offered Dixon her cheek for a kiss. "I hope my bags make it to the hotel. I paid that driver enough he should unpack for me and iron everything. I wish you hadn't been in such a hurry with the funeral, Dixon. The rush totally *shattered* me."

"You were supposed to be here last night."

"You know how tight connections are these days." Dixon had told Aubrey that his mother had a habit of missing flights. She refused to be rushed.

He reached into his pocket and held out a CD case. "The service is recorded here. We can watch it together if you'd like."

"I guess that will have to do." She took a breath, ready to say more, but Dixon spoke first. "Mom, you remember Aubrey? Brianna's sister?"

She turned to Aubrey. "Of course. We talked at the wedding. I'm sorry about your sister. She was a love and so devoted to those girls. God needed another angel, that's all I can say."

Aubrey almost laughed. Dixon's mouth twisted, fighting a smile. Aubrey had warned him someone might say that, and it had turned out to be his own mother.

Lorraine addressed Dixon. "I can't believe Howard is gone. He was our rock. Now we're all alone in the world."

"That's hardly true," Dixon said. "We have friends. We have the girls. There's no point making it sound worse."

"I feel things deeply, Dixon. I'm not stoic like you." She turned to Aubrey, smiling politely. "What is it you do again, dear? You're a travel agent, right?"

"No. I travel, but—"

"She does adventure races and reports on them online," Dixon explained. "She has a popular blog."

"Yes, blogs are all the rage these days. Do they pay much? Never mind. Now you'll have the insurance settlement."

"The insurance settlement?" What was she talking about?

"That money's for the girls, Mom," Dixon said. Dixon and Aubrey had gone through all the financial papers and figured out that the couple's life and car insurance would provide decently for the girls through college.

"But you'll be managing it for them." Lorraine was still looking at Aubrey. What was she getting at?

"I didn't have the luxury to quit work," Lorraine continued. "When your husband abandons you, you have to make your way in the world on your own." She sighed. "Even with money, being a single mother is not easy, I must warn you."

With a jolt, Aubrey realized what Lorraine meant.

"I'll be raising the girls," Dixon said quickly, shooting Aubrey an apologetic look. "Aubrey's going back to L.A."

Lorraine blinked at him. "But the girls need a mother."

"They need a parent," Dixon said. "They'll have me."

Lorraine smiled uncertainly. "I'm sure that will be fine. There are plenty of Mr. Moms these days." She faced Aubrey. "If your career is important to you, by all means stick to it. That's what we all worked for, isn't it? Women being equal to men."

"It seemed the most sensible," Aubrey said, her throat so parched it burned to swallow. "Dixon lives here. I'll visit, of course."

That sounds so lame. Like a divorced father making grandiose promises when he planned to escape to Barbados. This was the first time she'd explained the situation to anyone, and her cheeks flamed. She usually didn't care what other people thought, but somehow, because it concerned Brianna, this bothered her.

Before Lorraine could comment, Brianna's friend Rachel reached the porch, the first of a steady stream of arrivals, and Aubrey was relieved when Lorraine went inside. Rachel threw her arms around Dixon. "I'm so sorry."

"We're fine. Thanks." He pulled away, clearly not wanting a fuss, and motioned at Aubrey. "Rachel, you remember Aubrey?"

"Of course. We met at the girls' parties. Brianna talked about you all the time. She missed you so much—" Her gaze flickered, and she changed tack. "Anyway, your talk made me miss her even more." Her face threatened to crumple, but she gathered herself. "The girls are so lucky to have you." She glanced up at Dixon, her smile warmer, lingering. "And you're lucky to have a nearby babysitter. Dixon is great with the girls."

Aubrey felt like she'd been punched in the stomach. Rachel assumed that Aubrey would raise the girls, too. She couldn't speak.

"I'll be taking care of the girls, Rachel," Dixon said, thankfully covering for Aubrey's silence. "It makes the most sense. Aubrey's in L.A. She travels for her blog. She's about to get a sponsor, which is a big deal…." He glanced at Aubrey, who still couldn't speak.

"Oh, of course," Rachel said, clearly flustered. "I'm sorry. How stupid of me. I didn't realize…."

"It's in Brianna's will," Aubrey finally blurted. "Brianna wanted me to keep going with my career." She wasn't helping herself at all.

"Well, there you go!" Rachel said brightly. "Brianna was so proud of you. And she would want the best for everyone. Of course, I'll babysit whenever you need me, Dixon."

"Thank you. For now, could you keep my mother company? She's in the hat at the bar. Her name's Lorraine."

Aubrey saw that his mother was accepting a glass of wine and making the bartender laugh.

"I'd be happy to." Rachel touched Dixon's arm and gave him an intimate smile. "Anything else you need, let me know."

Hmm. Had they dated? Aubrey experienced a stupid stab of jealousy. As if her emotions weren't already tangled enough.

"Sorry about that," Dixon said quickly, before the next group reached them. "My mom's clueless and Rachel's clumsy."

"It's a natural conclusion. I'm her sister. Women raise children." She tried to smile, to act like it didn't matter, but she still felt off-balance, like the floor had tilted.

"Who cares what anyone thinks? We're doing what's best for the girls."

"You're right." Parenthood wasn't for everyone. And there was the breast cancer issue. Ghoulish as it seemed, if Aubrey died, the girls would only lose an aunt, not a parent.

A number of people from Bootstrap arrived together and gathered around Dixon to offer their condolences. Grace, the day care manager, spoke to Aubrey, her dark eyes full of compassion. "You holding up okay? This must be overwhelming, all these strangers."

"Everyone has been kind." Her cheeks ached from smiling so much, and nervous perspiration trickled down her sides.

"After we're gone, you have yourself a nice glass of merlot and close your eyes. Maybe play that song on the tape you played for us. It brought tears to a lot of eyes, let me tell you."

In Brianna's *Stuff to Save* box, Aubrey had found a cassette tape of a practice they'd done for the fifth-grade talent show. Brianna had played the piano while they'd sung Stevie Wonder's "You are the Sunshine of my Life," Aubrey's tentative alto supporting Brianna's ringing soprano. Aubrey had always loved the sweet purity of Brianna's voice, so she'd had the tape played at the funeral.

"That little spat you two had at the beginning was cute. I could just see it."

Not so dramatic, Brie, Aubrey had complained. *It's Lincoln Elementary, not Star Search.*

It says forte, so there. Brianna's obsession with the rules had driven Aubrey nuts when they were young. "I wanted the girls to hear that we argued, but we were best friends, too."

"Very smart." She squeezed Aubrey's hands, the affection steadying Aubrey, restoring her balance. "The girls did a good job at the church," she added.

"I think it's not quite real for them."

"It'll be up and down for a while. You know we've got

your back at Bootstrap. Maggie's circulating a sign-up sheet for driving the twins to their classes. Dixon needs every minute to save us." She smiled, but there was worry in her eyes. She moved away, replaced by a blonde in a clingy black dress holding a casserole dish. "Should I put this in the kitchen?" she asked Aubrey.

"I'll take it, thank you," Aubrey said.

"You're Brianna's sister. I'm Belinda Wilder from next door. I couldn't be at the service due to my job, so I took my lunch break to stop by to support Dixon."

"How kind of you."

"Anyway, this is my special cranberry chicken. Gets raves. Set some aside for yourselves." She winked. "And if you need help moving in, I'll be happy to pop over on the weekend."

Moving in? Her stomach twisted again. "I won't be moving here. Dixon will be taking care of the girls." She left it at that, too tired to recite the excuses. Besides, Belinda had caught Dixon's attention and he moved closer.

"So I hear you've become a single dad," she said.

"It made the most sense." He glanced at Aubrey, *sorry* in his eyes.

"One of these nights, we'll let Jessica watch the girls and I'll take you to a movie to forget all this. Jessica would be here now, except she's the star of her volleyball team."

"I'll be fine, Belinda. Thank you, though."

"I'll keep the meals coming, no worries." She patted his arm. "You're a saint, Dixon."

She waltzed off, swaying her hips, clearly hoping Dixon was watching. Jealousy struck Aubrey again. What the hell was wrong with her? It had to be because they'd slept together. Wasn't there a bonding hormone that kicked in after sex?

"Good lord," Dixon muttered. "She doesn't quit."

"She wants us to save some of this for later." She lifted the cranberry casserole.

He groaned. "I've got to get her to stop doing that without hurting her feelings."

"You could keep tossing them over the fence or buy a deep freeze."

"You're not being helpful."

"Sorry. I'll set this out. Maybe the guests will gobble it up. It gets raves, she says." She was glad she'd managed to joke.

People had finally begun to leave when Aubrey found herself staring out the kitchen window at the girls sitting on the swings of their cedar play set talking to Constance.

Dixon came up behind her.

Aubrey glanced at him. He looked exhausted but he had a smile for her and it warmed her.

"I'll be glad when this is over," he said. "You were right. People don't know what to say. Mostly they need us to make them feel better."

"I almost burst out laughing when Lorraine gave the angels line."

"My own mother." He shook his head, then smiled. "Speak of the devil, here comes Lorraine. She's taking the girls to her hotel to swim."

"That's nice of her."

"It is."

"Could one of you drive me to my hotel?" Lorraine said when she reached them. "I'm totally jet-lagged, and that wine went straight to my head."

"Why don't you nap in the guest room?" Dixon said. "You can take the girls in the van, since it has their booster seats."

"Take the girls?" She blinked.

"Swimming," Dixon prompted. "You promised, remember? They're excited. They've already packed suits in their backpacks."

"Tomorrow would be better, Dixon. We'll all be fresher."

"The girls have been let down enough, Mom."

"They're outside playing. They've probably forgotten."

"Believe me, they don't forget things like that." He was holding back anger, Aubrey could see.

"How about if I drive you and the girls to the hotel?" Aubrey said to Lorraine. "I can watch them swim while you take a nap in your room."

"That would be lovely," Lorraine said. She shot a look at her son. "You act like I don't love those girls with all my heart. Why do you assume the worst about me?" She turned to Aubrey. "He keeps a list of all the ways I failed him, but I keep trying. That's what mothers do." She looked at Dixon. "You know I'm still here for you. Always remember that."

"I will," he said, his anger gone, his voice kind.

"I'll go get the girls," Lorraine said and left them.

"I guess I don't cut her much slack," Dixon said. "It's probably not fair."

"She let you down when you needed her most."

"Howard managed to forgive her."

"He was older than you. More mature."

"It's more than that. He's better about people. He told me she was hurt and scared when Dad left, and she coped by turning inward, being more protective of herself."

"It had to feel like rejection to a child, Dixon. I'm impressed Howard would be so understanding. He always seemed kind of…" She stopped, not wanting to call Dixon's beloved brother *judgmental*. "He had strong opinions about people."

"You think he disapproved of you. Maybe you mistook his silence for criticism. He didn't say much."

She didn't want to tell Dixon about the time Howard had refused to let her watch the girls. He'd told the mourners that Howard was his hero. *I have big shoes to fill, but I'll do my best.* "Maybe you're right," she said.

"It's kind of you to take Mom and the girls. You have to be as exhausted as I am."

He seemed totally done in. "You should sleep while we're gone. I'm glad to have more time with the girls. I'll be fine."

THE GIRLS SWAM and swam, stopping only to eat dinner at the restaurant when Lorraine woke from her nap, then swimming more after a debate about how many minutes they had to wait so they wouldn't get cramps. They slept in the car coming back, and Dixon helped her carry them to bed. They let them sleep in their clothes.

"Looks like you wore them out," Dixon said to her.

"I did. Wore myself out, too." Her eyes burned from all the chlorine, and her arms from tossing the girls into the water.

"Thanks for all you did today…through all of it."

"We did it together. We made a good team."

"I agree." His gaze held warm affection. "On top of everything else, you saved me a useless fight with my mother."

"The girls enjoyed her. They even let her smother them with hugs."

"I know she loves them. She does her best."

"So tomorrow I was thinking we could have a picnic at that park where the girls had their third birthday party. The one with the train and merry-go-round? I'll make sandwiches with the leftovers."

"Sounds good."

"Afterward, we'll drop Lorraine at the airport. She's got a big practice for a ballroom dance competition on Monday."

"She's a busy woman." He shook his head, but there was kindness in his voice. He'd let his resentment go.

They smiled at each other, standing close, as if neither one wanted to walk away. She'd stayed mostly numb during the funeral, but now that it was over, sadness swelled in a dark tide. Brianna was gone and buried. Aubrey could picture the flower-covered casket, hear Brianna's sweet voice singing on the tape that she'd *always be around.*

She wished she could walk into Dixon's warm arms and escape again, but that was no longer an option. It wasn't even safe to try for a comforting hug. It would switch to something sexual right away.

"Good night," she said, backing down the hall.

"'Night," he said, longing in his eyes as he watched her go.

CHAPTER EIGHT

IN AUBREY'S ROOM, Scout meowed from the middle of the bed, where she'd been sleeping. Sleep was what Aubrey needed. Her muscles ached, her brain sizzled with white noise. She dressed in her nightclothes, hoping to drift off quickly, but she was wide-awake, afraid of her thoughts, of the sadness they would bring. She grabbed her laptop from the bureau, thinking to distract herself with research. As she did that, she noticed a small photo tucked into the frame of the mirror. It was a picture of her mother and father, the only one Brianna and Aubrey had. Faded with age, it showed the two young people in hiking gear in front of Machu Picchu. They were so young, so full of life, so happy. In love, too, she guessed.

The thought reminded her that she'd promised herself to look for her dad's parents. Back in bed, she pulled up DexKnows, typed in Seattle and "Metzger." A number of names came up, some with initials. She could call them one by one. First she'd see if she could narrow down the list at all by finding a photo. She typed the first name in the *image* search on Google. There were historical photos, some unrelated pictures, a young child, a picture of the Metzger Building in Cincinnati, nothing useful.

She tried a few more names. On the tenth name—Henry Metzger—she hit pay dirt with a newspaper photo of a tan, white-haired man holding up a big fish and a trophy. The face looked so much like her father's, even in that small, faded photo, that it took her breath away.

Clicking to the source of the photo, a newspaper article from three years ago, she read that Henry "Hank" Metzger, sixty-five, had won a bass-fishing contest sponsored by a Seattle fishing club.

Oh, my God. She'd found her grandfather!

Her heart raced and her mind jumped every which way. If only she could talk to Brianna. She had to show someone, talk this through. Before she knew it, she'd carried her laptop down the hall and was knocking on Dixon's door.

"Come in." He was in bed with his own computer, bare-chested, sheets at his waist. She received a jolt, remembering being in bed with him.

"I'm interrupting you," she said.

"It's fine. What's up?"

"I think I found my grandfather."

"Show me." Setting his computer to one side, he fluffed a pillow, put it against the headboard, then patted the mattress for her to join him. She crawled onto the bed and leaned against the pillow, her legs straight above the covers, his beneath.

They were in bed together again and in their night-clothes. She assumed he wore boxers, but he might be naked.

Lust swooshed through her, erasing her mission, so that she wanted to shove the computers out of the way and get under the sheets with him.

"You wanted to show me…?" he prompted.

"Yes. Right." She pulled herself together, shifted the laptop half on his thigh, half on hers and clicked open the newspaper photo. "What do you think?" She held the hiking shot beside the screen.

Dixon studied both. "They look alike. Same startling blue eyes that you and Sienna have."

"You see it, too." Excitement surged. She wasn't just imagining this. "Should I call him, do you think?"

"You have the number?"

"It's in the phone book. It could be out of date, but it's a place to start."

"So do it."

"He was estranged from my father back then. What if he doesn't want anything to do with us? I doubt he even knows we exist."

"The only way to know is to make contact."

"I know. I will. Maybe my grandmother's still alive. There could be uncles and aunts and cousins. A whole family for the girls. It's what Brianna wanted. I wish I could tell her."

"Yeah. That's hard."

"When things settle down I'll make the call."

"Sounds like a plan."

She leaned against the pillow, feeling a burst of optimism.

She noticed Dixon watching her. He had dark circles under his eyes. "I should let you sleep. Thanks for listening to me." She shifted as if to leave.

"Stay a bit," he said softly, touching her leg. "I'm not that sleepy." His gaze traced her shape beneath her sleep shirt.

Neither was she. "To tell you the truth, I'm afraid to try to sleep. I know I'll feel so sad."

"I know what you mean." Their eyes locked, sharing their sorrow. "It's good we'll both be busy." He cleared his throat. "I'll be scrambling to keep the doors open at Bootstrap. You must be looking forward to all that's coming up for you."

"I should be, but it doesn't seem real yet." She'd been so focused on getting through the funeral and having to leave that she hadn't let herself look forward.

"You're going back because of a podcast, right? What's it about?"

"Yes. It's video this time. ALT got me a special guest. Actually, it's Rafe."

"Your old boyfriend?" His eyebrows lifted and he tilted his head at her.

"Yeah. He's a wing-suit flyer."

"Where they glide in just a suit made of parachute cloth?"

"Yeah."

"That's impressive." He sounded surprised.

"Rafe's a travel writer. He specializes in extreme outdoor sports. Kite-surfing, tow-in surfing, extreme snowboarding—where they helicopter you to the top of a mountain?"

"He's an adrenaline junkie like you."

"I'm a wimp compared to him. I get a rush from swinging on a trapeze."

"So how will it be to see him again?"

"We haven't talked in a while."

"And...?" His eyes dug in. "You're not thinking of getting back together, are you?"

"No. And why would that be so terrible?"

"It's not my business, but I picture you with a guy who pays more attention to you, one who hangs on your every word."

"Is that so?" She smiled, flattered that he'd thought about her this much.

"Absolutely."

"Is that what you did with Tommi?"

"I was classy about it, but more or less."

She laughed. "One thing for sure, Dixon, I was wrong when I said your social life would suffer because of the girls. You'll have no trouble dating."

"Why do you say that?"

"Come on. All the women flirting with you at the funeral?" She remembered how jealous she'd been.

"What? You mean Belinda?"

"Not just her. Rachel, for example."

"That's different." Dixon looked sheepish. "Brianna had us over for dinner a year ago. It was sort of a blind-date ambush. Nothing came of it."

"Not for lack of interest on Rachel's part, I'm sure."

He colored. "She's nice, but she dates a lot, goes to parties and clubs. That's not me these days."

"Dixon, women date until they find a guy worth sticking with. Trust me. She'd want to settle down with you."

"You don't know that." His face was bright pink.

Was he attracted to Rachel? This jealous jab was fresh and razor-sharp. "Oh, yeah. You're a catch. You're handsome, kind and smart, and a good person." *And an amazing lover.* She wished *to hell* she didn't know that. "Women think you're heroic for raising the girls."

"They feel sorry for me."

"And they're dying to comfort you. You're a helpless single man trying to be a father. Talk about plucking a woman's heartstrings. Why do you think guys troll for chicks carrying puppies in the park? A man who loves kids and/or dogs is golden." Her voice had hiked up a register. Why was she going on like this? Dixon wasn't about to *troll* for a woman. He was trying to survive a loss and care for the girls as best he could.

"Where's this coming from?" He locked gazes, reading between her lines again. "You're not...*jealous?*"

She let out an awkward laugh. "Why would I be?" Her cheeks burned like she'd stuck her face in an oven.

"You tell me."

For some reason, she did. "Because we slept together probably. There's that bonding hormone you get."

"What?" He looked puzzled.

"Never mind. It's stupid. We aren't together. We never will be together. But I guess I feel kind of possessive."

"I know what you mean," he said softly.

"I want you to be happy, Dixon. I want you to find the right woman and live happily ever after. For your sake... and the girls."

The girls. The new woman would love them, care for them, become their second mother...*and replace Aubrey in their hearts*.

Her skin turned to ice, as if she'd been shoved out of a cozy cabin into a frozen snowbank in her undies.

"What is it?" Dixon asked.

"I don't know...." She swallowed against the knot in her throat. "The woman you find will love the girls, and they'll love her, too, and...I'll be out."

"Out? That makes no sense. You'll still be their aunt."

"I know. My brain gets that. But down deep where it's squishy? Not so much." She sighed. "I shouldn't have told you that."

"I'm glad you did. Come here." He pulled her to him, wrapping his arms around her, holding her close. She rested her cheek on his collarbone, breathing in his great smell.

Without thinking, she put her arms around him, too. His back was bare and she pressed her palms against his flesh, felt his muscles slide beneath her fingers, and her body went on full alert.

He ran his hand slowly down her back. It could have been to soothe her or to arouse her. It was doing both.

Not again. You can't do this. You made a responsible decision. Stick with it.

Gathering whatever strength she could find, she pulled out of his embrace, her pulse surging in her ears. "I should go."

"Probably smart. We're nearly naked here." His gaze rolled longingly down her body, slow as syrup.

"And in bed."

"That, too," he said softly.

It was all she could do not to melt on the spot, but she made herself get off the bed and stand on wobbly legs, clutching the laptop against her chest like a shield as she backed toward the door.

"I hope you can sleep, Aubrey," he said.

"I hope the same for you," she answered. For a second, she almost ran back to him, but she made herself stay strong.

Back in bed, she thought about what she'd said about losing the girls to Dixon's girlfriend-to-be. Yes, she'd still be their aunt, but every time she visited, they'd have to get used to her again. And when she left, they'd miss her. It would be a sad cycle they'd go through over and over.

She felt so alone, so hopeless. *Brianna, help me.*

Her hand fell onto the old photo of her mother looking so happy and excited. She'd loved adventure, as had the man at her side, Aubrey's father.

Write a blog, she told herself, and the idea was a blessing. She couldn't blog about Brianna's death, but she could write about her mother. She found the scanned copy of the photo she kept on her computer and pasted it into her blog.

That snap is my mom and dad on the hike to Machu Picchu where she got pregnant with me and my twin sister. My mom was totally intrepid. Having babies

*cramped her travels, but she loved us like crazy.
Our bedtime stories were about her adventures—
climbing Pike's Peak, biking the Yucatan, going on a
Native American Vision Quest. We lost her to cancer
just after we graduated high school. Mom taught me
to go after my dreams, to grab life and shake every
thrill out of it. That's what I've been doing. I've been
ticking off her bucket list one by one. I'm proud to
follow in her footsteps...and my father's.*

*I hope I've made her proud. If there's a Heaven,
I know she's up there cheering me on. Who knows,
maybe she's got her own blog.*

Brianna would be there, too, cheering with her mother.
After that, Aubrey felt more sure she was on the right path.
Checking email, she caught a message from Tabitha say-
ing that a possible ALT partnership with an RV company
meant that instead of sleeping in tents at Utah Adventure
Fest, Aubrey and Neil would be in a brand-new luxury
Voyager RV. That would be nice because of the length of
the race, which began and ended at separate campgrounds.
The festival included activities for kids and non-racing par-
ents, and evening entertainment after the racers returned.

Tabitha was right that the race was perfect for reaching more ALT customers, since there was a popular non-
competitive track for more casual athletes, one of ALT's
key markets.

Tabitha had also mentioned that if the sponsorship came
through, Aubrey would be speaking on ALT's behalf to a
national conference of P.E. teachers.

A national conference? Aubrey's heart leaped. Through
teachers, she could get her message to thousands of girls,
building their confidence, inspiring them to challenge

themselves. That was a far more important payoff than the cash that would save her career. That lit a corner of her sad heart.

THE NEXT DAY went as Aubrey had planned, which pleased her. After church, the girls swam at Lorraine's hotel, they had the picnic at the park, then drove Lorraine to the airport.

To keep the girls cheerful, Aubrey hunted down the indoor tightrope and trapeze, and Dixon helped her set it up. The girls were enthralled until bedtime.

All day long, Aubrey kept catching Dixon's eyes, full of affection, concern and longing. She found that, far from bothering her, all that attention felt good. It warmed her, made her feel important to him, and made it even more difficult to tell him goodbye.

The next day, Aubrey's last day with the girls, Dixon headed to work and Aubrey stayed with Sienna and Ginger. They had face pancakes for breakfast, watched the girls' two favorite movies—*Aladdin* for Ginger, *Spy Kids* for Sienna—then returned to Bucky's, ordering the correct pizza this time and turning in the girls' tickets for prizes.

Home again, they played nonstop—swings in the backyard, tightrope and trapeze in the house, then hide-and-seek. When Dixon got home, they were finishing up Toxic Swamp. They ate leftover pizza for dinner, practiced Skype on the two laptops, and Scout did all her tricks one last time.

It was so hard to tell the girls good-night. Sienna wanted Aubrey to stay for their yellow-belt test in martial arts on Saturday. Dixon promised to send her the video. She could hardly get out a word, but she managed to hold back the tears until she left their room and spent one last night in her sister's bed. If only she could hear Brianna's voice in her head, feel her spirit again in her hollow heart. That would take time, as she'd told Sienna, but that didn't make it hurt one bit less.

THE NEXT MORNING at 5:00 a.m., dressed and packed, Aubrey tiptoed down the hall, hoping she could give the sleeping girls a quick kiss and be gone.

Dixon met her in the hall. "I can make coffee," he said sleepily, then rubbed his face.

"I'll grab Starbucks on the way out of town. I've got to fly to make the meeting." Emotion gathered behind her eyes and she tightened against it. This early it was hard to keep the barriers up.

"We'll all be fine, Aubrey," he said, reading her face. "Like you said, it takes time."

She nodded, grateful to him. "I'm going to say goodbye to the girls."

She pushed open the bedroom door. They looked so peaceful. Sienna lay flat on her back, arms wide, Ginger curled up, her face barely visible above the covers, her thumb in her mouth.

Aubrey leaned down to kiss her, breathing in bubblegum shampoo and the powder-soft scent of her skin, memorizing her for the lonely weeks ahead.

Scout jumped onto the bed, surprising Aubrey. Usually, her cat hung by the carrier when Aubrey got packed to go.

"I'm leaving now," she said softly to Ginger.

Ginger's thumb fell away. "Mommy?" she murmured, her eyes still closed.

"It's Auntie Aubba," she said, forcing her voice to stay steady. "And Scout, too. You just sleep. I'll call tonight."

Aubrey stood and leaned over the top-bunk rail for Sienna. Scout leaped up the ladder to perch on the top rung. Sienna rolled toward the wall, feigning sleep, which was exactly what Aubrey would have done in her place. "I love

you, Sienna," she said, her heart a clenched fist. Scout meowed. "Scout, too. We'll talk tonight."

There's no easy way to do this. They were doing what
was best for the girls. Aubrey headed out of the girls' room,
surprised to see Scout still on the ladder, tail whipping the
way it did when she was royally irritated.

Aubrey motioned for the cat to come on.

Scout stared at her, stubbornly staying put.

"Okay," she said, slowly shutting the door. Scout could
not stand a closed door. At the last second, the cat zipped
through the crack and jumped into her carrier, clearly feeling abused.

Dixon was waiting for them in the hall. "Go okay?"

"Sienna was pretending she was asleep. Ginger didn't
quite wake up. Be sure she knows I said goodbye like I
promised."

"I will." Dixon walked her to the car and loaded her
roller bag into the cargo area. Once Scout was situated on
the passenger seat, Aubrey stood to tell Dixon goodbye.

"Drive carefully," he said. "You haven't had much sleep,
so pull over if you get tired." They stood inches apart.

"I will, don't worry."

"I'd wish you luck, but I know you'll do great."

"Thanks, Dixon."

"I'm glad you were here, Aubrey. For the girls…and
for me."

"Me, too." Her lip trembled, so she bit it into submis-
sion.

"It's good we had time as a family." He caught himself.
"That came out wrong. I don't mean as a family family
or anything—"

"I know what you mean. I agree. You're a good man,
Dixon. You'd better be. I'm leaving my nieces in your
hands." Tears spilled down her cheeks.

"Ah, hell." He pulled her into a quick hug, patting her back a few times, like someone unused to emotional outbursts.

When he let go, he said, "I'll miss you, Aubrey." He swallowed. "I've enjoyed your company."

"I'll miss you, too." That fact registered down deep with the solid truths she knew by heart.

Silence beat like wings fanning the embers of their unspoken feelings. There was more between them than chemistry, but there was no point saying so. It had happened because of what they'd been through together. If not for that, it would evaporate like the champagne mist from a popped cork.

It's good we had time as a family. The words lodged in her head. They could never make it work. Dixon would want a quiet, settled life—spaghetti for dinner on Tuesdays, *SNL* in bed on Saturday nights, football and bean dip on Sunday afternoons, and Aubrey couldn't imagine anything more soul-killing.

It was only the girls who made it seem worthwhile. You couldn't become a couple just for the children. Could you?

At that moment, the screen door banged and Sienna ran down the sidewalk, her face red, eyes frantic. "I don't want you to go," she cried and threw her arms around Aubrey's legs.

Aubrey struggled to stay upright, finally dropping to a crouch to hug her niece, her tangled hair tickling Aubrey's nose. "I know it's hard," she choked out, fighting to stay strong for her niece. "I'll be back before you know it. You'll be so busy. You have gymnastics and martial arts and the kids at Bootstrap and Uncle Dixon, plus the trapeze and tightrope..." Her throat locked.

"Aubrey has to get on the road or she'll be late," Dixon

said, pulling Sienna back with a gentle hand, so Aubrey could get in the car.

"I can't wait to see the video of your belt test," she said out the window. "Don't use the trapeze without Uncle Dixon spotting you, okay?"

Sienna nodded.

Aubrey drove off with a wave, but she had to park around the corner until her eyes cleared enough to drive. Scout meowed, impatient to get moving. *We're doing the right thing for everyone,* she told herself. It was all that would sustain her through the painful weeks to come.

Just eight weeks. I'll visit in eight weeks. She'd already marked the days on her Google calendar.

DIXON STOOD ON the sidewalk with Sienna until Aubrey turned the corner, feeling totally shredded. It was just too much—Aubrey fighting tears, Sienna, the soldier, falling apart. And there he stood swallowing lump after lump in his throat. He clenched his jaw against the misery.

He'd been this close to telling Aubrey to hurry back, to hell with giving them time to adjust. They already missed her too much.

A stupid idea lodged in his brain. What if they could be a couple? Mom, Dad, two little girls, all living under the same roof?

On what planet? Aubrey would never stay for the long haul. Her whole life took place on the move. She lived for her adventures. The two of them had leaned on each other to get through this tragedy. That was all there was to it.

Still, Aubrey had looked so desolate as she'd said good-bye.

She'll be fine. She'll get caught up in her career and be fine.

They'd done the right thing and now he had lunches

to pack and a business to save. For a second, he dreaded entering the house, empty of Aubrey's ringing laugh and fierce energy.

"What would you say to face pancakes for breakfast?" he asked Sienna when they got inside, determined to stay positive.

"You can't make them like Aunt Aubrey," she said sadly.

"Then cereal, I guess. You can have the sugar kind if you want." Once he was alone, Dixon pulled Howard's letter out of his wallet to read again.

Dix,

I hope to God you never see this letter, because if you do it means that Brianna and I are gone.

Brianna wanted to write a note to her sister explaining why we didn't ask her to keep the girls if we kicked off, so I figured I might as well write one to you.

Brie feels guilty, I guess. Aubrey's her twin. She's the obvious choice to take over. We all know that Aubrey's not the mother type. Brianna would kill me for saying that. She swears that Aubrey could be Mother of the Year if she so chose, but we can't take that chance. Not with our girls.

And you can be sure we didn't choose you because you're all that's left—Mom being Mom.

The girls need someone who will always be there, who will do what's best for them no matter how difficult or painful or sad. That's you all the way, Dix.

You're a strong, solid guy. I know you think you have to prove yourself to me. You don't. You had some bad breaks as a kid and you reacted like any tenderhearted tyke would.

So raise the girls right. I know you know how. I love you. Even when you were a pain in the ass, I

loved you. Not to get sickening about it, but if I'm
dead, I'm still with you. Always.
Your bossy big brother,
Howard

I'll do my best, he silently told his brother. They'd get
through this, and they would be all right. He'd make damn
sure they were.

BY THE TIME she reached the ALT flagship store where the
photo shoot was being held, Aubrey had shoved her sorrow into a corner of her mind, riveting a manhole cover
over it. Or tried to.

Every time she remembered Ginger calling her *Mommy,*
smelling of bubblegum shampoo, Sienna's desperate plea
that she stay, or Dixon's sad eyes, she cranked up the volume on her radio.

By the time she parked in the studio lot, her ears rang
like she'd been at a rock concert. She was pretty sure she'd
blown a speaker.

She'd had no choice. She could never be a soccer mom.
She wouldn't be any good at it, and she'd make the girls
miserable trying.

The shoot went well, though Tabitha wasn't present.
Scout rocked the pet life vest, demonstrating its use swimming the length of the pool where ALT sponsored scuba
lessons.

They were finishing up when Tabitha walked in. Aubrey took one look at her and knew something terrible had
happened. The perky marketer seemed slumped, shorter
somehow, her usually sparkle squelched to gloom.

"What's wrong?" Aubrey asked.

"Percy's freaked. Our CEO questioned the money ear-
marked in the budget for *Extreme Girl.*"

"What does that mean?" Aubrey's lungs locked down in the middle of an inhale.

Tabitha leaned in and spoke quietly, "It means Percy's got no balls. The CEO doesn't believe in blogs and Percy shrivels up if the guy so much as breathes funny at him."

"So…it's over? Is that it?" There went the PE conference plus the cash she required to keep her blog alive.

"No. God, no." She closed her eyes and inhaled, as if for strength. "I shouldn't have told you. It's my job to worry. All you have to do is rock Utah Fest. We'll post video as we go, offer prizes, do mini challenges. The hits to your blog will boggle Percy's mind. I'm positive."

All you have to do is rock Utah Fest. That sent a flare of panic through Aubrey. She hadn't exercised in a week, let alone trained. Even thinking about a gym session exhausted her. She felt heavy, as if she wore a scuba tank on her back, and her heart was a lead lump resting on her diaphragm.

That was the depression. Knowing didn't make it any easier. She had to fight it, push through it. She'd walked away from the girls to pursue her dream. She didn't dare give it up.

On top of being depressed, she ached for the girls. And, if she were honest, for Dixon. She'd grown to depend on his comforting smile, that hang-in-there way he looked at her, how closely he studied her face.

Her main hope was that Primal Quest Camp that weekend would be so engrossing she'd forget everything else. The thing about physical challenges was that they narrowed your focus to your body, and how to outsmart the mountain, wave, rapids, or ski slope, as well as your own fears. She loved that. She lived for that. Since her mother died, adrenalized serenity was what saved her, and kept saving her.

It would save her now.

After Tabitha ran down the plans for Utah Fest, Aubrey headed for the chichi bistro Neil worked weekdays so they could plan their trial run. She had to tell him about the ALT sponsorship and she wasn't sure how he'd react. Neil wasn't big on change.

It was his meal break, so they huddled in the restaurant office with the clang of pots and shouts from the kitchen in the background. Six feet tall, blond and built like a Nordic god, Neil dwarfed the space as he hunched over the table inhaling soup and pita chips. His go-to Halloween costume was Thor. Aubrey's friends had all been heartbroken to learn he was gay.

"I'm happy for you about ALT and all," he said, "but you know this will complicate the race. I gave up a trip to Cabo to meet Pierce's parents for Utah Fest, and Pierce is *Not Happy,* capital N, capital H."

"ALT won't interfere. They want us to win more than you do. We'll do the ALT promo spots before the race starts and at the end of race days. Tabitha and her camera guy will try to keep up with us during the race, but we'll be wearing lightweight cameras on our helmets and on a chest strap as backup. You won't even know they're there."

"You better be right. I could lose my main squeeze over this. Though, frankly, if I have to go to one more dog show I'm going to hang myself by a dog leash. Never get serious with a person who has a hobby that conflicts with your own."

"Duly noted."

Neil was her perfect teammate. He was totally fit, obsessively organized and nearly psychic with a compass. That was vital, since navigation was Aubrey's weak point. She was the resourceful one, good at adapting equipment or finding fresh solutions to problems that flustered Neil.

They were a two-person team, rather than four because Neil wanted more control. The entire team had to finish together, and Neil didn't want to risk two more sets of possible problems.

Neil could squeeze in the trial run the weekend after Primal Quest Camp. They decided where to do it, and went over the equipment they needed. Finished, she gave him a quick hug, then raced to make the five o'clock studio time they'd booked for the video podcast.

They were putting on her microphone when Aubrey heard her name called. She looked up to see Rafe striding toward her. Ignoring the tech with the wire in his hand, he grabbed her up and swung her around, then set her down. "Damn, girl. How are you?"

"I'm good. You?"

"Spectacular, now that I see you." Rafe was always happy to see her, but easily said goodbye. He said it was the Buddhist ideal of non-attachment—not clinging to outcomes or things or people. He mixed his version of Buddhism with Native American spiritualism and a dash of nature worship.

He was handsome, with the angular face, high cheekbones and olive skin of his Cherokee grandfather. He managed to look both muscular and wiry at once. His shoulder-length hair was blue-black and shiny, and he wore a bead-and-leather choker.

She was glad to see him, but the attraction was totally gone. That was a relief. She'd been so unexpectedly wrecked by the breakup she'd had a sliver of doubt that she was totally over him, no matter what she'd told Dixon.

Rafe winced, rolling one shoulder, and she remembered he was coming back after an injury. He must still be in pain.

"Mr. Simón...we'll need to get a mic on you." The producer, who'd been barking orders from the moment Aubrey arrived, spoke to Rafe in the tender tone of a woman who'd fallen under his spell. That happened a lot.

"Yeah. Sure." He fished a key drive out of his pocket and gave it to her.

The sound engineer called to Rafe.

"Dinner after?" he said to Aubrey. "We'll catch up."

"Sure." She'd have to break away to call the girls and say good-night, of course. She'd set an alarm on her phone to be sure that no matter how crazy the evening got, she would make that call. She'd rather die than disappoint the girls.

A few minutes later, they got the green light and Aubrey kicked off her podcast. The interview flowed as easily as Rafe's glide into the canyon in his wing-suit. He narrated the video, making it sound as easy and safe as a walk in the park, though she knew any mistake could have sent him plunging to his death. It took years of paragliding and razor-sharp instincts to do the sport. He looked like a superhero looping his way to the canyon floor, staying dangerously close to the mountain in order to catch the thermals that kept him aloft as long as possible.

After she signed off the show, Rafe drove her to his current favorite restaurant in his Porsche, with the top down, grinning at her every few seconds, his enthusiasm infectious.

She was surprised she'd imagined that Rafe had been falling in love with her when they were together. When he looked at her, there was distance in his gaze. He held himself back. The months away had given her perspective, but it was also having Dixon look at her as intently as he did. The difference was dramatic. Maybe she'd be wiser the next time she fell in love.

CHAPTER NINE

THE HOSTESS FLICKED an appreciative eye over Rafe before leading them to *his* booth. When Rafe lowered himself to the bench, he winced then grabbed his side, forcing a smile.

"You're hurting from your injury?" Aubrey asked.

"No big thing," he said, clearly not wanting to dwell on it. After the waiter took their wine order, he studied her face. "You look tired. Dark circles. Your smile kind of droops. What's up?"

She took a breath as the reasons washed through her. "It's a long story."

"I've got time and wine's on the way if your throat gets dry."

She was grateful when her confession was delayed by the waiter bringing the wine, followed by the restaurant's chef-owner—a ski buddy of Rafe's, who promised to send out a new dish for Rafe's opinion.

When they were alone again, they lifted their wine-glasses to each other and Rafe gave his usual toast. "To what comes next."

"To that," she said, hoping it was good for both of them. "So what happened in Denver? You were injured?"

"It was a snowboard fly-in late in the day. I was beat, but I didn't want to waste the helo, so I took one more trip. Lost it on a jump and slammed into an outcropping. Scapula, collar bone and three ribs."

"That sounds horrible."

"Not fun, that's for sure." He sipped his wine, then added, "But it brought good things." An expression she'd never seen before came over his face—boyish and bewildered, like a kid surprised by a birthday gift he hadn't deserved. "I fell in love."

"Really?"

"Really. With my physical therapist, can you believe it? Her name's Shari Cooper."

"That's great, Rafe. I'm happy for you."

"Yeah." Then his features drooped and his smile faded. "Except she broke up with me last week. Or tried to anyway."

"I'm so sorry. What happened?"

"She says we're not compatible. She's into yoga and meditation and natural foods."

"That doesn't sound like you." Rafe trained like a maniac so he could eat the fast food he loved.

"I got into some of that. It was good for me. The real problem is that Shari doesn't like to travel. She's more into quiet nights by the fire. And get this…she *knits!* Really pretty scarves in fuzzy wool."

"Wow." Rafe was all about adrenaline and action, caffeine and thrash rock. Shari seemed to have a point about their differences.

"We were okay until I got better. I booked a couple trips—a mountaineering thing in Nevada, surfing in Australia—and she flipped out that I was leaving." He scowled at the table, then lifted his gaze. "Maybe I got a little stir-crazy. The chimes, herbal tea and Japanese flute music got to me after a while. I tried to keep it together. And I was getting into her scene. I did yoga with her."

"But it wasn't enough?"

"She wants me to stay in Denver and become a personal trainer. I feed stories to three outdoor magazines,

Aubrey. They don't want *Fat-Burning Workouts to Get You into a Bikini.* Plus, a friend is putting together investors for a movie on extreme sports in California. He wants to feature me."

"That would be cool."

"I know. But Shari doesn't see that. She thought I'd changed, that my injury taught me a lesson. It did—quit before you get hurt—but that's not enough for her."

Aubrey sipped her wine.

Rafe was quiet for a few seconds and seemed to be struggling with his emotions. "I miss her so much. At first, I figured, okay, detach, this is the universe telling me to let go, to flow with the mountain."

"But you love her." He looked the way Aubrey had felt after their breakup.

"I do. I even miss her kid. Cecily. She's sixteen and a real smartass, but we got along." He swallowed. "I want to make it work, Aubrey. I'm thirty-five. It's time to lock a few things down. I want steady people in my life. People I can be steady for."

"Could you both give a little? Compromise?"

"I thought we were. I did yoga, like I said, and I learned couples massage. That was fun." He grinned fleetingly. "She did a gym wall climb with me and we ride bikes, but she doesn't want to try anything major. She could do it, too. She's totally buff from the heavy-duty yoga she does. She was a gymnast in high school, on the swim team in college." He shrugged. "She says my stuff is too extreme." He shook his head.

"I'm sorry, Rafe."

"Yeah. I know. Anyway, enough about me. It's your turn. Explain why you'd have to check those bags under your eyes, since they're too big to carry on the plane."

She told him about the car wreck and losing her sister.

He was shocked and saddened. He reached for her hand. "I'm so sorry. You were close to your sister, I remember. What about the little girls? Who's going to take care of them?"

"My sister's brother-in-law. Dixon. You met him at the birthday party."

"That's right. Tall guy. Built like a tennis player?"

"Yeah. He lives in Phoenix and spends a lot of time with the girls. I travel so much...."

"Sure. Plus, you'll be the cool aunt. They'll think you walk on water. They probably already do."

"They were sad when I left. It was...hard. I miss them. I had to leave early because of the podcast ALT set up."

"What's the story with ALT anyway?"

"That's the good part. I'm close to getting a sponsorship...." She told him about the plans, about the Utah Fest test.

"That is huge. I've talked to athletes with endorsements. Some work, some don't. Sounds like you and ALT are a natural fit."

"I hope so, though the marketing director's hinky and the CEO doesn't have a clue."

"Corporate suits never get it. They surfed a couple swells on spring break and think they're *totally gnarly*. You just shine your light like you do and you'll rule."

"Thanks, Rafe. You're making me feel better."

"Good. That's what friends are for." They drank more wine. "So you'll know for sure at the Utah race?"

"Yeah. They want to use it because it's big, and there's the festival, so there are casual people, too. There's a fun track besides the competitive one. It should give ALT and my blog more exposure."

"Sounds like fun. You'll nail it."

"I hope so. It's not too intense—kayaks, mountain

bikes, easy climbing routes for newbies. I'm kind of worn out, though, to tell you the truth."

"You'll get fired up once you're there. You bring a lot of people into the outdoors who would otherwise cower in the gym. I wish you could talk to Shari...." He lifted the bottle to refill their glasses, then set it back down with a clunk. "Wait. What if I brought Shari to Utah Fest? We could race as a team."

"Would she come?"

"You said it's not extreme, right? We could practice with the kayak, do a few climbs. The social part would appeal to her."

"I hope you don't expect one race to change her mind." That would be a set-up for disappointment.

"No, but she can see how fun it can be. Maybe cut me some slack. It's worth a try." He tapped the table, shifting in his seat, restless as always. "Do you think people can change?"

"In small ways, I guess. If they want to badly enough. If it's worth it."

"It's worth it for sure for Shari. I just wish it wasn't so hard. You and I were great together. No strife."

"You weren't in love with me, Rafe. You're serious about Shari. It's different." She was pleased that she wasn't the least bit jealous.

"When did you get so wise?"

"It's easier to see when it's not you."

Aubrey hoped Rafe could work things out, but it sounded like he and Shari were too far apart in personality and interests. They'd been forced together because of his injury, just as she and Dixon had been by the deaths of loved ones. Without that bond, their differences would be glaring.

If Aubrey ever found a guy to settle down with, he'd

have to love travel and outdoor sports, and be fun and easygoing. Like Rafe in many ways, except he'd love Aubrey as much as she loved him.

What if she didn't really want that? Down deep. It seemed so risky. So much could go wrong. People got hit by cars, they died of cancer, they let each other down, gave up on each other. It all seemed so *fragile*. What could be so good it would make up for the risk and the inevitable pain?

She saw it was getting close to time to call the girls, so she gave Rafe the details about the race and had him drive her to her car. As soon as she was alone, she called the house number, wondering which sweet voice would answer, eager to tell Aubrey all about her day.

The phone rang and rang, then went to voice mail. At least the message was in Dixon's voice. Aubrey would have been heartbroken to hear the one Brianna had recorded with the girls shrieking—*I get to say the beep part. No, I do. Me, right, Mommy?*

Aubrey didn't want to leave a message, so she dialed Dixon's cell. Voice mail. *Damn.*

They were probably in the bath. She'd call again when she got to her apartment.

A half hour later, she let herself into her place. It was bright and lively—crammed with her roommate's Hollywood memorabilia and Aubrey's sports equipment, the walls covered with movie posters and photos of snowboarding and underwater caves—but it felt…lonely with her roommate at work.

Aubrey usually loved having the apartment to herself. But then she'd still had Brianna's company in her head and heart.

Brianna, where are you? A terrible sadness bloomed in her brain, like a monster behind the door jumping out to scare her. She dropped onto her bed and wrapped her arms around herself.

If she could talk to the girls and Dixon, she'd be saved. Fingers shaking, heart squeezed tight, she dialed Dixon's cell phone again. Voice mail.

No bath takes that long.

Had something happened? Where would they be at this time of night? Had one of the girls gotten sick? Were they at the hospital? The panic was irrational, but after losing Brianna, she knew worst-case scenarios actually came to pass.

She dialed again, breathing too fast, feeling faint. This time, a muffled voice whispered, "Yeah?"

"Dixon? Are you okay? What happened?"

"Fell asleep…working."

"Are the girls okay? I called to say good-night but no one answered."

"Sorry. They drifted off watching a movie on the laptop in Ginger's bed and I let them sleep. They were up early seeing you off."

"Oh. Sure." She fell back against the headrest, relieved that nothing bad had happened. She should let Dixon sleep, but the panic of being alone seized her again. If he could tell her a little about the girls, maybe she'd get through the lonely night….

All day, she'd carried them in her head, pictured them dressing, going to Bootstrap. She'd hoped Sienna didn't get put in time-out and that Ginger hadn't cried. She'd imagined them on the ride home, arguing about who got the better booster seat, eating one of those nasty casseroles for supper—or maybe throwing it over the fence for the heck of it.

"How did they do today?" she asked.

"Huh? Uh, fine. No problems."

"That's good." *Was there tension in his voice? Over what? Had they missed her? Had they forgotten her?* She realized either answer would make her sad.

She had to leave Dixon alone. The poor man was half asleep. "Tell them I called, okay? That I kept my promise? I'll call in the morning before you leave for Bootstrap. Say seven-thirty?"

"Sure. Whenever."

"Maybe bedtime's too late. After supper? Say six?"

"Supper's hectic, but you can try."

"How about if you call me when it's a good time?"

"I can do that." He sounded so weary of her. She understood, but her eyes burned with the stupid urge to cry. "Good night," she said over a knot in her throat.

"'Night." *Click.*

That was that. She stared at her phone, dotted with sweat from how tense she'd been. *They're settling in without you. It's what you wanted.*

Even if they'd been awake, the call would have been like it had been with Brianna, when she'd put the girls on the phone, coaching them on what to say, telling them no when they wanted to watch TV or eat a snack instead of breathe at their faraway aunt through the mouthpiece.

She'd been clinging to them in her mind, holding them like the string of a kite in a hard wind. On top of that, she was supposed to be there for *them,* not the other way around. It wasn't their job to fill the emptiness left by Brianna's death.

It was…just…so…hard. A sob started deep in her belly and filled her chest until she let it out in gulping bursts, feeling like a fool, but grateful her poor roommate didn't have to hear her.

When she'd finished, she felt spent, but still wired. She needed something to do. *Look ahead. Think of the future.*

She went online to research adventure races in Arizona for when the girls were older. There were mountain races around Flagstaff and desert ones in the south, usually involving mud. The girls would love that.

Next she wrote a blog post:

My nieces totally rock. I can't wait to adventure with them. We'll be building a new generation of intrepid girls....

It was tough to be so positive and perky and optimistic when she felt like warmed-over dog-doo. Scout gave an irritated squeak. She wanted Aubrey to shut the computer down and go to sleep. "I'll try, but no promises." She set her alarm so she could call the girls at breakfast, and curled around her cat. At least she still had Scout, who began a comforting purr.

THE THIRD NIGHT after Aubrey left, Dixon removed the casserole dish from the microwave with two hot pads, then scooped small servings onto each girl's plate, the steam smelling of noodles and tuna. His stomach churned. It was a long shot that the girls would eat more than a bite, but he had to try.

He seemed to be living in a haze.

At work, he put out brush fires, fought to hang on to their clients while the remaining staff juggled tasks and duties. He'd set up interviews with a half-dozen social workers, at least, nearly finished the big grant application and had a callout about a temporary job counselor.

Meanwhile, he hadn't touched the job bank. Soon it would be out of date, nearly useless to the clients.

"Come and get it, girls," he called. He'd been letting them watch too much TV so he could work in the evenings. He would have to hire Jessica to sit with them on weekends so he could go into the office for a few hours. As it was, he spent a lot of time spotting the girls on the trapeze and tightrope Aubrey had set up. What a ridiculous thing to put inside the house. Totally Aubrey. Wild, impractical and irresistible.

He missed her. He couldn't deny it. He had to admit he'd wondered how her reunion with her ex-boyfriend had gone. She hadn't mentioned it when she'd called, and now it seemed stupid to bring it up. Maybe she'd get back together with him. He hoped not. The guy wasn't good enough for her.

Not that it was any of his business. All in all, it was good that she'd gone back to L.A. for a couple of months. He didn't have to fight his attraction or dread the girls' misery when she left again.

This departure had been torture enough. He'd lied to Aubrey when he'd said the girls were doing fine. Ginger kept bursting into tears, Sienna had tantrums over nothing, and they both had trouble at night—Sienna had wet the bed twice. The first night, Ginger had sleepwalked, the next she'd had a night terror. Constance had told him that wasn't unusual, even for children who hadn't experienced a death, but it had scared the hell out of him. She'd held a counseling session with each girl, and told him they'd both been deeply upset by Aubrey's departure.

He wasn't about to make Aubrey feel any worse than she already did by telling her that. She'd been calling at breakfast and bedtime every day. They'd tried Skype, but when the image froze, the girls got as upset as if Aubrey had hung up on them. Frankly, it was a relief not to see her face. Her fake-happy voice was bad enough. Seeing her sad blue eyes above that plastered-on smile about broke his heart.

The overall situation sucked. Handling the clash of emotions from the people he cared about with his own had strained his abilities to their limits. Constance had noticed. *You look pretty ragged, Dixon. You're no good to them exhausted. Get some help. Grief's a long-haul thing.*

No kidding. He selfishly wished Aubrey were here to play Toxic Swamp or hold a water fight in the tub or sing that weird frog song. Truth be told, he was as miserable without her as the girls were.

You're just lonely. Get over it.

Aubrey needed to get on with her life as much as they did. This morning, she'd reminded him again to send her the video of their belt test on Saturday, even though she feared there would be no cell coverage at her boot camp. She'd been afraid to disappoint the girls if she couldn't make the daily calls while she was there. He almost hoped she couldn't, since her calls upset the girls more than soothed them. If she didn't call for a while, maybe they would miss her less. No way could he tell her that.

His only hope was to let time and distance do its healing work.

"Girls! Supper!" he yelled again. They came into the kitchen and instantly made faces at their plates. Constance had warned him their appetites would suffer, and that all of them would be more sensitive and irritable.

Oh, yeah. In spades. "I give," he said. "Peanut butter with honey or marshmallow crème?" If he ever made it to the market, he'd buy wheat germ and bananas to add a little nutrition to the meal. Damn. This parenting stuff was not for wimps.

For a brief moment, he flashed on his old life, when he was free to work sixty hours, then come home to pizza and a game, a good book, a hot series on HBO, a long run or a gym slam. Weekends, he'd have beers with friends at a sports bar, sleep till eleven, then stagger out for bagels and espresso at his favorite coffee bar, ending up at Howard's for a Sunday barbecue, where he loved every second he'd spent with the girls, when they were happy and secure with two healthy, loving parents.

All that was over…gone forever.

He had the girls and he'd do anything for them, lay his life down if he had to. In fact, that was kind of what he'd done. He didn't regret it one bit. But that didn't make it any easier to endure.

AUBREY WENT TO bed early Thursday night, since she'd head to Primal Quest Camp early the next morning. She X'd off the day on her laptop calendar. *Day three of exile.*

That was how she felt—like she'd been banished from the girls for two months. *And Dixon? No. Forget Dixon.*

She'd been worried about calling the girls from the camp, but learned there was a satellite phone for emergencies. She doubted singing the frog song to two little girls qualified, but she didn't give a damn.

She fell asleep then, later, fought her way to wakefulness to answer her cell phone, which had to have been ringing for a while. She squinted at her clock. Midnight.

"Yeah?" she said, trying to clear the brain fog.

"Aunt Aubrey?" It was Sienna, her voice scared.

Aubrey jerked upright, instantly alert. "What's wrong?"

Sienna let out a sob. "I did it again. I wet the bed."

"I'm so sorry, sweetie." Aubrey's heart squeezed with anguish. *How can I help her? I'm so far away and she sounds so scared.* She got out of bed to pace, Scout at her heels.

"All the clean sheets are gone. Uncle Dixon has to buy soap to wash them. He said to wake him, but I'm scared to. Ginger walks at night and screams in her sleep, so he gets up a lot. He went to bed early to catch up." The words tumbled from her usually taciturn niece.

"Ginger screams?" Aubrey asked, the thought a stab of ice in her chest.

"It's called *night terror*. It's like a nightmare, but it doesn't hurt and she doesn't remember it. Uncle Dixon looked it up on the computer."

"That's good," she said, but she was alarmed. Dixon hadn't mentioned sleepwalking, night terrors or Sienna's bed-wetting when they'd talked. *We're all fine.* He hadn't wanted to worry her, she assumed, but that wasn't right. He was shutting her out. "Maybe we can fix this without waking Uncle Dixon. Do you have a sleeping bag?"

"No, but Mommy does. It's in the laundry room."

"Perfect. Sleeping bags are fun and cozy."

"They are?"

"Oh, yes. And the best thing about sleeping bags is they're waterproof, so if you have another accident, it won't get on the mattress."

"Really?"

"Oh, yeah. I've slept in rain and snow in a sleeping bag and stayed dry as toast. I'll stay on the phone while you go get it."

"Okay." There was a clunk as Sienna set down the phone.

Aubrey waited, her heart in her throat, as her niece went after the bedroll. It seemed to take forever, but finally she returned and Aubrey listened as she untied the string, un-rolled the bag and got into it.

"It smells like clean clothes in here. I like it."

"So, you're all zipped up, snug as a bug in a rug?"

The little girl sucked in a breath. "Mommy always said bug-in-a-rug when she tucked us in tight."

"That's because your grandma used to say it to us."

"Oh."

"Do you think you can sleep now, sweetie?"

"I don't know." She sounded panicked.

"How about if I stay on the line until you get sleepy?"

"That would be good." She breathed out in a whoosh of relief.

"When we couldn't sleep, your grandma used to tell me and your mom about her adventures. Shall I tell you one of mine? I'll try not to sound like your mom."

"It's okay if you do. I'm used to it now."

Aubrey felt such a rush of love. Her niece had called her because she was scared and thought Aubrey could help. *She trusts you. She needs you.*

And just like that, Aubrey was throwing clothes into a suitcase, phone pressed to her ear, rattling on about a ski trip when she'd seen a bear catch salmon, when she'd camped overnight in an ice cave, while she got ready to drive to Phoenix.

She was totally wired, wide-awake. She'd be there by breakfast. She'd make the girls' martial arts belt test on Saturday after all.

Between adventure tales, Sienna told Aubrey how much she and Ginger had missed her, along with details about how they'd been getting on with Dixon. Everything she said made Aubrey sure her nieces needed her. Dixon did, too, no matter what he told her. He was their guardian, but she was his backup.

She would miss Primal Quest Camp, and that would make ALT unhappy, but it couldn't be helped. The girls mattered more. She would have to return to L.A. the following weekend for the trial run with Neil. She wouldn't let him down. If meetings with ALT came up, she'd fly back and forth. Forget two months of settling in. This was the right thing to do. She knew it in her bones.

She was merging onto Highway 5, telling Sienna about biking down the Maui volcano, when Sienna whispered, "I'm sleepy now."

"Good girl," she whispered back. "You sleep well." *See you soon,* she thought, but she kept that to herself, wanting to surprise the girls. Her only regret was that the Date Ranch Market wouldn't be open so she couldn't bring the girls the red licorice they loved.

After that, she drove as fast as she dared, staring ahead through the dark, blasting her most frenetic playlist at full volume, singing along until she was hoarse, talking to Scout to keep from drifting off.

Outside of Indio, she gave up the fight and pulled into the rest area for a nap, which helped.

At seven-thirty sharp, Aubrey parked in front of her sister's house, so excited to see the girls she couldn't stand it. On the way, she'd come up with a great plan. It made her breathless and eager and a little scared.

Dixon might not like it, but she wasn't taking no for an answer. She didn't care what the experts said. She might not be mother material, but she was an aunt and aunts had instincts, too. Hers were firing off like her sense for the flow on a mountain climb, clip to foot-hold to hand-hold to clip.

She got out of her car, grabbed her bag and pulled the strap of Scout's carrier over her arm. Standing on the walkway, she remembered driving here ten days ago, when she'd expected to hug her sister, drink champagne and celebrate their separate successes. The house had looked bright and cheerful, colorful with flowers and full of life.

Now it seemed to slump, its paint paler, its cheer dimmed, its geraniums drooping. The house seemed to be grieving like the people inside.

Aubrey was here to make it better. Brimming with con-

fidence, she dashed up the sidewalk, Scout's carrier bumping her hip, the suitcase bouncing behind her.

Reaching the porch, she heard the shrill shriek of an
alarm, along with muffled yells. She caught a whiff of
smoke. God. She tried the knob, which opened, and rushed
into the house.

CHAPTER TEN

THE AIR IN the living room was gray, and smelled of burned pancakes. Aubrey set down her bag, but kept Scout with her as she hurried to the kitchen. No one heard her over the smoke alarm and the girls shrieking, their hands over their ears.

"Calm down, would you?" Dixon yelled as he swung a broom at the smoke alarm and knocked it to the floor. The abrupt silence almost pulsed.

"You broke it, Uncle Dixon," Ginger said in horror.

"Aunt Aubrey never burned the pancakes," Sienna said, sounding totally outraged.

"Aunt Aubrey's not here, is she? You're stuck with me." He sounded weary and exasperated.

At that moment, he saw Aubrey standing in the doorway, and his eyes widened. "Aubrey?" Amazed relief filled his voice, and her heart lurched with happiness. "How did you get here?" He sounded like she'd appeared by magic.

"How do you think I did? I drove."

"All night?" He blinked.

Ginger squealed, a much happier sound than her smoke-alarm shriek, then ran to hug Aubrey around the knees.

"You came back," Sienna said as if it were a dream come true. "But it's not enough X's." She pointed at the refrigerator where a printout of two months labeled *Aunt Aubrey Comes Back* had been taped to the fridge. Three days had been crossed off in a child's shaky hand. So Aubrey hadn't been the only one counting the days of her exile.

"I couldn't wait that long." She dropped to her knees, Scout's case clunking to the ground, and drew both girls close. Scout meowed, so she reached back to free her. The cat twined around the three of them.

The girls' hair smelled of smoke, cooking oil and bubblegum, and Aubrey breathed it in like the sweetest perfume.

Ginger pulled back. "It's my turn for the sleeping bag, isn't it? Tell Sienna. She thinks it's hers. It's not, is it? Tell her, Auntie Aubba."

"How about I get you both your very own sleeping bag?" They would need them for the plan.

"Yes! We want our own bags! Can mine be pink?" Ginger asked.

"Why not?" Aubrey said.

"Sienna told me she called you. She shouldn't have," Dixon said. He'd recovered from his delight and now sounded grumpy. "She knew she could wake me. This is totally unnecessary. We're fine."

Aubrey gently freed herself from the girls and stood to face him. "No, you're not fine."

"He burned the pancakes," Sienna added as if to prove Aubrey's point.

"But you have that boot camp...." He frowned.

"This is more important."

They stared at each other. She sensed the girls' eyes on them, waiting for the outcome of this disagreement.

"Go brush your teeth and get your backpacks, girls," Dixon said, not taking his eyes from Aubrey's. "We'll go out for breakfast. They don't burn their pancakes at I-Hop."

With shouts of *yay,* the girls ran off.

"I don't know what she told you, but—"

"She told me there were no clean sheets because you ran out of laundry soap, that she's been wetting the bed, and that she didn't want to wake you because you were exhausted by Ginger having night terrors."

"So...she told you everything." He grimaced sheepishly.

"You said they were doing great, Dixon."

"I didn't want you to worry."

"You can't shut me out. We're in this together."

Anger flared in his eyes, but he kept his voice level. "No, we're not. I'm the one who has to soothe them after you call and upset them."

"My calls upset them? You didn't tell me that." Her heart lurched.

"Why hurt you, too? You shouldn't have rushed out here. You can't act on impulse with kids. All the experts say that. You have to prepare them."

Screw the experts. She wanted to shout at him, but he was speaking out of pain, exhaustion and frustration, so she held back. "Maybe I'm not an expert, but I know the girls need both of us."

"And how long will you be here? Until you have another race? A podcast? An urgent meeting? When you leave, you'll break their hearts again," he said, his voice cracking. "And I'll be the one who has to deal with that, not you."

His words struck like blows, but she steadied herself, determined to talk this through. "If we prepare them for when I have to go and when I'll be back, they'll be better able to handle it. Like that calendar you made." She nodded at the X's on the fridge. "They'll see that someone they love can leave, but still return."

"You're only guessing, Aubrey."

She remembered Sienna's scared voice on the phone, and how she knew she had to come. She was right, experts be damned. "We're all guessing, Dixon. And you could use the help. Admit it. You don't have time to go to the grocery store. Sienna says you've been feeding them peanut butter sandwiches for supper and you ran out of juice boxes."

"They should drink more milk anyway," he said. "We're adjusting. It's only been three days. I'm doing all I can to ease their way. They're sad. I'm sad. We're all sad. We just have to muddle through."

"You don't have to do it alone, Dixon. That's my point. And you shouldn't protect me from the girls' pain—or your own. I'm part of this. I can help. Or at least I have to try."

DIXON STARED AT Aubrey. She was standing her ground, which surprised him. She had fire in her eyes and in her voice. The call from Sienna had sent her flying here from L.A., giving up a training camp she'd told him was a big deal. Her sacrifice moved him, but it was still impulsive, and it hurt more than it helped. She'd leave again—another wrenching loss to endure.

When she'd appeared, it was as if he'd conjured her out of the smoke of the burned pancakes, and his heart had leaped in his chest. As glad as he was to see her, he was also mad as hell that she'd come. He'd hurt her by saying what he'd said, but he was too worn out to hold back.

He hated feeling so torn. He liked things simple and clear. He didn't have the energy to fight an inner war. From the minute Aubrey had showed up, she'd brought confusion into his life.

"I'll be here most of the three weeks until Utah Fest," she said firmly.

"Most?"

"Next weekend I have a trial run with Neil for the Utah race. I can't break my word to him, but I'll be back after that."

"And then what?" he demanded.

She took a deep breath. "Then I'm taking the girls with me to the race."

"Are you out of your mind?" She'd truly lost it if she thought she could drag the girls along on an adventure race.

"Hear me out. It's a festival in addition to a race. Families come with RVs and campers, and there are food booths and bands and games and daytime activities and sing-alongs at night. The girls will have fun."

"But you'll be in a *race*. What are they supposed to do while you're zip-lining across Bryce Canyon?"

"I'll bring someone to watch them. Jessica, I hope. I have to clear this with ALT, first, but that's my plan."

"You want to take four-year-old girls who just lost their parents camping in the wilds of Utah?"

"It's hardly wild. It's at a campground with bathrooms and showers. ALT is hosting me in a fancy RV anyway, so there should be room for all of us."

He forced himself to stay calm. She was clearly talking off the top of her head, making it up as she went along. "Be realistic, Aubrey. Ginger hardly eats. She walks in her sleep. Sienna wets the bed."

"We'll take precautions," she said, a hesitation in her voice, which reassured him that she hadn't lost all sense. "We'll put a rubber liner on the bed, bring spare sheets, and make sure the RV is locked at night. I'll be right there if Ginger gets up. They'll be playing all day in the fresh air, so they'll sleep better. Probably eat better, too. Don't forget, after three more weeks, they'll likely be doing better in general."

"We don't know that. The girls need a predictable, consistent schedule."

"You can't wrap them in cotton batting, Dixon. They need to experience life, try new things."

"They lost their parents, Aubrey. The bedrock of their lives turned into quicksand. They need solid ground under them, not a raft in white-water rapids. This is your dream, not theirs."

"They need to get away. They need a break from their sadness. You and I both know that helps. We had that night, remember?"

"That's not the same." But it hit him low, the memory of being with Aubrey, of forgetting his sorrow and just enjoying the physical moment, the comfort, the release and relief. He'd carried it in his head ever since, soothing and arousing at the same time. Confusing, like everything else about Aubrey.

"It'll be good for them, I think."

"You want to take them away for days, surrounded by strangers, and in the hands of a teenager who's never spent more than a couple hours at a time with them?"

"Why are you fighting?" Sienna's voice was shrill with shock. Dixon and Aubrey turned to see the girls standing in the doorway, dressed, backpacks on, ready to go. With the promise of breakfast in a restaurant, they'd gotten ready faster than usual. "We're not fighting, we're discussing," he said.

"You don't have discussing faces," Sienna pointed out. "You have fighting faces. And you yelled, Uncle Dixon. You did."

"I shouldn't have. I'm sorry."

"You're taking us away?" Ginger's eyes were wide and scared.

"Not taking you away," Aubrey said, shooting Dixon an angry look. "Taking you *along*."

"With strangers?" Sienna asked.

"You'd be with me and probably Jessica," Aubrey said.

"Don't," he warned Aubrey, not wanting her to tell the

girls what she had in mind, not until he could talk her out of it.

"You scared them," she snapped. "They deserve the truth."

"Not now," he said, but he knew she wasn't about to stop. She had fire in her piercing blue eyes.

Aubrey crouched down to the girls' level. "I want to take you girls with me on my next adventure. What do you think about that?"

"You will? You'll take us?" Sienna said, excited because she had no idea what that would entail. This was so unfair.

"I have to find out for sure, but if it works out, yes. Jessica will come with us, if she can, to watch you during the day while I do my race. There will be food and games and other kids to play with, and we'd roast marshmallows over a campfire. We'll sleep in a big RV—that's a home on wheels with beds and a bathroom. Does that sound like fun?"

"Yes! We want to go, don't we?" Sienna turned to Ginger.

"We do. We want a 'venture!"

"Next year would be better," Dixon said, trying one last time to stop this train wreck.

"Now. Not next year," Sienna said. "Aunt Aubrey invited us."

"You don't know what the trip will be like, Sienna," he said.

"There are videos I can show them," Aubrey said. "We can even check out the RV online."

"You don't have permission to bring them. Jessica's got volleyball. That means weekend games and—"

"So why don't you come?" she said to him. She'd clearly surprised herself, as well as him, with the blurted words.

"Yay! Uncle Dixon can come!" Ginger said. "We'll all be together."

"Won't that be great, Dixon?" Aubrey was digging at him and daring him at once, just as she'd done on that cliff—a dare that had ended in her own twisted ankle. "That way you can keep everything safe, steady, stable and routine like you want." Now she was mocking him.

"You know I'm busy at Bootstrap."

"It's only five days, mostly the weekend. Bring your laptop and cell phone. You can work from the campground."

"See? You can work!" Sienna echoed.

"Please, please, please, Uncle Dixon?" Ginger bounced up and down, eyes desperate, as if her life depended on this. Since they'd lost their parents, the girls had extreme reactions to everything—dissolving into tears, giggling hysterically or throwing fits over the smallest thing. Like Aubrey had told Sienna that first night, grief made you react strangely.

Now she'd put him on the spot with the girls. *Thank you, Aubrey.* But he couldn't be angry because he'd caught something else in her eyes. She was scared. She wanted him along to back her play.

Damn it all to hell.

In three weeks, the grant would be in and he'd have hired the social workers. Maybe a couple days out of the office wouldn't kill him....

If you don't go, you'll worry the entire time. He realized he was as leery of Aubrey's ability to handle the girls as his brother had been. Maybe that wasn't fair, but his brother was right about one thing. *You can't be too careful.*

"Don't get your hopes up, girls," he finally said. "There are lots of reasons why this might not happen. There will be other times."

But the girls took his answer for yes and jumped up

and down, hugging each other, dancing around the room, shouting that they were going on a 'venture.

When the girls had bounded out of hearing range, he turned to Aubrey. "Asking me in front of them was low. You don't even know you can bring them."

"You freaked them out by yelling. I had to tell them. And all ALT cares about is me being in the race. How could they mind if my family came along to cheer me on?"

"It's done now. They know. But we're going over all the logistics and looking at the videos of the festival, and if it looks the least bit flaky, it's off."

"Look," she said, her whole body bristling. "I'm as concerned about the girls' well-being as you are. I would never endanger them. You're as bad as your brother. And I don't care what you say, he disapproved of me and—"

"You're fighting again," Sienna said, hands on her hips.

Dixon and Aubrey stared at each other.

"A little," Aubrey admitted. "But it's arguing, not fighting. We both love you and want the best for you, but we have different ideas about what that is."

"Like when Mommy lets us get on the highest monkey bars, but we can't tell Daddy or he'll have a holy fit?"

"Exactly," Aubrey said, a smile teasing her lips.

Dixon found himself smiling, too.

"If you yell, it's fighting," Sienna said.

"Then we promise not to yell," Aubrey said.

"Pinkie swear?" Sienna added.

"Pinkie swear." Aubrey held out a hooked finger.

Dixon linked his with hers, met her gaze and sighed. What the hell were they doing? He kept holding her finger, glad she was here, despite the fact she'd swept in and created chaos. Arguing would be a constant between them, though they'd have to manage it in whispers and away from the girls. On top of that, her continuing presence meant more personal torture for him. Just holding one finger had sent a charge through him.

Maybe this would all go away. The trip might prove impossible and Aubrey would see that running from Phoenix to L.A. would be too much upheaval for the girls and too much hassle for her.

But what if she wants more? What if she wants shared custody? What if she tries to haul them to L.A. for weeks at a time?

That would never work. Life would be one continuous disagreement over homework, snacks, bedtimes, plane flights, video games and on and on—worse than the worst ex-spouse custody conflict.

They couldn't do that to the girls. He had to convince Aubrey to do the right thing before anyone got hurt more than they were already going to be.

WHEN HE ARRIVED home that night, Dixon opened the door to a living room shrouded in blankets and towels, and smelling deliciously of something baking. Aubrey had picked up the girls from Bootstrap in time to take them to gymnastics, freeing him to do a couple extra hours at work. He had to admit it was a relief to not have to rush home and swing into action dealing with complaints and meals.

"Shh, Uncle Dixon," Ginger said, her face streaked with chocolate, a huge cookie in her hand, hair in crooked ponytails. "Auntie Aubba is asleep."

"We were playing hide-and-seek in Camping Town and she went asleep under the table."

"Where's your sister?" Dixon asked.

"Making ice cream sandwiches with the cookies we baked."

"Don't eat any more of that. You'll spoil your supper."

"For supper we're having a buffy."

"A buffy?"

She shrugged. "It's what Auntie Aubba said."

"Is that right?" He got on his hands and knees and crawled into the dim tent, which smelled of fabric softener. He realized that meant Aubrey had done the laundry, which had required a trip to the market for detergent and, evidently, ingredients for cookies.

Near the wall, through an orange sheet, he saw Aubrey's silhouette. He crawled under the cloth and found her asleep, a flick of chocolate on one cheek, a strand of hair stuck to her lips. In the light through the orange fabric, her face glowed. She looked young and peaceful and so pretty. Carefully, he pulled the hair from her lips. He'd dreamed of them just the night before and had woken up sweaty and frustrated.

He was still studying her when her eyes opened, their sharp blue soft with sleep. She blinked, smiled slow and sexy, as if she expected him here, close enough to kiss.

He felt the urge to do it, until she jolted, and sat up, nearly banging his forehead. "Where are the girls? I was hiding. I drifted off!"

"They're spoiling their supper with cookies bigger than their heads."

"Whew." She lay back against the corner of the sofa, her shirt gapping so that he had to avert his gaze. "Those are supposed to be for dessert. We're making ice cream cookie sandwiches."

"Ginger says we're having *buffy?*"

She laughed, a soft musical sound. "Buf*fet*. I figured we'd take one more swing at the crap in the freezer. I'm going to set out bite-size samples, like a tasting menu, describe them with a French accent, make it fancy and fun. Whatever we can't get them to eat, we'll toss over the fence."

He laughed. "I hope it works. They've had enough peanut butter sandwiches to last a lifetime. You did the laundry?"

"I grabbed soap when I was at the store."

"Thank you."

She tried to push up from the sofa edge, but couldn't get traction, so he clasped her hand and pulled her upright, their faces inches apart. Desire roared through him. One little tug of their clasped hands and their lips would meet in a kiss they almost couldn't help.

"I wanted you to be glad I came."

"I am," he said, "but for all the wrong reasons."

"It's a start." She smiled again and it was so sexy he almost threw her onto the floor and tore off both their clothes.

Instead, he crawled out of "Camping Town" and went to the kitchen to spoil his supper with one of those amazing-looking cookies, right along with the girls.

FALLING ASLEEP IN the sheet tent gave Aubrey back some energy, so she was able to perform her culinary act with flare, showing off the sample dishes, one by one, doing her bad French accent, scribbling the names on the girls' whiteboard with markers, putting a smiley or frowning face next to each dish after the girls voted.

She liked seeing the amazement on Dixon's face as the girls wolfed one icky-looking bite after another. She felt as proud as if she'd won first place in a race.

With a flourish, she held out a forkful of Belinda Wilder's nasty Chinese noodle casserole. "Who eez to try next, hmm?"

"Uncle Dixon!" Ginger cried.

Aubrey leaned closer, holding out the fork. Dixon braced her hand and bit into the food. She fought the thrill that washed through her, totally wrong with the girls watching. He seemed to hesitate, too, a spark of attraction lighting his eyes. *I'm glad to see you...for all the wrong reasons.*

She knew exactly what he meant. When he'd woken her from her nap, she'd been dreaming they were in bed together. She'd almost pulled him down with her.

Dixon chewed the food, then said, *"Magnifique!"* and kissed his fingers. The girls went nuts laughing at their serious uncle being so silly.

This is working. In a burst of delight, Aubrey used the pen to make two flicks on Dixon's upper lip—a moustache—and one on his chin for a beard. "You look *very* French," she said, rolling her r's.

"Now me! Now me!" Ginger cried, so Aubrey applied the marker to her face, adding a curlicue to the end of each line, then did the same for Sienna. The girls ran to see themselves in the mirror.

"I could never have gotten them to eat that much," Dixon said.

"That's why I'm here. To do the stuff you can't." She was determined to prove to Dixon she'd been right to come back. Next week, when she left for the trial run with Neil, she'd have the first test of her theory that if the girls were prepared, they could handle her departures. In the meantime, all she had to do was get the okay from Tabitha on the Utah Fest trip and it would all flow from there. She had all her fingers and toes crossed that it would.

IT TOOK FOREVER to get the girls to bed that night. Aubrey had gotten them to eat more, but she'd also riled them up. They kept raving about the 'venture and asking Aubrey questions and getting more and more excited. Dixon had to keep being the buzzkill, reminding them it wasn't for sure yet.

Honest to God it was exhausting. *You're as bad as your brother,* she'd said. Howard could be a wet blanket when it came to fun. That was true.

She came into the living room, saw him and held up her hands. "Don't say it. I know. I let them get too excited before bed." She looked totally wiped out. He remembered that she'd driven all night and been up all day entertaining the girls—except for that nap in "Camping Town." He felt a rush of gratitude to her, and his irritation evaporated. "How about a drink?" he said.

"I bought beer." She started for the kitchen.

"You sit. I'll get them."

He fetched two bottles, pausing to appreciate the fully stocked refrigerator. That *was* a relief. He held out a beer to her. She'd curled up on the sofa in her sleep clothes, which didn't leave much to the imagination.

Hell, he didn't need any imagination. He had memories. He'd held her naked body, been inside her, heard her cry out as she climaxed…

The memory made him want her even more, which was bad, though he wouldn't take back those moments for anything in the world.

"You okay?" she asked, tilting her face at him.

"Fine. Uh. Great." He'd been standing there like a slack-jawed horndog. He carried his beer to the *far* end of the sofa.

She took a long pull on hers, the muscles on her pretty neck twining. "That hits the spot," she said.

"Right. Yeah." *Quit ogling her, you ass.* He swigged a drink. It was quiet in the room, lit only by two lamps. He liked looking at her, watching her shift positions, fold her legs beneath her, her hands always in motion. She began to rub one ankle, then winced.

"That's your bad ankle, huh?"

"Yeah. It's a little weaker than the other one."

"Give it here and I'll rub it." *Way to make it worse.*

She unfolded her leg, the lamplight flashing off her smooth skin, and put her heel in his palm. He used his thumbs to stretch the ligaments in her instep, noticing the bruise from the casserole crash was nearly gone.

"Ohhh, that's so nice." She closed her eyes and sighed so deeply it was erotic. But then everything about her was erotic to him. Her body beneath the thin clothes, her mouth, the way she moved, her arms, her fingers, the gap between her shorts and her inner thigh... *Focus, man.*

"You never told me how your podcast went," he said to keep his thoughts in line. "With that guy...Wing-Suit Man."

"You mean Rafe? Wing-Suit Man's kind of mean, Dixon." She smiled. She was right. He'd mocked the man. He wasn't sure why. "It went well. I got good comments afterward. ALT was pleased. Thanks for asking." But he could tell she knew his real question was about her ex.

He kept rubbing her foot, jealousy rumbling in his belly like hunger pangs. Finally, he couldn't stand the tension. "So how was it...seeing him again?"

"Nice. We went to dinner to catch up. Why do you ask?" She was full-on teasing him now.

"Just curious." He shrugged.

"I see." She sipped her beer, maddeningly silent.

"Well?" he finally had to ask.

"Since you're *curious,*" she said, mocking him, which was only fair, "I'll tell you he's in love."

"With you?" He spoke too quickly and with far too much interest.

"He was never in love with me."

"Then he was an idiot," Dixon said.

"Thank you." She seemed surprised by the compliment.

"He fell in love with his physical therapist after his accident. Her name's Shari. They kind of broke up because now that he's recuperated, he wants to travel and she'd rather sit by the fire and knit."

"They don't sound like a good match."

"That's what I thought. He's going to try to bring her to Utah Fest to show her how fun outdoor sports can be."

"For someone who knits?"

"She does yoga and was a gymnast. The race isn't that difficult. You could handle it easily." She ran her gaze down his body, setting his equipment on fire.

"So he thinks she'll catch the adrenaline addiction?"

"No. It's sort of a compromise. He does yoga with her, for example."

"You think it'll work?"

"Hard to say. She wants him to become a personal trainer. But that's not him. If he gives up what brings him joy, he'll resent her, don't you think?"

"And she'll feel like his jailor." He knew that cold. "If Tommi had given up that Chicago job for me, it would always have stood between us."

"Exactly." She sipped her beer, thinking it over. "On the other hand, if you love someone, you're supposed to make sacrifices. They say it's worth it."

"Depends on how big the sacrifice is."

She gave a quick nod. "I mean even when two people are compatible, it's not easy to live together. Brianna and Howard had things to work out and they adored each other."

"That's true." And Dixon and Aubrey were as incompatible as Wing-Suit Man and his lady. Not that that was up for discussion—important to keep in mind.

"Anyway, if they come to Utah Fest, you can see what you think their chances are."

"*If* I come. If it works out."

"It'll work out. I'll talk to ALT tomorrow. I'm taking the girls to pick out sleeping bags, too. Do you need one?"

"I'm set." He groaned internally, realizing he'd been dragged into her plan, despite his objections. Aubrey was back, crazy chaos and all. He liked it and hated it at the same time.

He realized he was still rubbing her foot. She had cute little toes and he had the insane urge to kiss each one. Thank you, Aubrey.

CHAPTER ELEVEN

SATURDAY MORNING AT six, Aubrey hung up the phone, equal parts psyched and freaked. The girls could come to Utah Fest, but Tabitha wasn't happy about it. *No way am I telling Percy,* she'd said. *And you can't let them distract you. You totally have to nail the race. Total focus.*

Aubrey had promised, but worry had begun to trickle through her confidence. She had a lot to juggle. She had to keep her head in the race so they'd finish strong, do all she could to promote ALT gear, while making sure Neil didn't get upset. On top of that, she had to make sure the girls had a good time and that Dixon felt more confident about her judgment around them. *Don't panic. This is what you wanted. There will be bumps along the way, but you'll make it work.* One good thing was that Tabitha had promised to ask for a bigger RV to accommodate the girls and Dixon.

She found Dixon in the hall bathroom, shaving, the door ajar. Steam wafted around him, fragrant and warm from his shower. She watched, transfixed, as he dragged the razor though the last stripe of cream, his forearm muscles twisting, biceps swelling.

Water had beaded on his chest. He had a towel tied low on his hips—loosely—and she could see those sexy diagonal muscles, and a thin line of dark hair leading down to a part of him she'd had inside her body. *Oh, dear.*

She was steamier than the bathroom.

He noticed her staring in the mirror and stopped shaving midstroke. "Did you need something?" He looked amused.

You...out of that towel and into me. "Uh, yeah, um, I have news." *Pull yourself together. Stick with the point.* The more time they spent together, the less control she seemed to have over her response to him.

"News?" His eyes twinkled, clearly getting why she seemed so distracted.

She forced herself back on track. "Yes. Good news. The trip is on. I wanted to let you know before I told the girls."

"Oh." He didn't seem pleased. He set his razor on the counter and wiped off his face, buying time. "I really wish you'd think this through a little more. The girls are still pretty shaky...."

"We made a deal," she said. "They're going and so are you." He was doing his Howard bit, frowning at her, all serious and judgmental, and it irritated the crap out of her.

On the other hand, the more he reminded her of Howard, the less attracted she felt. He could drop his towel right now and she'd hand it right back to him. Maybe before the month was out she'd be totally sick of him and his fuddy-duddy, stick-in-the-mud, you-can't-be-too-careful ways.

She could only hope.

SATURDAY AFTERNOON AT the martial arts meet, Aubrey was so proud of the girls she thought her heart would burst. She kept catching Dixon's gaze, seeing the same gleam of pride that she knew shone from hers.

The girls kicked and punched and blocked and shouted their *kihai*'s at the tops of their lungs. And when they stood before the sensei's table to answer the philosophy questions, their responses were loud and clear. They both earned their yellow belts.

Aubrey videotaped the girls for her blog, telling them

they would be famous with all her fans. They were thrilled. Already, she was building the girls' athletic self-esteem. She was right to be here as much as she could, no matter how complicated it seemed at times. The trip would be good for them, too, she was sure.

One of the mothers smiled at her and Dixon. "You should be so proud of your daughters," she said. "They are the cutest things. How old are they?"

"Four," Aubrey said, "but they're not our—"

"Thank you so much," Dixon said, squeezing Aubrey's arm to stop her from explaining. When the woman had gone, he said, "The less fuss people make about the girls losing their parents, the better for them."

"That's true," she said. It was a natural mistake to make—assuming Dixon and Aubrey were a couple. Aubrey was having a lot of trouble not making it herself. "I wish Brianna and Howard could have been here to see them." The familiar knot formed in her throat when she thought about her sister.

Dixon put his arm around her waist and squeezed. "Who knows? Maybe they were."

She smiled up at him, grateful and comforted. *Don't make too much of this. Don't get used to this.* Sometimes she was just too tired to fight it.

DIXON WAS SURPRISED that Aubrey's return didn't turn out to be as disruptive as he'd expected. In fact, the days settled into a reasonable routine. He took the girls to Bootstrap in the mornings, while Aubrey worked and trained for her upcoming adventure race. Dixon set her up as a guest at his gym, and she went on hikes, bike rides, did some rock climbs and rented a kayak at Tempe Town Lakes.

At noon, she brought them all lunch—takeout or sandwiches she'd made—and they ate together at a nearby park.

She took the girls with her for the afternoons, driving them to their classes and activities, even a few playdates.

The girls still quarreled more than normal, got into altercations in day care and burst into tears easily, but they seemed more settled. Ginger's appetite had returned. Days passed between sleepwalking incidents, and there'd been only one night terror in ten days. Sienna had only wet the bed twice.

Aubrey seemed to be right that preparing the girls for her comings and goings would make it go easier. When she'd gone to California for the trial run with Neil, there had been a couple of outbursts, but the fact they only had to mark three X's on the calendar before she was due back seemed to help.

So far, so good on that score at least.

Dixon tried to avoid being alone with Aubrey at night when his guard was less sturdy. He was hyperaware of her, picking up her scent from across the house, noticing her shape, how fluidly she moved, how good she looked after a workout—her hair tousled, her color high. He seemed to constantly fight the urge to stare at her lips when she talked.

Crossing paths in the mornings, fresh from the shower, conjured all kinds of possibilities in his mind. At night, picturing her alone in bed, while he tossed and turned down the hall was pure frustration.

Sleeping with her would be a mistake, making it that much harder when she left. And she *would* leave. There was no question about that. He could feel her getting restless. She seemed jumpy, exhausted and, frankly, *bored*.

She must miss L.A., her own gym, her friends, her hangouts, her privacy and her freedom. She had to be itching to be on the move.

The minute he got home, she took off for the gym for

a second workout, returning late, her face red, clothes drenched in sweat—part of her training, she told him, but he'd bet she was working off the frustration of taking care of the girls for so many hours. He felt guilty when he worked late because he knew she had to be chomping at the bit to escape.

All the while, despite all his precautions, he felt himself falling for her, sliding into a false sense of intimacy, a fantasy that they were becoming a family. It was the same thing he'd done with Tommi, and he surely should know better as a result.

He had to constantly smack himself around with the cold facts. They were not a good match. She belonged with a better version of Wing-Suit Man. She could no more sit around knitting sweaters than he could put on the guy's suit and fly.

Aubrey was working hard at taking care of the girls. He'd give her that. One day he came home to find a tent set up in the living room, outfitted for a campout, the air smelling of roasted marshmallows. They were *practicing,* the girls had told him, holding marshmallows on straightened hangers over a hot plate, the fixings for s'mores waiting on the counter.

The scene brought back memories of camping trips he'd taken with Howard, who'd been an Eagle Scout, and that had sent a new surge of grief through him. He still wasn't sleeping. He had no energy and suffered from dark moods only relieved by the joy of seeing the girls and talking with Aubrey.

In a way, preparing for the trip provided a worthy distraction. Dixon shared camping tips from Howard: *don't bother the skunks and they won't bother you.... Don't leave out food to attract bears and raccoons.... Be safe from rattlesnakes by never putting your hands or feet where your eyes can't see.*

The girls listened with wide eyes.

Aubrey rolled her eyes during his lectures. She focused on the cool RV they'd be staying in, which supposedly included a flat-screen TV, DVD player, popcorn popper and a Wii.

He'd believe it when he saw it. Aubrey had the girls so psyched about the trip they were bound to be disappointed. He hoped the girls wouldn't get homesick or scared at night. He hoped Sienna wouldn't wet the bed and Ginger wouldn't sleepwalk.

Stop thinking like Howard. Maybe it'll be great.

Dixon had gradually been moving more of his belongings to the house. His plan was to rent his condo—furnished—for a while. Eventually, he would sell it and the girls' house to buy a bigger one with a pool—a fresh start in a new home without so many sad memories.

At Bootstrap, he'd begun to make headway. The two social workers he'd hired were inexperienced, but eager, and that put the agency at about half capacity. He'd gotten word that they'd made it to the second round on the grant competition. So far, so good.

The employees had walked into his office as a group and offered to take a ten-percent pay cut until the grant money came through. He'd been so touched he'd had to feign allergies to hide his tears.

They had faith in him, though he knew they all missed Howard and Brianna, felt the huge hole the couple had left at the agency's core.

He came in every day with a smile on his face and something to eat—bagels, crullers, and once, bacon-sprinkled doughnut-holes, which were a big hit. It wasn't much, but it was something.

Ten days after Aubrey's return, Dixon was on the sofa working on a proposal when she came in from her night's workout. She limped, shoulders down, seeming totally beat up. When she noticed him, she pulled herself upright and tried to hide her limp. "You're up late," she said.

"That must have been some workout. You're limping."

"I pushed myself pretty hard."

"I thought the Utah race wasn't that demanding."

She shrugged. "I have excess energy to burn."

"You must be getting restless," he said. "You're tied down with the girls, away from home. It's got to be hard." If he let her know he understood, she'd be more likely to confess she wanted to leave.

"Not at all." She threw her shoulders back. "I enjoy the girls."

"Child care is boring, Aubrey. I feel that way, too."

"You do?" Relieved, she dropped onto the sofa.

He motioned for her to give him her foot.

She started taking off her shoe and sock. "What drives me crazy is how much the girls fight. And compete over everything—who gets to put out Scout's food, who Scout loves more. It got so noisy, Scout hid under the bed. And Scout's not afraid of sled dogs, for God's sake."

She set her heel on his lap. Beneath the hint of shoe rubber, he picked up the scent of the lotion she used. It filled the house after she showered, driving him crazy.

He squeezed her instep.

"Oh, that feels *so* good." She let out an erotic moan.

He cleared his throat and focused on the conversation. "Constance said that's typical when children lose a parent. They're more irritable, more sensitive to slights and more competitive."

"So, we're taking Extreme Parenting 101."

"Yeah." He laughed. "Good way to put it."

"Oh…wow.… You are *so good.*"

That was a hellishly sexy thing to say. She leaned her head back, looking for all the world like she was about to come.

He braced himself against biology, but it was no use. Desire surged, and he moved her foot so his hard-on wouldn't nudge her heel. After all this time, he'd expected to be immune to her, but, if anything, it was worse.

"Before this, did Sienna have all these rules about not making mistakes?" Aubrey asked. "If we miss a beat on the ABC song, we have to start over."

"Oh, yeah. Be glad she's out of her *Miss Mary Mack* hand-clap phase. It was way too easy to miss a clap, let me tell you."

"You mean like this." She held up her hands and recited the rhyme as they clapped it out, ending with a miss. They laughed, and the knot in his chest loosened, he felt like himself, like life was easier…nearly normal.

"How are you holding up, Dixon?" She leaned closer to him. "Are you as steady as you seem?"

He smiled. "Not even close. Sometimes it's all I can do to get out of bed in the morning."

"I have the same problem." She stretched her fingers along the back of the sofa. He wanted to take her hand, but the resulting electricity would ruin the moment. "It's depression, you know—part of grief."

"It's been three weeks. I figured we'd feel better by now."

"The ripples roll out for months, and there's an ebb and flow. Just when you think you're better, another wave hits. It takes a while to smooth out. At least it did when our mother died."

"Good to know," he said, noticing the dark hollows under her eyes. He wanted to pull her into his arms and somehow make her feel better, the way she was helping him, but that would only lead to trouble. "The one benefit to the insomnia is I found a couple new grant possibilities online."

"That's good."

"Yeah, but I have no concentration, so I barely handle the daily stuff, let alone dig into new grants."

"I have to flog myself to get out a simple blog post. It's not easy to fake perky, believe me."

"I believe you." Their eyes met, soldiers in the same foxhole. He'd stopped massaging her foot, but it rested on his thigh. Their connection snapped into place, a line of hot energy, urgent as ever. The room was dim and quiet, moonlight through the window glinting off her cheeks, her bare legs, her teeth.

"This is weird, isn't it?" she said. "The two of us sitting around after the kids go to bed talking about our days? That woman at the martial arts test who thought we were together? That's kind of how we act. Like a couple...but without the benefits."

"Yeah," he said hoarsely.

"It's...*frustrating.*"

"Definitely."

"Why do you think I've been doing extra workouts?"

"It's not because the girls are driving you nuts?"

"No. It's you...looking so good all the time...smelling so good...being so *there.*"

"I know what you mean." He experienced a physical longing for her so strong it qualified as *yearning*—his entire being seeking her out, like a plant hunting the sunlight it needed to survive.

Of course, the need for sex was hardwired into their bodies, plus denial had heightened the urge. On top of that, Aubrey brought out his reckless side, the what-the-hell, go-for-it part of him that had arisen out of the anger and loneliness of his youth, the sense that what he did didn't matter because *he* didn't matter. He understood that, but it didn't make this any easier.

In fact, if she said one word, if she leaned in, touched him, shifted her body, breathed that sexy way she had, he would not be able to stop himself. He'd carry her to bed and that would be that.

AUBREY COULDN'T BREATHE. Dixon was staring at her like a starving man at a feast. Rather, a starving man gazing through a window at a feast…with a rock in his hand. His body was tense, every muscle contracted. His jaw muscle twitched and he was taking shallow breaths.

She didn't dare move. Already, he thought her too impulsive. If anyone was going to start something, it had to be Dixon.

The seconds ticked by.

Oh, for God's sake, do it. Give in. Why fight it? It'll be good for us. We need it. Plus, we'll sleep better afterward. We both need sleep, right?

Who was she kidding? If they went to bed together, they wouldn't sleep one wink. And then what?

Then it would get complicated.

There would be expectations. His and hers. Dixon didn't do casual, and they certainly weren't going to get serious with each other.

But sex could be lovely and head-clearing and healing and life-affirming and—

"No."

"Excuse me?" She blinked. It was like he'd read her mind and wanted to stop the runaway train of excuses.

"We can't do this," he said through clenched teeth.

"No, we can't," she said, letting that fact sink in. "The

carnival left town. We had our ride." They had to stick with the agreement. She'd had enough trouble forgetting the first time. If they went for more, it would get confusing and someone would get hurt. They had a lot to get through together with the girls. They couldn't take their eyes off the ball.

She swung her foot off his thigh and jumped to her feet. "Thanks for the foot rub." She'd taken a cheerful tone, but the words came out shaky.

"No problem," he said, looking at her, almost as if he'd wanted her to argue. "Hope you sleep well."

Fat chance now. "You, too." She headed off on legs as trembly as her voice.

In bed, nestled into the pillow, she let her thoughts wander through impossible possibilities. What if they *could be* together? A couple in love…raising the girls…a real family. That would make everything so much easier.

And harder. She pounded the pillow. *Picture it: you're packing for a trip. Dixon's stuck with the girls. Again. You miss a parent-teacher conference, a soccer game, a gymnastics meet. You feel guilty, so you get defensive.*

He withdraws. You try to compromise, but you end up resenting each other. You argue. You fight. The girls cry and beg you not to fight so much.

No. The girls' frightened faces when Aubrey and Dixon had had that mild argument about the trip had been awful. The girls were too important, too vulnerable to risk the inevitable conflict she and Dixon would have.

They weren't compatible. They wanted different things. She couldn't tolerate the boredom and routine that Dixon seemed to crave. It felt okay now because there were limits. They were helping the girls and each other get through the worst of their grief. After that, all bets were off.

She rolled over again, wide-awake. Scout meowed in disgust and jumped off the bed, giving up on sleeping with Aubrey.

"This is no luxury RV. There must be some mistake." Aubrey stared in horror at the pick-up with a camper-shell to which the *Team Extreme Girl* banner had been tied. *No way. This can't happen. I promised the girls and Dixon.*

"Where's the big bus?" Sienna demanded. "With the popcorn maker and the bunk beds and the *Wii?*"

"Yeah, the *Wii,*" Ginger echoed. Scout meowed from the carrier Ginger held.

"I'm not getting a signal," Dixon said, holding his cell phone high. He was tense over the work he'd left when they'd taken off for Utah Fest. He was expecting an important phone call.

"I'll go find Tabitha," Aubrey said, her already high anxiety spiking into the red zone. She sprinted toward the registration table. This was not good at all. The girls were hardly talking to her after she'd made a last-minute trip to L.A. for the grand opening of a new ALT store, barely returning in time to pack for the trip. They'd done all right when she went to train with Neil because of all the talk in advance. The surprise trip had upset them. A lot.

Dixon had been right that her schedule was tough to predict, at least until the ALT sponsorship was confirmed and she could calendar her commitments. Her plan to run back and forth between Phoenix and L.A. would be tough to pull off.

Already, cracks had begun to show in how well she was managing in both worlds. After she'd posted the girls' yellow-belt test on her blog, Tabitha had sent her a private email saying the girls were sweet and all, but mothers weren't ALT's target market, so *cool it on the kiddie posts.*

She'd noticed a drop in hits to her blog, and she had lost some followers. She'd been preoccupied with the girls, and low on energy, so she hadn't been as present or as enthusiastic as usual. And she hadn't even done much research on her next adventure.

She spotted Tabitha at the far end of the registration booth. Decked out in ALT's new line of fluorescent hiking gear, she was impossible to miss. Aubrey trotted to where she stood. "There's been a mistake," she said, hoping it was true. "There's a pick-up truck with our banner on it—"

"Not a mistake," Tabitha said. "That's what we got. There was a miscommunication with the Voyager people. The bigger model wasn't available, but by the time we found out, they'd sent the original one to an RV show in Vegas."

"You're kidding." She stood there, stunned, everything in her resisting this news.

"I wish I was. I borrowed the truck from my brother and grabbed a bunch of camping gear from an ALT store on the way out of town. Worse than that, we got stuck with Rocky as camera guy. He's pissed about not getting the bus, so I figure we'll give him the camper to sleep in and we'll use tents. The last thing I need is a hacked-off videographer. Plus, he has terrible B.O."

"The girls will be heartbroken. They were so excited about the RV." And Dixon would never let her hear the end of it. Neil would be bummed, too. Her head began to pound.

"We've got bigger problems, Aubrey." Tabitha lowered her voice. "Percy's hopping mad about you bringing the kids. He found out."

"Oh, dear."

"He's mostly mad at me for screwing up the Voyager deal. Now the RV promotion might fall through. It's bad.

If my uncle wasn't on the ALT board, I'd be doing free-lance sportswear catalogs this very minute."

"I'm sorry to hear that." Her mouth went dry.

"It's not totally your fault," Tabitha said. "We'll deal with it. What is it you say on your blog...*make the best of every challenge?* That's what we'll do. Come on. I'll show you the camping crap I nabbed."

Aubrey followed Tabitha to the camper, where Dixon stood with the girls. She met his gaze and gave a tiny headshake, telling him the news was bad. "Would you help Tabitha unload the gear while I talk to the girls?" she asked him in as positive a tone as she could manage.

She led the twins away, dropped to her knees and took one of each girl's hands. How to say this...

"There's been a little change. We get to do some real camping. Remember how we practiced at home? This time it will be real tents, and you get to use your new sleeping bags."

"There's no bus?" Sienna asked. "We have to sleep outside?" She sounded scared.

"We *get* to sleep outside. That's more of an adventure."

"But you promised! It had a bathroom." Her chin quivered and tears filled her eyes.

"There's a bathroom over there." She pointed toward the campground facility. "And there are showers." It made her ill to let them down. They were easily upset already. In a strange place with strange people it would seem worse.

"There's no *Wii?*" Ginger asked faintly. "We can't watch *Aladdin* or make popcorn?"

"No, but we'll roast marshmallows and sing songs. And I can read you the *Aladdin* book by the light of a lantern, which will be so cool and cozy."

Ginger's face crumpled and she burst into tears.

Sienna yanked her hand away from Aubrey.

"I know you're disappointed," Aubrey said. "I am, too, but we'll have fun, I promise." Could she promise? God, she hoped so.

Tabitha backed out of the camper, noticed them huddled on the ground and said, "Hey, what's with the tears?"

"Girls, this is Tabitha. She's helping us with the trip. Tabitha, these are my nieces, Sienna and Ginger."

"Are you *sure* these are your nieces?" Tabitha asked in a big dramatic voice. "You said your nieces are *adventure girls.* Adventure girls don't *cry.* Adventure girls *kick ass.*"

The girls stared at her. "You said *ass,*" Sienna said.

"That's because I'm an adventure girl, too. Adventure girls can say the *A* word. Try it. Say *adventure girls kick ass.*"

Sienna managed a smile, but she wasn't recovered enough to test out the swear word.

Dixon came over with a tent under his arm. "I'm going to set us up over there." He pointed toward an open area near some trees.

Tabitha looked him up and down. "You should be on the team. If you can handle a camera, you can be my videographer."

"My job is to watch the girls," he said.

"There are moms all over the place. I'm sure they'd be happy to add the girls to their kids."

"We're set," Dixon said. "Thanks."

Aubrey noticed that Sienna was watching children playing on a small playground at the far side of the campground. There were swings, a slide and an old metal merry-go-round. "You girls want to go play?" Maybe if they made friends they'd cheer up.

Sienna nodded. Sniffling, Ginger took her sister's hand, and they walked toward the equipment. Nearby there were festive booths offering food, carnival games, sundries and camping equipment. The registration table was swamped with people.

Neil would text her soon. They liked to register early, do their skills check before it got crowded, and get the kayak and climbing gear loaded on the race vans so they could scope out the competition before the route reveal, which would happen in the huge fire pit with rows of logs for seats. Normally, she'd have time to post a blog before the reveal.

Instead, she had to help Dixon set up the tents and keep an eye on the girls. *Roll with it. Be flexible. You can make this work.* Flexibility was one of her strengths, but when it came to the girls, she doubted herself. She grabbed her backpack, let Scout out for her usual recon, then headed over to Dixon.

They were nearly finished when she heard her name and turned to see Rafe striding her way, trailed by a woman and a teenage girl. The woman had to be Shari, the girl her teenage daughter. It seemed like a good sign that she'd brought Cecily along.

Rafe hugged Aubrey and whispered, "This better work." After the hug, he turned to introduce them. "Shari and Cecily, this is Aubrey. She writes the blog I told you about. Aubrey, this is Shari and Cecily."

Shari was petite and pretty with blond dreads. She wore a gauzy shirt, loose tie-dyed pants and jute sandals.

"I'm glad you decided to come," Aubrey said, shaking Shari's hand.

"I hope I will be." Shari shot Rafe a look. *Uh-oh.*

"Are you going to race, too?" Aubrey asked Cecily, who had to be boiling dressed in all black. The high-desert sun could be intense. Her long-sleeved shirt said *Die, Yuppie Scum,* and her expression was as black as her outfit.

"God, no," she said, rolling her eyes.

Shari sighed. "I thought we could do the Family Fun Track, but evidently, Cecily doesn't believe in fun."

"Cecily's going to chill, while Shari and I do the competitive track," Rafe said.

"I had to come or I'd be grounded all summer," Cecily muttered.

"The fun track seemed fine to me," Shari said with a rigid smile, "but Rafe insists competing is the only way to go."

"The race is pretty low-key," Aubrey said to reassure her.

Dixon joined them, breaking the tension. "This is Dixon Carter, my brother-in-law," she said to Shari. "Dixon's going to watch our nieces while I race. We thought they'd enjoy the festival."

"Good to see you, man," Rafe said, offering a fist for Dixon to bump. "I hear you're going to raise the kids. That takes guts."

"I'm sorry for your loss," Shari said, leaning in to shake Dixon's hand. "And yours," she added to Aubrey. "It must be so difficult for you both."

"We're managing," Aubrey said, touched by her kindness.

"I'll check on the girls." Dixon clearly wanted to avoid the topic. He headed toward the playground.

Aubrey's phone buzzed and she saw Neil had sent her a text. He was at the registration table. "My teammate's looking for me," she said. "I'm sure we'll see each other later." She hurried off.

When she reached Neil, Aubrey was shocked by how bad he looked. His face was gray, there was sweat on his upper lip and his eyes were bloodshot. "Are you hung over?" Neil rarely drank, and never before a competition.

He shook his head. "Food poisoning. I threw up half the night. It's just cramps now."

"If you want to rest, I can cover the route reveal for both of us."

"If I don't get the orienteering details, we're screwed." He gave her a quick smile. "I'll be okay."

Despite being sick, Neil took the RV issue in stride. He'd brought his camping gear just in case. They registered, did their skills check, and she led him to their campsite and introduced him to Dixon. Dixon said he had to drive into town for missing supplies and left the girls in her care.

He wasn't back before the route reveal, so Aubrey had to bring the girls with her. They fidgeted and argued, until Aubrey let them climb the empty benches at the far side of the amphitheater.

The race director uncovered the race map and went over the course. They would cover two hundred miles over four days. The first day would include a forty-mile mountain bike ride, followed by fifteen miles in kayaks, then an obstacle course, which would likely include a net climb, rope swings, a tunnel crawl and balancing on logs over a stream. At the end of the day, they'd hike to camp.

Unlike more hardcore adventure challenges, where teams could push through the night to improve their positions, Utah Fest required eight-hour sleep breaks until the final overnight.

The second day involved a mountain climb, a steep hike on a narrow trail, an obstacle course and a whitewater swim. Because the swim was downstream, it was considered a "break."

The next day's race, mostly climbing and hiking, was an orienteering challenge. Shortcuts were possible if you could find them. Neil's navigation skills would give them an edge. The last day included bits of all they'd done, and ended at the second campground with a big party and closing ceremonies with prizes for the top six teams.

The girls were bothering some of the racers, so Aubrey had to go after them, missing some route tips the official was giving. That wouldn't have been a big deal, except Neil had been in the bathroom.

Heading back to camp, they ran into Rafe and Shari, so Aubrey asked if they'd go over the tips she and Neil had missed. Shari invited them to join them for dinner over Rafe's mesquite grill, which Aubrey appreciated. Sharing a meal together might give Aubrey a chance to encourage Shari about the race, which could help Rafe rescue their relationship. The race tips might rescue Aubrey and Neil's chance to finish well, too.

CHAPTER TWELVE

As THE SUN went down, Aubrey sat with Dixon and the girls on Rafe's camp chairs, watching their hot dogs sizzle next to Shari and Cecily's tofu burgers and Rafe's T-bone steak.

Feeling weak, Neil had gone to bed after drinking an herb tea Shari made for him.

Aubrey and Dixon drank beer, Shari hot tea and Rafe drank whiskey from a pint bottle. That wasn't normal behavior before a race, she knew, so he had to be upset about how Shari was reacting to the event.

Halfway through dinner, Scout returned from her recon mission, and the girls showed Cecily all the tricks the cat could do, thrilled by the older girl's attention.

When they'd finished eating, Dixon took the trash bag to the Dumpster near the restrooms. "There's some kids with guitars at a bonfire out there," Cecily said to Shari. "I'm going to check it out." She seemed to be resigned to making the most of her imprisonment.

"Can we go, too?" Sienna asked Aubrey.

"I'll walk them over if you want," Cecily said with a shrug.

The girls cheered and grabbed Cecily's hands, so Aubrey could hardly say no.

"Where are the girls?" Dixon asked when he returned.

"They went with Cecily to a bonfire," Aubrey said.

"Cecily used to babysit all the time," Shari said wistfully. "Now it's not cool. In ten years, you won't recognize those sweet little girls," she said to Dixon.

"I'm not looking forward to that."

"Memorize them now and keep the videos handy. They'll give you hope."

They all smiled, but Aubrey felt a twinge. With Aubrey so far away, the girls might become even more distant from her. On the other hand, maybe they would confide in her because their uncle didn't understand them. It was impossible to know and that made her feel worse.

"What got you interested in physical therapy?" Aubrey asked Shari, who seemed to need cheering up.

"Personal experience," she said. "When I was seven, I fell off a horse and broke my leg. When the cast came off, I was afraid to walk. My physical therapist was magic. She talked me through it, showed me I could conquer the pain. I wanted to do that for people."

"She's very good," Rafe threw in. "She fixed me." He extended his arms, as if to prove it. He was clearly feeling the whiskey.

"I hardly *fixed* you," Shari said.

"You fixed what was fixable, babe." He put his arm around her.

"I don't know how you expect to race with a hangover," she said, going for a jokey tone, but she clearly disapproved of him drinking.

"Hell, I could do this race in my sleep," Rafe said, but he put the bottle on the ground, chastened by her comment.

"I wish I felt that confident," Shari said.

"You'll do fine," Rafe said. "You nailed the skills test."

"They only made me climb a few feet."

"Tell her she doesn't have to worry, Aubrey," Rafe said. "She does *power* yoga, not that wimpy relaxation stuff."

"No yoga is wimpy, Rafe." Shari shot him a smile, easing up on him a little it seemed.

"Plus, she was a gymnast and a swimmer. Tell her the skills carry over."

"They do," Aubrey said. "Definitely."

"I'm okay on the kayaking and biking. It's the climbs that scare me."

"Yoga gives you core strength, balance and flexibility," Aubrey said, "which will really make a difference for you. They chalk an easy route for beginners, too. If you're concerned, you could practice on the skill-test rock face."

"Maybe we can do that." Shari looked at Rafe.

"If it'll make you feel better," Rafe said.

"I understand your concern," Aubrey said. "I'm not a natural athlete myself, so I practice as much as I can, do research and talk to experts before I try a new activity."

"Do you have any other tips?"

"Let's see.... Don't stretch for a clip. That was a mistake I made at first—trying to save time by doing as few clips as possible. I ended up doing what amounted to a lot of pull-ups and exhausting myself. Clip a lot so you use your stronger leg muscles more. What you lose in time, you'll gain in endurance."

"That makes sense," Shari said. She seemed calmer, too, which Aubrey thought was a good sign.

"She's got better muscle definition than you, Aubrey," Rafe threw in. "I'm not kidding."

Shari blushed at the compliment.

"You've got a strong partner," Aubrey added. "That's an advantage. Lean on Rafe. Neil's more organized and better at navigation than I am, so I count on him for that. Of course he's stronger, too."

"You seem pretty strong," Shari said. "And brave. I saw that reindeer race on your blog."

"That was scary, I have to admit. I fell pretty hard a couple times."

"You should see the bruise on her backside," Dixon threw in, then stopped short, probably realizing how intimate that sounded. "It's, um, up here. At the hip." He motioned on himself, clearly embarrassed.

"I'd bet you're braver than you think you are," Aubrey said to Shari. "I hear that from my readers a lot. They get inspired by my blog to try something that intimidates them and succeed at it."

"Really?" Hope lit Shari's eyes for the first time.

"Yeah. It carries over, they tell me. I've had people succeed at one of my challenges and then go on to stand up to overbearing parents or apply for a new job."

"Yeah?"

"Yeah. Actually, Tabitha Styles, the PR person from ALT, got the nerve to apply for her job after she got over her fear of closed-in spaces by exploring caves after she saw me try it."

"There aren't any caves to crawl through on this race, are there?" Shari asked.

"I doubt it," Aubrey said.

"At least that." Shari managed a quick smile.

"You'll do great, Shari," Rafe said. "I'm totally confident."

"I'm glad somebody is." She turned to Aubrey. "It must be rewarding to get feedback like that."

"It is. Very."

"She's got thousands of fans," Dixon added. She felt his gaze on her, as supportive as his hand had been on her back at the funeral.

The firelight lit his features, added dramatic shadows, making him sexier than ever. She realized she was happy, excited about the race to come, thrilled to have Dixon and the girls with her.

It seemed too good to be true somehow.

The music started up then. People all around cheered. Many moved toward the sound. The band was clarinet, fiddle, and an accordion, and they started with a fast folk song. Already, people were holding hands and moving in a snaking line.

"Come on, let's dance," Rafe said to Shari, jumping up, reaching for her hand.

"No, thanks. I want to be rested for tomorrow."

"How about you, Aubrey?" Rafe said. "You like dancing."

"We should get to bed." She looked at Dixon as she spoke, then realized that gave the impression that the two of them were sleeping together. *Whoops.* "I mean the girls. Get the girls to bed."

"Right," Dixon said. "Time for bed…for the girls." He seemed as embarrassed as she did. They said good-night and set off.

Aubrey looked at Dixon, as they walked side by side. He was a solid guy, clearly built to be part of a couple. He had the emotional stamina, the devotion, the faith required to make a life with someone, and then a family. For just a second, under the wide-open star-filled sky, she wished it could be her.

They found the girls sitting cross-legged among older kids, jaws hanging, totally intent on the college-age guy who was telling a story. "Then they heard a noise…and a *scream!*"

The girls gasped, turned toward each other, eyes wide as saucers.

Ghost stories? On their first night camping? *Uh-oh.*

"You said Cecily was watching them." Dixon frowned.

"I thought she was." Cecily was a few yards away talking to some boys, smoking a cigarette and holding a beer.

Dixon leaned down to the girls. "Time for bed."

Ginger jumped up and grabbed his hand, clearly relieved to escape.

"No. There's more stories," Sienna cried.

"Not for you, there's not," Dixon said. "Come on."

"I'm going to speak to Cecily," Aubrey said.

"We'll hit the bathroom and meet you at the tents."

Aubrey met Cecily's eye. Startled, the girl tossed her cigarette, set down her beer and hurried over.

"You were supposed to watch the girls. They're too young for ghost stories."

"I just walked them here. You didn't ask me to babysit. Sorry." She clearly felt bad that she'd let them down.

"I should have been clearer," Aubrey said, mortified by her laxity. Dixon would have been far more careful, she knew.

When Dixon brought the girls back from the bathroom, Aubrey got them into their pajamas and sleeping bags, which she'd placed on cots, while Dixon went to organize his own tent.

"Isn't this cozy?" she said, kneeling between them.

The girls were wide-eyed and totally alert. An owl hooted nearby. "What's that?" Ginger asked.

"Just an owl," Aubrey said. "Isn't that cool? We get to hear wildlife."

"Do owls attack people?" Sienna asked.

"Heavens, no," Aubrey said. "He's just saying goodnight, sleep tight."

Leaves rustled from the wind.

"Is that a bear?" Sienna squeaked. "I might have left a juice box out there. Did it come for that?"

"That's wind in the leaves, sweetie. I love that sound. It makes me sleepy."

"I'm afraid to sleep here," Ginger said, starting to cry. "I want to go home."

"Don't be scared. Scout would growl if anything was wrong, but she's already sleeping. Look." Scout was curled in her bed, perfectly content, eager for the race to come.

"I have to go to the bathroom again," Sienna said. She was likely afraid she'd have an accident in the sleeping bag.

"Let's go, then." Aubrey walked her back to the facility, Ginger going along because she was afraid to be alone. The entire way Sienna shot her flashlight here and there in the dark. "I see eyes. Is that a skunk? Will it spray us?"

"That's a dog, hon. Remember all the dogs people brought?"

In the sleeping bags, Sienna complained that her mosquito bites itched too much. Aubrey had forgotten repellent and was out of calamine. "You could rub ice on them."

"No. I'm too cold. My nose is freezing."

"Tuck deeper into your bag, then." She fought impatience. She wanted to touch base with Dixon before he went to sleep, think through tomorrow's route and run down her backpack inventory, especially with Neil not feeling well, but she couldn't do that until the girls were settled.

"I think I have to go to the bathroom again," Sienna said.

"You're just nervous. You hardly peed at all. We're protected, remember?" She patted the bag, making the rubber liner crackle.

Sienna nodded, but only a little.

Aubrey made sure the zipper pull tab on the tent was on the outside in case Ginger tried to sleepwalk, though Aubrey would wake if she got off the cot.

"What if the hook-hand man comes for us?" Ginger blurted.

"The hook-hand man?"

"Jason told us the man with a hook for a hand *haunts these very woods to this very day.*"

"He said that to scare you. There's no hook-hand man. It's all made up." If only she'd anticipated this possibility before she'd blithely sent the girls off to their imaginative doom.

"What about the Viper?" Sienna asked. "He said the Viper is coming…."

"The Window Viper? That's a joke. It's Window Wiper. *I am the Viper…. I've come to Vipe your Vindows.* Get it? He's the window *wiper,* not the *viper.*"

"Oh." But her eyes stayed wide and frightened.

"How about we cover up those bad stories with a good one?" She pawed through the books in Ginger's backpack, pulling out *Aladdin.* She read a few pages, interrupted by more complaints. They itched, they felt sweaty, the sleeping bag was too tight, the cot too squeaky, the zipper dented their cheeks, their noses were cold.

"Look, girls," she said finally, exasperated. "When you go camping, you have to put up with a few irritations in exchange for the fun of being outdoors."

"It's not fun outdoors," Sienna said.

"I hate outdoors," Ginger added. "You said we would have a popcorn maker and a DVD player and bunk beds in a motor home."

"You lied," Sienna, ever the hard one, said.

"I didn't lie. I didn't know we didn't have the RV. We have to make the best of it, okay?" The edge in her voice silenced them for a few breaths.

She'd barely read another page before Ginger said, "My stomach hurts."

Aubrey froze. Ginger hadn't thrown up all week. "Is it a nervous hurt or a throw-up hurt?"

"Throw-up hurt."

"That's because you ate two s'mores and hardly any hot dog," Sienna said.

"It tasted burned."

"It tasted *roasted*," Aubrey corrected wearily. "That's the best part of cooking outdoors." Her brain was about to explode. It was the first night and the girls were miserable. Maybe this had been a mistake. Maybe they were too young, too unsettled for this.

"I think Uncle Dixon bought some Pepto-Bismol in town. I'll go get some and be right back."

It was a relief to get out of the tent and into the open, where she could breathe. The breeze sent the smell of campfires and pine to her nose, which she loved. Normally before a race she'd be excited, eager for the morning. Instead, she was worried sick.

Aubrey found Dixon looking up at the stars, hands at his hips, his strong shape outlined by moonlight. He belonged on the cover of a self-help book about leadership, heroism and overcoming adversity.

For just a second, she felt insignificant, inadequate, outshone. Chiding herself, she forced confidence into her stride, took a big breath and joined him.

"Tell me you bought Pepto-Bismol in town," she said, her voice a little high, her tone a little brittle.

"Why? Who's sick?" He tensed, alert for trouble, eyes searching her face.

"Ginger's stomach's upset. I think it's nerves, but just in case."

"I bought some. Hang on." He ducked into his tent and returned with two bottles. "I got calamine, too. I noticed they both had mosquito bites." Dixon had saved her butt without even thinking about it.

"My fault. I forgot the repellent." She took the two pink bottles from him.

"Other than Ginger's stomach, the girls okay?"

"Sure, if you don't count the fact that they're homesick, scared of bears, owls, skunks and the wind, and it's too hot, too cold, too tight, too squeaky, too itchy. Mr. Hook-Hand might nab them. Sienna's afraid she'll wet the bed and they both think I lied to them about the RV."

She was dizzy from the rant. It had all balled up inside her and she had to let it out. Her foolish idea that they'd all have fun together had been cruel. She'd caused the girls more turmoil, not less.

"You were right. The girls are too shaky for this. Hell, they burst into tears because they couldn't make popcorn or play *Wii*. This is my dream, not theirs. Like you said." She paused. "I just hope I haven't ruined the outdoors for them. One of my bloggers said her parents pushed her to swim too early and she was afraid of water for years. If I did that to them…" She couldn't hide the wobble in her voice. "You should take them home in the morning."

"What?" Dixon looked honestly puzzled. "It's not the end of the world, Aubrey." He smiled at her. *Smiled.* How could he take this so lightly?

"It is to them, believe me."

"Kids get homesick the first night in a strange place. That's normal. If I take them back, they won't learn they can conquer it. That's your motto, right? Feel the fear and do it anyway?"

"Like you said, they're only four. Too young to wrestle alligators." The joke almost hurt her throat.

"It's true that I didn't think the trip was a good idea," Dixon added. "But being here I've changed my mind.

They're out in nature, getting exercise, which is good for the blues. They're meeting kids, having fun, doing new things. They could have done without the ghost stories, but…" He shrugged.

"I wasn't clear with Cecily that she should watch them."

"Live and learn. The girls will be fine, Aubrey."

"You really think that?"

"I'm not always a wet blanket."

She wanted to throw her arms around him and laugh at herself, bury her face in his neck and rest there.

"So go back in the tent, coach, and give one of your great pep talks." He motioned with his hand. "Speak from the heart."

"Now you're giving me my own advice."

"Somebody has to." His smile warmed her, steadied her, pulled in her scattered energy like a flock of birds returning to a favorite branch.

She crawled into the girls' tent and applied the pink liquids as required. Once the girls were settled, she said, "I know you're both homesick—"

"What's homesick? Is it like upchucking?" Ginger asked.

"No, sweetie. It's that funny feeling you get when you're in a new place and you wish you were in your own bed."

"I have that," Ginger said softly.

"Does the pink medicine fix it?" Sienna asked.

"What fixes it is remembering you have your home with you wherever you go. It's in your heart and your mind and in the people you love—your sister, me and your Uncle Dixon."

"That doesn't fix me," Sienna said.

"Not at first, no. This medicine takes one night to kick in. I feel homesick, too, you know. So does Uncle

Dixon. We know we'll feel better tomorrow, so we're not so freaked out. It'll be like that for you, too."

"You promise?" Sienna asked.

"Yes, but you have to *try* to feel better. That's your part of the cure. Can you do that?"

Both girls sighed at the same time.

"Think about the fun you'll have. Hikes and games and junk food. Uncle Dixon will probably take you swimming in the river."

They were quiet, thinking, but Aubrey felt their tension dissipate like smoke on the night breeze.

"I'm sorry I disappointed you about the RV," she said. "I know that's part of your upset. I shouldn't have promised until I was sure."

"Just do better next time," Ginger said. "That's what Mommy says."

Aubrey smiled, imagining Brianna's kind voice gently correcting her girls. "I will," she said and leaned down to kiss her forgiving niece's forehead.

"Sorry we were babies," Sienna said.

"You weren't babies. You're brave adventure girls, just like Tabitha said. I get scared, too, you know."

"You do?" Sienna's eyes glittered at Aubrey, totally intent.

"You bet. But I don't let that stop me. I keep going, and I learn that I'm braver and stronger than I thought I was." She could hear her mother's voice as she talked, feel Brianna's arms around her, and it was like having them both with her. "You'll do that, too."

"Okay." Sienna relaxed into her sleeping bag, the rubber pad crackling beneath her.

"You think you can sleep now?" Aubrey asked, holding her breath for the answer.

"Will you read us *Aladdin?*" Ginger asked.

"Absolutely." But she'd barely finished a page when she heard the slow, heavy breathing of two sleeping girls. She eased out of the tent and found Dixon sitting close by in a canvas chair.

"I listened in. Hope you don't mind."

"Backing my play in case I blew it?"

He shook his head. "Are you kidding? I figured you'd make me feel better, too. You did. You said some good stuff again."

"Thanks." Her heart filled with sudden, fervent emotion. "I love those girls so much. I know it's barely a shadow of how Brianna loved them, but it's almost more than I can hold."

Dixon's accepting gaze erased any embarrassment she felt over the admission. "I know what you mean." His eyes shone in the moonlight, full of shared love for the girls, admiration for her and an extra heat that made it hard for Aubrey to breathe.

"I've said it before, but I have to say it again. There is nothing ordinary about you, no matter what you say on your blog."

She was surprised how relieved she felt that he didn't think of her the way Howard always had. "You don't think I'm a frivolous travel junkie living on adrenaline?"

"Oh, that, too." He grinned. "But you have a spark," he continued more seriously. "People light up around you. I couldn't even blame Wing-Suit Man for staring at you. We all were. I was ready to clock him if he'd tried to drag you into a dance. What an ass."

"He's not a bad guy. He never drinks before a race. He's upset about Shari and—"

"He's all right." Dixon grasped her hands in his, warming her. "It's not him. I just couldn't stand the thought of another man holding you in his arms."

Electricity zipped along her nerves, lighting her up inside. The way he looked at her made her woozy enough to need some of Ginger's Pepto-Bismol. His gaze slid over every inch of her face, finally steadying on her mouth.

"I wanted to be the one."

Her lips parted to speak, but Dixon's mouth covered them in a soft kiss. He waited there…for her to kiss him back or pull away, she wasn't sure which. What happened was heat slammed into Aubrey, the way Dixon had kicked open that hotel room holding her in his arms. She clutched his face and he took hers between his palms. They held on like that, breath hot between them, not moving their bodies, as if they knew any shift would break the spell that allowed this brief and urgent contact. Everything but Aubrey's mouth seemed to be melting away.

After a time that seemed both too long and too short, they separated. Dixon's hands fell away, leaving her cheeks chilly. They stared at each other, gasping for air. "I don't know how to stop wanting you," Dixon said.

She nodded. "I know. Same here."

His eyes burned with the question neither of them had dared ask out loud: *Can we do this? Can we be together?*

"The girls need both of us. You were right about that," he said.

Aubrey's heart quivered, eager for his next words. *Does he think we can? Does he want to try?*

Then she saw that his face held anguish, not hope, and a fist closed around her fluttering heart, stilling it.

"I can't afford to feel any more for you than I already do," he said. "Breaking up with Tommi tore me up. Losing Howard…dealing with that… I can't handle any more."

"I understand," she said because she did. They were both vulnerable.

"I feel close to you," Dixon said, the words slow, as if

he fought to say them. "I want to be with you…but I know it's not real."

"It's wishful thinking," she replied. "It's because of the girls, and because we're both going through this together."

"We have to be careful for the girls' sake," he said.

"They can't take any turmoil or false hope." And neither could either of them. It had been the girls who had brought them together and it was their concern for the girls that would keep them apart.

"So we agree," he said. "It's for the best." He'd said that when she'd stopped arguing about him being guardian. She hadn't liked it any better then.

For a moment, she was sick of doing what was best. She ached for Dixon, and she could see he wanted her, too. She peered at the golden moon, felt the breeze ruffle her hair, inhaled a breath of cool air, and said what was needed. "Right. It's for the best."

STRADDLING HER BIKE, Aubrey lowered her backpack to the ground, earning a complaint meow from Scout, who was eager to get moving. They had a half hour before the race started and Tabitha wanted a staged equipment check so Aubrey could talk about the ALT gear she would be riding, wearing and using. Neil waited for her near the starting line.

"Now sound natural," Tabitha said, so perky it hurt. Rocky wasn't up yet, so Tabitha was holding the camera. Aubrey had never started a race so beat-up, but she did her best to sound lively as she listed the items—lightweight shoes, padded socks with wicking action, space-efficient backpack, sleek cargo shorts, slim-line hydration bag and her ALT mountain bike.

"Got it," Tabitha said, capping the lens. "I need to hustle

Rocky or we'll miss the start and be stuck with your body cams for footage." She sprinted away.

"I bet you could use some caffeine."

She turned to see Dixon holding out a steaming mug, and the smoky aroma filled Aubrey's head. "God, yes." She accepted the cup and sipped. *Mmm.* "Much better," she said, though it might have been the sight of Dixon that had given her the lift. He looked so good with his hair tousled, face soft from sleep. It was all she could do not to kiss him.

"You sleep okay?" Dixon asked, studying her.

"I was up some. Sienna had to use the bathroom." After that, she'd lain awake reliving the kiss, fighting the stubborn desire for more. She had all these *feelings* for Dixon. She knew why. She'd explained it to herself, and to him, but her heart didn't give a damn. Her heart needed a smack upside the head.

"You look great," he said, checking her out, head to toe, giving her another zing.

"It's the new ALT gear," she said.

"It's more than that. It's you, Aubrey."

They held each other's gazes for what seemed like forever. Dixon wore a goofy smile that rivaled the one straining her mouth muscles. Her exhaustion had evaporated. She sparkled, alive, practically crackling.

Two sharp clicks made her blink. Tabitha had snapped her fingers in Aubrey's face. "Hello? We need some pre-race footage at the starting line. Rocky's set."

"Good luck!" Dixon called to her. Aubrey and Tabitha rode their bikes to the edge of the crowd, where they met Neil and a rumpled Rocky.

Neil handed her a sticker with 24—their team number— and she applied it to her sleeve. Noticing how gray Neil looked, she said, "You okay?"

"I will be soon," he said. "Rafe gave me some Tylenol with codeine."

"It's that bad? You need pain pills?"

"Shari's herbal remedies don't cut it." He put a finger to his lips. "Don't tell her, though."

"If you're not well, Neil…"

"I'm here, aren't I? This is a race, isn't it? I don't quit." She loved how committed he was. It was a thing they shared.

"We need more emotion this time," Tabitha said. "Give us fear…doubt…excitement… Go big."

Rocky rolled his bloodshot eyes, Neil his dark-ringed ones.

"I don't know about *big*," Aubrey said.

"We need big. Have to have it."

"Yay, Auntie Aubba!" Ginger's voice made Aubrey turn to see Dixon and the girls standing with the people who'd gathered to cheer the racers. Ginger sat on his shoulders and Sienna held his hand. Both girls were in their pajamas.

"Win the race!" Sienna yelled.

"I'll try," she called back.

"All you can do is your best," Ginger called in her reedy voice, repeating advice Brianna must have given her. Aubrey's heart throbbed at the reminder.

"You're right," she called back.

With the girls and Dixon fresh in her mind, it was easy to give Tabitha all the emotion she needed. Aubrey ran down the challenges of the day's race, sharing her excitement, nervousness and determination. Satisfied, Tabitha uploaded the video onto a laptop. She and Rocky would try to keep up for the mountain bike leg of the race, then hitch a ride with a race van to where the kayaks were set up. At day's end, Aubrey would do a voiceover of the body-camera footage she and Neil got in between.

As the seconds ticked down toward the starting gun, Aubrey got the rush she loved, every nerve and muscle firing, ready to explode into action. This was her bliss. It was even richer because her family was cheering her on. She was lighter than air, wide-awake, and invincible. Feeling like this, how could she lose?

CHAPTER THIRTEEN

LATE THAT AFTERNOON, just as the racers were due back in camp, the sound of a helicopter made Dixon look up from his laptop. He'd meant to be at the finish line to greet Aubrey, but he'd gotten lost in his work.

Not so lost that he wasn't tracking the girls, who were at the playground with Cecily. She'd begged to babysit them to make up for the ghost-story screw-up, so he'd allowed it, keeping a close eye just in case.

That morning, the twins had made friends with two girls, and been invited to their travel trailer to play. Dixon had iced tea with their mother, an elementary-school principal, who offered to keep an eye on the girls so he could work. He found a nearby bench and made a lot of progress on the budget.

The helicopter was close enough he could see *Air Ambulance* in red letters on its white side. Wait a minute. Had one of the racers been hurt?

He shut his laptop and ran to tell Cecily he was going to see what had happened, but she was running toward him holding the girls' hands. They all looked scared. The rotors got louder and he could see the helicopter was landing nearby.

"Someone got hurt," Cecily said. "It's Team 24."

Aubrey's number. God, no.

He handed her his laptop. "Take the girls to our tent," he said, and ran to where the crowd had gathered. He pushed through to where paramedics were helping someone on a stretcher. He couldn't see who it was, but Aubrey's fluorescent green hydration pack lay on the ground beside one of the EMTs.

Aubrey was hurt. How badly? Very badly if it required a helicopter. He bobbed and dodged and craned to see her, but the EMTs blocked his view.

Then someone who'd been kneeling by the stretcher stood. *It was Aubrey.* He'd never been so happy to see her face. She was all right. Relief crashed through him so hard he nearly dropped.

She saw him, saw his expression, and ran to him.

"They said Team 24," he said, his ears ringing. "I thought it was you. I saw your water pack on the ground."

"It's Neil. I gave him my pack when his ran dry. It's his appendix, they think. He gutted it out to the end, can you believe that?"

He couldn't believe she admired Neil for that. Adrenaline-charged fear turned to fury and he said, "You think that's good? His appendix could have burst. He risked his life and for what? A stupid race."

Her eyes widened at his ferocity and she stepped back. "The pain wasn't severe until the last mile. He's getting help, Dixon. I'm sorry I scared you."

He tried to calm down. There was no use yelling at her. "It's the girls you should worry about."

"You told them I got hurt?" Now *she* was angry.

"Of course not, but they heard it was Team 24, so what else could they think?"

"Where are they? I have to tell them I'm okay."

They set off running for the tents. He noticed she favored one leg.

"You're hurt," he said, but she waved off the arm he offered her.

"It's just my ankle." She'd pushed through the pain to finish the race just as Neil had. Not good.

Spotting the girls with Cecily outside the tent, Aubrey sped up, calling and waving as she ran. "I'm okay, girls. See. Nothing's wrong."

When they reached the group, Cecily said, "We heard. Tabitha told us it was Neil's appendix."

"Did you win?" Sienna asked.

Aubrey grinned. "Not yet. Today's just the first day. We're in fifth place. Neil made it to the end of the race before—" She stopped, remembering Dixon's reaction, no doubt. "Before the pain got bad and he had to stop," she finished. She was resting her bad foot on the instep of the other.

"Will you win tomorrow?" Ginger asked.

"I don't know, sweetie." She paused, and her smile disappeared. "If I can't find a partner, I'm out of the race."

"But you were almost winning," Sienna said.

"I have to be on a team to participate," Aubrey said. The ALT sponsorship depended on her doing well in the race, he knew, so she had to be troubled.

"That's not fair," Sienna said.

"It's the rule. If someone else had to drop out, I can join their team." She was clearly trying not to despair.

"How about Uncle Dixon?" Sienna said. "He can be on your team."

Aubrey locked gazes with him.

"I'm taking care of you girls," Dixon said.

"Cecily can take care of us," Sienna said. "She baby-sitted us today."

"She did?" Aubrey said, clearly doubting the wisdom of that.

"I can watch the girls while you two race," Cecily said,

stepping closer. "We had some plans for tomorrow anyway."

"Yes!" Ginger said. "We're going on a treasure hunt and swimming and making friendship bracelets."

"We appreciate the offer," Aubrey said, "but it won't work."

"I'm totally certified as a babysitter, if that's what you're worried about. I know CPR and first aid. I did a good job, didn't I, Dixon?"

"You did fine," he said to her.

"See?" she said to Aubrey. "When I'm in charge, I'm in charge."

"Please, please say yes," Ginger said to Aubrey.

"I'll only charge like $50 a day," Cecily said. "And I'll throw in the overnight for free, since we'll mostly be sleeping."

"The overnight?" He'd forgotten about that. No way could he leave the girls overnight.

"No," Dixon said before this could go further. "I'm not racing. It's not happening."

"Why not?" Sienna started in. "It's not fair."

"It's not fair," Ginger repeated.

"Enough," he said. The idea was crazy in too many ways to list, but when he looked at Aubrey, he saw she was still thinking about it.

What the hell?

Before he could say anything, Shari, Rafe and the ALT PR person joined them. Shari looked tired, but happy, so she must have done all right during the race. Cecily and the girls joined Rafe and Shari.

Tabitha marched up to Aubrey. "We're totally screwed. You can't race solo and no team is down a girl. I'd do it, but teams have to be coed. Rocky's useless. He couldn't hike a mile without needing oxygen."

"So I'm disqualified," Aubrey said quietly.

"Yeah. It's over. Percy will have my head."

"It's not your fault," Aubrey said faintly, obviously devastated by this news.

"As far as Percy's concerned it is. And don't forget the RV deal."

"Couldn't we try another race? It'd be smaller, I know, but—"

"We've been through this. It's this race or nothing."

They stood in silence, letting the bad news sink in.

Shari joined them. Dixon saw that Cecily and the girls were walking away. "I sent them to shuck corn for supper," Shari said to him. "Cecily told me she offered to watch the girls so you could race with Aubrey."

"That was kind of her, but it's not necessary. I won't be racing."

"You can trust her," Shari added. "I complained about her, but she really is a responsible girl. And she likes your nieces a lot."

"I'm sure that's true," he started, but Tabitha cut him off.

"This is a brilliant idea, Dixon! You're Neil's size, so his gear will fit. You'll totally save the day. It's perfect."

"No," he said sharply. "It's not happening." He'd raised his voice and everyone stared at him.

"He's right," Aubrey said, though it had taken her far too long to agree with him. "Camping is new for the girls and they need one of us close by."

"You've got GPS spotters on your straps and cell phones," Tabitha said. "The vans can fetch you if the girls so much as skin a knee."

"The overnight is impossible," Aubrey said. "Period."

"Then do a test run tomorrow. One day's race. Maybe someone else will drop out," Tabitha insisted. "There were some pretty thrashed chicks at the aid station. Maybe we can turn two days of the race into enough momentum to convince Percy to do the sponsorship. You can't give up so soon."

Aubrey looked at Tabitha, then at Dixon. He didn't know whether she wanted him to refuse once and for all or go along with the relentless woman.

"All you have to do is sign waivers and pass the skills test," Tabitha said. "Obviously, you'll pass. Anyone can see that." She studied him again. "What do you say? One day—that's all we're asking. There's a lot at stake here."

"There is," he said. *The girls' well-being...my peace of mind.* He glanced at Aubrey, willing her to put an end to this, but he could see she wanted him to say yes. Her color was high, her eyes bright, hope flickering there. She'd let her partner risk a burst appendix for the sake of the race. She'd go along with this in a heartbeat. He hated that about her.

"I'm sorry, but we can't do it," Aubrey said, surprising him completely. "It's too much to ask of the girls, of Cecily and, most of all, of Dixon. We have to do what's best for the girls."

Wow. His jaw dropped. The woman was constantly surprising him.

"Talk it over, why don't you?" Tabitha said, clearly not giving up. "Talk with Cecily. Talk to the girls. You know they're on board. I'll see if anybody's got the sniffles or a hairline fracture or would take some ALT gear in exchange for their spot." The woman was indomitable.

After she'd gone, Aubrey said, "I'm sorry about all that. I know you can't do it. You need to stay with the girls." Her lip trembled, but she meant what she was saying.

"I do. I'm sorry, Aubrey. I know how much this meant to you."

"Don't be sorry." He saw that the light had gone out of her eyes. What would happen to her blog without the influx of cash from ALT? "It didn't work out. I'll get over it. Something else will come up."

He wanted to help her, but not at the girls' expense. His gut twisted, his mind torn by divided impulses. *Why can't this be simple? Right or wrong. Yes or no. Why does it have to be gut-wrenchingly hard?*

One day. What harm could there be? Cecily had been good with the girls. The principal with the two little girls the twins liked would probably oversee the situation. Dixon and Aubrey *would* be reachable. The race organizers were careful about safety and had spotters everywhere.

Damn it all to hell. Looked like he had some checking to do.

SITTING OUTSIDE HER tent, Aubrey went through her gear methodically, as if she were preparing for the next day's race. She didn't know what else to do. She felt numb. Her journey was over, the sponsorship dead. When she'd lost Neil, she'd lost it all. It wasn't quite...*real.*

Hope flickered, a little blue pilot light not ready to be snuffed out. Maybe another team would need a woman. Maybe they'd let her go solo. Maybe Percy would give her another chance. Tabitha was still out scouring the festival grounds for someone to bribe with ALT gear, so she wasn't dead yet.

You're done. Get used to it. Move on.

She was glad for these moments to herself. The girls were with Shari and Cecily. Dixon had disappeared. She wasn't sure why.

When she told Tabitha no, Dixon had looked *amazed.* He'd expected her to sacrifice the girls to stay in the race.

That had hurt. She loved the girls as much as he did and worried about them, too.

He wasn't as respectful of her career as she'd hoped. He'd been outraged that she'd allowed Neil to stay in the race when he was so sick. As if she could stop Neil from what he was determined to do. How was she supposed to know how bad off he was? Neil himself hadn't known.

She heard footsteps and saw Dixon, a grimly determined look on his face, as if he had an unpleasant but essential duty to perform. *What now?*

She stood to face whatever he had to say.

"I'll do the race tomorrow," he said. "But only one day. The overnight's out. That's all I can do for you."

"What?" She'd expected more bad news. She fought shock, letting his words sink in. "But what about the girls? I don't want them to be scared or unsettled."

"Neither do I." He blew out a breath. "I've been looking into this a little more. I talked with Cecily—laid down the rules—total focus on the girls, no sidebars with friends— and Shari backed me up. I asked a woman to supervise. The twins played with her daughters this morning. She's a school principal and I trust her."

"Wow." She was dumbfounded.

"I talked to a race official. They have good coverage for emergencies. We'll check in every couple of hours and if I need to go back, they'll get me there. The girls want to spend the day with Cecily and I think they should have a say. They've been powerless through all of this. If they feel independent enough to stay with someone other than us, then I want them to do it."

"You do?"

"Yes."

"Are you sure about this?"

"As much as I can be. Even if I were staying, they'd

likely end up with the principal's kids and Cecily anyway. I'm pretty boring as a playmate."

She was amazed and grateful that he'd gone through all that just to help her. "What about you? Are you up for the race? Tomorrow there are climbs, kayaking, hiking…"

"I'll do all right. I crewed in college, so I'm good on the water. I'd like to practice climbing, if you're up for it."

"I'd be glad to. We can do it now if you'd like." She struggled to get past her shock. He was putting himself and the girls through this for *her,* because of what the sponsorship meant to her. "Thank you, Dixon," she blurted. "Really, thank you. I know this isn't easy for you—"

"Don't thank me yet. You haven't seen me on a mountain." He gave her a wry smile she could tell he had to work to produce. Again, her heart squeezed with gratitude… and more.

"And before you ask, I'm good with a compass."

"Really?"

"Don't laugh, but Howard was an Eagle Scout. He took me camping a lot, taught me how to build a fire, use a compass, all that."

"So that's where all the camping rules about bears and snakes and getting lost came from?"

"Pretty much, yeah."

"Well, I'm glad, and believe me I'm not laughing. You're saving me."

"You still have the overnight to figure out, but this gives you one more day of the race."

"This means so much to me." She threw her arms around him. "You're such a good person, Dixon." When they separated, she could tell he was pleased to have made her happy. *If you love someone you make sacrifices. It's supposed to be worth it.* Her own words filled her head and she got another surge of connection with Dixon. They were together, a team, with the girls, with each other, and now on her race. It *was* too good to be true.

When Aubrey and Dixon reached the skills-test area to practice climbing, Rafe and Shari were there using one of the three top-roped routes. Shari had just begun her climb, with Rafe belaying her from below.

"Looking good, babe," Rafe called up to her.

Shari glanced down, noticed Aubrey and Dixon, and smiled nervously. "I'm taking your advice about practice," she yelled to Aubrey.

"Good for you."

"Look up, not down," Rafe said to her.

She nodded, bit her lip and moved her foot to a new hold.

Dixon was already pulling on a harness. Aubrey did the same, then showed him the double figure-eight knot she used to attach her climbing rope to the belt ring. When he'd tied his, they checked each other, tugging on the rope to be certain it was secure.

He yanked hard and she fell into him, laughing, loving the rush she got from the contact. The smell of Dixon mixed with outdoors was glorious. "Looks like you're tied in tight," he said with a slow smile.

For the first time since they'd conceived this plan, it dawned on her that it would be *fun.* She'd been so worried about Neil, about staying in the race, holding on to ALT and making sure the girls were okay, she'd forgotten how much she loved racing and how thrilling it would be to share it with Dixon. She was bringing him into her world, and it felt good.

"For the race, they'll either top-rope the routes like this or post a belayer," she told him, getting down to the serious stuff. The teammate on the ground "belayed" the rope for the climber using a pulley device. "I'll belay first, since

there's a knack to it." It took experience to properly manage the tension and anticipate the climber's needs. "But
I want you to practice, too, in case there's a bottleneck at
a climb and we decide to try a fresh route on our own."

"Right." Dixon moved to the rock face, looking upward, reading the chalked holds, already ahead of her,
which was good. He dipped his fingers into the talc sack
so he'd get a solid grip.

"Any advice?" he asked. She liked that he had no trouble
asking for tips. Some guys got their junk in a twist when
a woman knew more than they did.

"Every climb is a puzzle. Visualize three moves ahead,
but don't fixate because there are always surprises and
you'll have to adapt."

"Believe me, I get that." They shared a rueful smile over
the sad surprises they'd experienced in the past few weeks.

"The goal is to flow in a smooth, continuous movement."

"Got it."

A yelp made them both look toward the sound. Shari
had dropped from the wall. She hung from her harness a
few feet from the rock face.

"It's okay, babe," Rafe said. "Everybody falls. Swing
back to the wall."

"Bring me down. Now." There was a hysterical edge
to Shari's voice.

"Don't quit. You're almost there."

"I mean it. I'm done."

Aubrey knew the first few falls could be scary until
you learned to trust yourself and your equipment. Aubrey looked at Rafe, who clearly didn't understand what
was happening. Fear didn't stop Rafe, it spurred him on.
Shari was near paralysis. If she didn't work through this,
she might lose her nerve altogether.

Dixon unclipped from the climbing rope. "Help her," he said, motioning Aubrey to take his place.

She gave him a few quick instructions on belaying, then hooked in and climbed quickly up to Shari.

"It's no use," Shari said to Aubrey. "Make him get me down. Please."

"Look at me and take a yoga breath," she said, offering Shari a steady gaze. "Once you're settled, we'll talk."

Shari's eyes flitted nervously at first, then finally locked on. She inhaled deeply from the belly, exhaled through her mouth with a strong sound. She took three more breaths, each one giving her more color, easing the tension in her face.

"Better?" Aubrey asked.

Shari nodded. "I'm still done with this. I'm strong, but I'm not like Rafe. I'll never be like him. I'll never love this like he does."

"Forget Rafe," Aubrey said. "Think about you. What do you want out of this? For yourself?"

Shari stared at Aubrey, but her mind was racing, Aubrey could tell. "I'm not a quitter," she said finally.

"I can help you get to the top. Is that what you want?"

"I do. Yes." She settled into determination, calm, in charge of herself again.

"The first few falls scare everyone. Plus, you're tired and frustrated. Trust your body like you do in yoga with a tough posture. This is easier than that, believe me. Keep your eyes on your goal. The top."

Shari nodded and looked up. Aubrey could see her gather her courage, committed to finishing. Aubrey was so proud of her. She felt that way whenever one of her readers reported a new achievement.

"I'm ready." Shari leveled her gaze at Aubrey.

"Good. Start rocking as if you were on a swing. Aim

yourself at that ledge." Aubrey pointed. "I'll meet you there in case you need a hand."

Shari nodded and started swinging her legs.

Aubrey unclipped, grabbed finger holds and shifted to nudge her toes into small pockets in the rock. Once positioned, she clipped in and swung herself onto the ledge to meet Shari.

A few seconds later, Shari reached the spot. Aubrey braced her back, but Shari easily clipped in, totally balanced.

"You didn't need me," Aubrey said. "You've got this. You'll get to the top no problem." She could see that her words had registered with Shari. Aubrey coached her upward, climbing parallel to her, talking Shari through each hesitation.

At the top, Shari scrambled to her feet. "I did it! I can't believe it."

"I can," Aubrey said. "I knew you'd make it."

Shouts and whistles from Rafe and Dixon reached them from below.

"Thank you." Shari's eyes shone with pride.

"Belaying down's the fun part. You ready?"

"Absolutely."

Together Aubrey and Shari fended themselves away from the cliff so Rafe and Dixon could belay them down. Dixon seemed to be a natural at the task.

Once they were on the ground, Rafe picked Shari up and swung her around.

"You're *good*," Dixon said to Aubrey, his eyes full of admiration. It was a joy to hear him acknowledge her skills. She knew that Dixon would no more become an adventure racer than Shari would, but at least she knew he understood why she loved it.

They practiced for an hour, then went for supper. After that, Aubrey joined Tabitha to do a voiceover of the day's race, which they could upload for her fans. She explained what had happened with Neil. Rocky had gotten plenty of footage of the helicopter hauling him away. Earlier, Aubrey had called the hospital and learned that Neil's appendectomy had gone well.

Finally, she explained about her new teammate. As she talked about Dixon, Tabitha kept raising her eyebrows and poking Aubrey with an elbow. She wanted her to hint at a possible romance between Dixon and her.

Aubrey resisted, jabbing Tabitha back.

After, she said, "Forget it, Tabitha. Dixon is my teammate, period. He's helping me out of a jam because he's a good guy. That's all there is to it."

"Come on. I've seen how he looks at you. And you practically quiver when he gets close."

"I do not." But she couldn't deny the buzz of excitement knowing she'd race with him at her side.

"Think about the overnight," Tabitha said. "ALT sleeping bags zip together great, too."

"Dixon won't do the overnight," she said. "I wouldn't want him to. The girls are too fragile."

"We could set it up so he could sneak back to camp at night to check on them. How's that?"

"Just drop it. Please." Before she could argue more, she received a text from Neil—the first word from him since he'd collapsed—and all he'd written was *so sorry to let you down.*

He had nearly died and he was worried about her?

Get better. That's all that matters. Maybe she should have stopped him at the starting line when he told her about the pain pill. Thinking about that, she did a blog post.

*I lost my teammate today. Poor Neil thought he had
food poisoning, but it turned out to be appendici-
tis. He pushed, got us into fifth place before they
air-evac'ed him to the hospital. Talk about having
my back...*

*Loyal teammates are great, but there are lim-
its. Neil risked his life today, and that's going too
far. Luckily, all he'll walk away with is a tiny scar,
but he could have died. Please, friends, don't take
big chances. Stay safe, take care of yourselves...and
each other.*

Finished writing, Aubrey leaned against the canvas back
of her camp chair, her thoughts jumbled. She remembered
Dixon's harsh words: *he risked his life. And for what? A
stupid race.*

Dixon might admire the way she'd helped Shari, but
she couldn't get carried away thinking that he approved
of what she did. He'd picked up Howard's attitudes along
with his compass skills and Aubrey better never forget it.

CHAPTER FOURTEEN

WHEN AUBREY AND Dixon reached the first cliff climb mid-morning, she saw they'd caught up with the fourth-place team. The woman was halfway up the wall, belayed by a race staffer, her partner waiting for her at the summit. Dixon had turned out to be in even better shape than Aubrey had guessed. They'd held on to fifth place even after stopping every couple hours to check on the girls.

The next event was an obstacle course. "How good are you at net crawls?" Aubrey asked, peeling off her backpack to put in the carry basket for the race staffer. Scout jumped down to check out the surroundings.

When Dixon didn't answer, she looked at him. He was snapping a cell-phone shot of a red-rock bridge in the valley below. "You need to put your backpack in the basket so they can haul it up for us," she said.

He turned to her. "This is beautiful country, Aubrey."

"I know." She tried not to sound impatient. "If we hustle, we can pass this team at the obstacle race."

He pointed his phone at her. "A beautiful lady, too."

She held still for the shot, forcing a smile. But she did notice over his shoulder how right he was. The red and orange sandstone cliffs looked windblown, swirling like cake frosting in places.

Aubrey grabbed climbing gear from the bags against the base of the mountain so they'd be set when the belayer was available, while Dixon put his backpack in the basket.

Together they donned their harnesses. "I'll go first so I can alert you to any trouble spots," she said. "I'll be quick, so you'll have more time."

"No need to rush. That's when accidents happen."

"I know what I'm doing, Dixon."

"Better safe than sorry."

"Okay, *Howard*."

He tilted his head at her, puzzled.

"In Brianna's letter she called him Howard 'Better-Safe-Than-Sorry' Carter, and said that if she had a dollar for every time he said that, they'd have traveled to Reno by private jet."

"Too bad they didn't go by jet," Dixon said softly.

Sadness brought her up short and their eyes met. "Sorry to remind you," she said.

"It's okay. Everything reminds me."

"I know what you mean."

Above, the woman climber called, "Belay off."

"Looks like we're up," she said, adrenaline washing away the sorrow. "Remember, don't stretch for a clip, and don't cross-click. Visualize three moves ahead—"

"But be flexible. Go for flow. You told me all that."

She smiled. "You can't be too careful."

"Howard would be proud."

"Oh, I doubt that. He'd be pissed that I dragged you into this."

She was relieved when Dixon smiled.

With the belayer's help, she racked up her line, tied-in, dipped her fingers in her talc pouch, then looked up at the rock face she would scale. It seemed so impossible. How could she ever reach the top without falling? As usual, the rush of fear hit hard.

You can do this. You've done it before. You're stronger than you know. Her mantra was like a magic spell.

Instantly, Aubrey snapped back. Her vision sharpened so the route seemed neon-lit, the bolts glowing, the chalked holds bright white.

She shook out her arms and legs, flexed her fingers, then nodded at the belayer before she stepped onto a ledge three feet up. *Ready...set...move.* She shifted to the left, stretched for a finger hold, then flattened herself against the rough rock. Breathing in the earthy smell, she fitted her left foot into a crack and shifted her weight, raising her arm so she could slap the caribiner into the clip. *So good. So fun.* She gloried in the strength in her arms, the power in her body, her nimble fingers and strong legs.

Then she was off, flying over the stone, going from ledge to crimp to pocket to pinch, zigzagging her way upward, like a human lizard.

She was having so much fun that just before the hardest part of the climb—called the *crux*—she did some *dyno*—leaping from ledge to hold to ledge.

It was a thrill, trusting her body to carry her this way, knowing she had the training and the skill to pull it off.

When she reached the top, she called, "Off belay."

"Belay off," the belayer replied.

Dixon stepped up, ready to go next.

"It's straight on," she called down to him. "Stay flat against the rock when you hit the crux." She pointed to the spot. "You'll nail it."

Dixon surprised her with his speed and sure-footedness. He fell once—bouncing at the end of the slack a few seconds before swinging to re-climb to the anchor bolt he'd missed. She was relieved he'd remembered to drop straight down instead of trying to catch himself on the rock, a move that led to injuries.

When he got to the top, she held out his pack, hers already on, Scout on board and ready to go. "You're a natural," she said.

Dixon turned to look below. "It's hard to believe we did that. From here it looks impossible."

He was right. That was part of the thrill. She hadn't thought about that in a long time. Hearing his first-timer reactions reminded her of her first experiences, an added bonus.

Dixon pulled on his backpack and they set off at a trot for the obstacle course. They did well, but not well enough to pass the fourth-place team. Next up was another climb. The team ahead of them had made the summit, but the race staffer was off-loading supplies at the aid station.

Not willing to wait, Aubrey asked Dixon to belay for her. She would anchor a top rope for Dixon if the staffer wasn't ready to belay him.

She went fast, eager to bank time. Halfway up, she risked a stretch and missed, dropping into a fall.

Damn. "Leave it," she called to Dixon, so he wouldn't mess with her slack. She leaned forward, until she was nearly upside down, a quick way to start the hike-jump back up.

"I'll get you closer," he yelled, yanking up the slack. The move forced Aubrey to slam her head into the wall. She saw stars as pain burst inside her skull. Checking the spot, she found a little blood and the beginning of a lump. Not serious, but not fun.

"You all right?" Dixon called up to her.

"Fine," she said, clipping onto the bolt she'd missed. She was waiting impatiently when Dixon got to the top.

"Let me see your head. You hit hard," he said.

"It's fine." She avoided his hand. "We gotta roll."

"You could have a concussion. Let me check your pupils."

"My pupils are fine. My skull's fine. For God's sake, trust me." She shouldn't have snapped, but they didn't have time to waste on explanations. A quarter-mile later, they reached a narrow plank bridge. Aubrey took the lead, Dixon followed close behind. She was halfway across when a small gap caught one foot and she rocked forward and back. She would have easily caught her balance, but Dixon grabbed her, playing hero, and they both fell into the river.

The water was ice-cold, but she was too pissed to feel it. Weighed down by their packs, fighting a strong current, it took forever to reach shore. Dragging herself onto the bank, she whistled for Scout, who had leaped to safety, then began tromping back to the bridge, water squelching in her boots. She didn't hear Dixon behind her, so she turned and saw him *studying the map.*

At this rate, they'd be lucky to place at all. "Let's go!" she yelled at him.

"This way. Shortcut." He waved her over.

Blowing out a breath, she trotted to him. *You better be right.*

"A half-kilometer downstream, there's a steep trail that will intersect the main one." He showed her.

She didn't quite get it, but she figured he knew what he was talking about. "Let's go."

"Sorry I knocked you into the water. I thought you were dizzy from the blow to your head."

"When I say I'm good I'm good, Dixon. If you believed me, I wouldn't have a goose egg on the back of my head right now. Let's go." *The man's here out of the kindness of his heart. Don't abuse him.*

She was hurt, truth be told. Dixon didn't think she knew what she was doing any more than Howard had.

They pushed hard from there, nailing the white water

swim, Dixon whooping in triumph as they skimmed into calmer waters at the end. The shortcut had caught them up to the fourth-place team, and Dixon nailed a route later on that shot Team 24 solidly into fourth.

The last stretch was a hike, followed by a run across the finish line. When they were close enough to hear the air horns and cheers, they moved into a sprint, staying shoulder to shoulder as they ran.

As they neared the end, Aubrey saw the twins waving a hand-painted sign that said, Team Extreme Girl Rules!

Dixon noticed, too, and they both waved at the girls, who jumped up and down, ripping their sign apart in their excitement, but no one cared.

Aubrey's heart just about burst with tenderness. They met the girls for hugs. Their faces were streaked with poster paint and they looked happier than Aubrey had seen them since before the accident.

"Yay, yay, you are almost winning!" Ginger said.

"First is winning. Fourth isn't," Sienna corrected.

"But it's better than fifth," Cecily said. "Time for our song." She handed the girls kazoos and they hummed the frog song loud enough to silence people all around, who applauded when they were done. After that, Cecily took the girls back to Rafe's campsite. Aubrey was impressed with how responsible and upbeat a babysitter she'd turned out to be. Shari had been right about her.

She turned to Dixon. "Thanks for doing this."

"I'm glad I could help. It was fun."

"If this is the end for me, I'm glad I spent it with you." She realized suddenly how much she meant that.

"Good." Their eyes met and held, and she got a strange sense of peace, as if whatever happened from here wouldn't matter as much as this feeling between them.

"Here comes trouble," Dixon said with a groan.

She turned to see Tabitha heading over, trailed by a gloomy looking Rocky. "Maybe she worked a miracle for me and scored me a teammate for the overnight."

"If anyone could, it'd be her. She's relentless."

But Aubrey could see from Tabitha's face that the news wasn't good.

"We'll do post-race comments and a voice-over on your body-cam footage," Tabitha said. "If it looks good and the clicks spike, maybe Percy will come around." She didn't sound that hopeful.

They were about to head off to do the footage when Shari arrived, an urgent look on her face. "Can I speak with you two?" she said to Aubrey and Dixon. Aubrey could see she had tears in her eyes.

"You know where we'll be," Tabitha said, heading with Rocky for the camper.

"Are you okay?" Aubrey asked.

She smiled sadly. "In some ways. I'm proud of myself. I did well on the race. But this is where it ends for me."

"What do you mean? Is it the zip line tomorrow that worries you, because it's not—"

"No. It's me and Rafe. We're over." Her lip trembled.

"Oh. I'm so sorry."

"Don't be. It's right. We talked today. Honestly. For the first time since we've been together. It was while we were hiking."

"He loves you. He wants to work things out, I know." She glanced at Dixon, who looked concerned.

"I know he does. And I love him, too. I can't compete with the adrenaline he lives for. I tried to end it a month ago. I realized I'd been scrambling for activities to keep him interested because my life—the life I love—bores him to tears. This was one last chance, but it's not enough. We're too far apart."

"You can't compromise?" Aubrey's heart ached for them. "Both give a little."

"Sometimes a compromise makes everybody miserable. We deserve better than miserable."

"I'm so sorry," Aubrey said.

"Yes," Dixon said, clearing his throat, clearly uncomfortable. "It's, um, sad to hear." He'd turned beet-red.

"Anyway, there's good news for you," Shari said, forcing a smile onto her face. "That's why I wanted to talk to you. Cecily and I will head home in the morning, but Rafe is staying."

"He is?" Aubrey said, not getting the point.

"So he can be on your team and finish the race with you." Shari squeezed Aubrey's arm. "That way you don't have to worry about the overnight." She looked up at Dixon. "You can stay with your girls."

"You're kidding," Aubrey said.

"Not at all. It works out for everyone. Rafe is happier out here than he ever was with me."

"I don't know what to say," Aubrey said. It seemed terrible to benefit from their heartbreak, but she could see how this would save her.

"Say you'll win. That's what he needs right now."

"I'll do my best."

"Thank you for what you said to me up on that rock face. You made me think about what *I* wanted, apart from Rafe, for myself. These past months, I'd lost sight of that. I'll always be grateful to you." She leaned in and gave Aubrey a hug, then hurried away, clearly wanting to hide her tears.

Stunned, Aubrey just stood there.

"You better tell Tabitha," Dixon said, smiling, "before she shoves some poor racer off a cliff so you'll have a teammate."

"Right. I should." She headed off at a run, excitement soaring again. She was back in the race. Shari wanted them to win. If anyone could get Aubrey to first place, it would be Rafe.

Tabitha was thrilled, but immediately pressured Aubrey to say on camera how glad she was to be with Rafe again, that it was a *rekindled romance*.

She refused again. *Relentless* was the right word for Tabitha. Aubrey hoped that once the sponsorship came through, Tabitha would be less aggressive. *What if she isn't? What if she never eases up?*

But Aubrey wasn't going to spoil the triumph with new worries. She would zip line that canyon when she got there.

DIXON BENT TO kiss first Ginger, then Sienna, good-night, trading places with Aubrey, who was doing the same. There wasn't much room, so her hair brushed his cheek, his arm her elbow, his knee her thigh, each contact setting off a small charge in his blood, which was remarkable considering how every muscle in his body was in agony from the physical abuse they'd been through. Nevertheless, his equipment seemed raring to go.

"Good night, girls," Dixon said.

Both girls murmured a sleepy "G'night."

"I'll be at Uncle Dixon's tent for a bit." Aubrey held up her phone, into which she'd typed Dixon's number. "If you need me, push the green button and we'll hear your call on Uncle Dixon's phone."

"We know." Ginger yawned, not looking up.

"It's right here between your cots." Aubrey put the phone on the tent floor.

"Can we please sleep now?" Ginger asked.

"Sure. Good night." Aubrey smiled at Dixon, then they both backed out of the tent.

He got to his feet, hiding his grimace of pain, and held out a hand for Aubrey, who bounced up, not the least bit fazed by the day's physical demands.

He could tell how excited she was that she would finish the race. He tried not to think it was because Rafe would be a better partner than he had been.

Don't get your equipment in a twist. They'd lapped one team at least, so Aubrey was in fourth place. He had to admit he kind of wished he could be with her to the end. Despite the pain, he'd enjoyed it. It had been pure pleasure to see her in her element. She was amazing to watch.

Now they walked side by side to the canvas chairs in front of his tent. He lowered himself slowly, wincing as his muscles objected.

"You're sore?" Aubrey asked, grinning.

"A little." He was in agony. He'd considered stopping at the medic tent for an ice pack, but decided that wasn't dignified. He couldn't wait to take some aspirin, crawl into his bag and groan himself to sleep.

He noticed she was rubbing her ankle. "That bothering you? Give it here." She scooted closer, slipped her foot out of her flip-flop and rested it on his lap. He rubbed gently.

She sighed. "You have such great hands. If I were a cat I'd be purring." The low murmur of her words sent another charge through him.

"How's your head?" he asked, remembering the day's mishap on the mountain.

She felt around in her hair. "Down to walnut size." She turned, so he could see for himself.

"Looks okay." He was relieved he hadn't given her a head injury. "Sorry I hurt you and dumped you in the river."

"You were trying to help. I shouldn't have yelled at you.

You volunteered to race with me and it wasn't easy. I'm grateful to you. I really am."

"It was good to get out of my head for a while, do something physical. Making it up that first cliff, looking down from the top…it felt damn good."

"It did, didn't it?"

"After all the dark days, it was good to remember all the beauty in the world." He thought of the photos he'd taken, and pulled out his phone, clicking to the picture of Aubrey. "Take a look." He held it out, and Aubrey leaned in, sending her scent to his nose. Campfire smoke in her hair, camp-shower soap blended with the vanilla sweetness of her skin to make him feel light-headed, though that might have been exhaustion.

"I look sweaty and cranky," she said.

"Maybe a little."

"I've been too stressed over this race. Too worried about ALT, plus the girls, and the struggle to even get out of bed every day."

"That's a lot of pressure."

"But you reminded me how fun it is. When you whooped after we swam those rapids? It made me burst out laughing. It was like I forgot the joy of it."

"I could use a little more joy in my life, to tell you the truth." Trying to match Howard's sobriety and intensity, Dixon had given up, well, fun—that flash of discovery and surprise—in favor of keeping his nose to the grindstone, eyes on the prize. It was as if he feared that if he weakened even a little, he'd be lost forever. He didn't regret changing his life. But that didn't have to be all of it. Aubrey reminded him of what he'd given up.

After that, they talked through the day, their words overlapping, as they discussed the triumphs, the flubs, the branches ducked, the roots stumbled over.

He loved seeing her so excited, her eyes shining, her grin so wide her cheeks became small apples beneath her eyes. He'd thought, along with Howard, that her career seemed impractical, but he saw now that it was right for her.

"Hell, if there'd been a way to make it work, I would have liked to run the whole race with you."

"Really?"

"Yeah. You're pretty remarkable at what you do."

There was a beat of silence filled with a million unspoken things that wouldn't help either of them. He felt a rush in his heart, like the bubble and churn of the rapids they'd swam through. It was affection and caring and a double dose of desire.

He remembered that he'd hurt her feelings earlier. "And I do trust you, Aubrey." She'd read his failed rescue attempts as lack of faith in her abilities. "I couldn't stand the idea of you getting hurt. If anything happened to you, I don't know what I'd do." The possibility emptied him out inside.

"Because of the girls, right? The effect on them."

Like an idiot, he made it worse. "And on me."

What are you saying? Leave it alone. This can't go anywhere. You agreed. But the rush of feelings crashed through every barrier he'd thrown up. "I'm falling in love with you, Aubrey."

She blinked at him and her face softened. "Me, too. I'm falling, too." Their eyes locked and heat pulsed between them, stronger than ever.

What the hell...? This was not good at all. This made things worse. *Stop staring at her. Stop thinking about her. Stop feeling like this. It's useless. Someone will get hurt.* He moved restlessly, as if he thought he could run from this, but intimacy closed around them like the darkness surrounding the glow of the lantern he'd lit.

"What are we going to do?" Her eyes were wide.

"We've talked about this."

"It won't work, I know. We're on different paths. I travel all the time. You don't. And we can't risk the girls' sense of security."

"Exactly."

"It's difficult," she said softly. "When you and the girls waved me off on the race that first morning, I felt like I couldn't lose, like I had my family on my side, so I was invincible. I know it's not real..."

Her words trailed away, but he saw a comet shower of hope flash across her eyes.

Damn it all to hell, he felt it, too.

"It *is* real," he said, sealing his fate. "No matter how hard we fight it, it's there. Right now, all I can think about is taking you to bed."

That did it. That lit the tinder they'd been stacking up since the last time. He watched desire ignite in her eyes. She trembled, seemed to go boneless, so what could he do but catch her in his arms and kiss her with whatever strength he had left?

AUBREY MELTED AGAINST Dixon, ecstatic he was kissing her and that she was kissing him back, not caring one bit how wrong it was. She wanted this. So did Dixon.

Every word they'd spoken trying to deny it had dissolved in the air like a spark that hadn't reached the ground.

Dixon broke away and took her hand. "Come on." He pulled her out of the chair and toward his tent. "The girls have the phone if they need us."

She went with him, crawling into the tent as he held open the flap. He joined her. The two of them and their feelings for each other filled the space, strained the tent, whose thin fabric hardly seemed strong enough to contain all this desire and heat and need.

They undressed hurriedly and slid together into the sleeping bag, face-to-face, lying on their sides, the lining cool and slippery against her back, Dixon hot against her front. Dixon twined his legs with hers, the friction of his hair delicious against her skin. She breathed in the wood smoke in his hair, the musk of his skin mixed with the lime-scented camp soap.

"This feels right." Dixon's gaze was certain. He had no doubt and that filled her with confidence.

"It does," she said. Their lips met in a deep kiss that promised so much more. Their movements were restricted, but neither seemed to care. Dixon slid his hand down her body and found her, making her gasp, turning her entire body liquid.

Dixon gripped her bottom and hauled her tight against him, his hardness pressing into her belly, showing her how much he wanted her.

She wanted him, too—inside, where she was most needy—and she separated her legs and led him to her wet and ready place.

Holding her gaze, he pushed in slowly, watching her reaction, the light in his eyes flaring at each sound she made, each shift of her hips to draw him deeper.

Deeper he went, filling her, feeling so right. Each thrust brought his shaft against her, sending wave after wave of tingles and surges until she could hardly breathe. She wanted it to go on and on. They were climbing together, just as they had the rock face, in flow. He looked into her eyes as he drove into her, telling her they belonged together. She'd never felt so right in a man's arms.

THE NEED IN Aubrey's eyes as Dixon entered her was almost enough to send him over the edge. *Not yet. Hold on.* He wanted to savor every stolen moment. He hadn't known he could want a woman so much. Every touch or shift brought a sound, a flutter of her lashes, a shiver from her. Every few seconds, she would kiss him, as if for air or sustenance, or to be sure he was real.

He understood. This was like a dream, and he wanted it to last all night.

They had little room to move, but they hardly needed it. Every millimeter of motion seemed to make them burn hotter, like a bonfire that would incinerate a million marshmallows to ash.

They breathed together, groaned and cried out, faster now, hungry music in total harmony. At the end, just as he felt her quicken, she breathed his name into his ear in a way that made him feel like he'd been away too long from where he belonged.

Her shivering release drew him into his own. He surged into her, again and again like those white-water rapids they'd swum through, giving himself over to the emotions, giving himself over to her.

Spent, he rolled onto his back and pulled her onto him in the warm wrap of the sleeping bag. He needed this. He needed her. Holding her and all her happy energy filled the hollow place he'd felt since he lost his brother. At least for a little while.

He wanted to stay this way all night, bodies close, legs twined, her cheek on his chest, her soft breath against his neck, reminding him that love was possible, that human warmth could be his every day and all the long nights, warmth against whatever chill he faced—the pressure of saving Bootstrap, the need to make a safe life for the girls, all of it.

That's what you thought with Tommi.

As if she'd sensed that icy thought, Aubrey asked, "Can we do this, Dixon? Can we be together?"

He waited before answering, fighting his doubts, which swelled upward, demanding attention. "I want to try," he said finally, because it was the truth. They'd been cautious and careful, but their feelings had kept growing. *Aubrey wants this, too. Tommi didn't.* He had to cling to that.

Deep down, he knew how impossible it would be, but he refused to go there. He felt too good, almost whole, and he had to hope that wanting it to work would be enough to make it so.

A phone rang, startling them so that they stared at each other, as if they'd been caught committing a crime. Aubrey reached outside the sleeping bag to get her phone from her discarded shorts. They'd flung away their link to the girls as readily as they'd tossed their clothes.

CHAPTER FIFTEEN

AUBREY BLINKED AT the display on her phone. *Dixon Carter. But Dixon's here with me. How can he be calling?*

She snapped out of her haze as if she'd been slapped. "It's the girls," she whispered, grabbing her shirt as she clicked the phone to speaker, so Dixon could hear, too. Dixon got out of the bag and pulled on his shorts.

"Ginger's gone." It was Sienna, her voice small and so scared. "I had to pee, so I woke up and she wasn't there."

Aubrey's heart lurched. She looked at Dixon.

"She's not in the tent?" he asked Sienna, yanking on his shirt.

"No. And it's my fault." She started to cry. For Sienna to cry, it had to be terrible. "Scout wanted out and I left the zipper up so she could get back in, but Ginger sleep-walked. I'm sorry."

"Maybe she went to the bathroom," Dixon said.

"She's too scared to go alone," Sienna sobbed.

"We'll find her. Don't worry." Aubrey zipped her shorts. Dixon grabbed his flashlight and was out of the tent and calling Ginger's name.

Finding her flip-flops, Aubrey crawled out, too. Sienna stood in front of the tent, calling for her sister, too, her voice a small, sweet echo of her uncle's.

Dixon swung the light in a circle, but there was no movement, no little girl wandering in the dark.

"Is she lost?" Sienna asked mournfully.

"I doubt she got far enough to be lost," Aubrey said, feigning calm. They had no idea how long Ginger had been gone.

"The river's close," Dixon said quietly to Aubrey.

And the nearest trails followed it. *If she fell in...*

Surely the cold would wake her. "Get your tennies and your flashlight, Sienna, and we'll check the bathroom just in case," she said, amazed she'd managed to sound calm and confident.

"She might have gone to see Cecily or the girls she played with," Dixon said. "I'll check both places and meet you on the trail."

When Sienna emerged from the tent, Aubrey took the flashlight and swept the girl up into her arms, not waiting for her to put on her shoes. Her little body was feverish with fear. Aubrey set off at a fast walk, not wanting to alarm Sienna, but moving as quickly as she could.

"Is she scared?" Sienna asked, her voice wobbling with Aubrey's jouncing steps.

"Not if she's asleep." *But if she woke up and found herself lost...* Aubrey prayed they'd find her in the bathroom, calmly washing her hands.

You should have been with them, Aubrey. You belonged in the tent. She'd promised from the beginning to take precautions against Ginger sleepwalking. Instead she'd jumped into Dixon's bedroll with hardly a thought for the girls.

Ginger was not at the camp bathroom, so Aubrey headed for the trail to meet Dixon, running full out, flashlight wobbling as she scanned both sides of the path. Poor Sienna bounced in her arms. "I'm scared," Sienna said.

So am I.

But she had to make Sienna feel better, so she gave her something else to think about. "Remember when Ginger sleepwalked to the kitchen?" she asked. They'd found her staring into the fridge, face aglow, as if there was a golden treasure inside.

"That was because of Mickey," Sienna said.

"Mickey?" Aubrey repeated, her mind racing ahead to what they would do next. Take the trail along the river? Split up? She could see Dixon's flashlight in the distance. If he'd found Ginger he'd be waving and shouting by now.

"In the Night Kitchen," Sienna said.

"The kitchen?" What was she talking about?

"The book. That's why she went there."

"Oh. Right." *In the Night Kitchen* was a Maurice Sendak picture book about a boy who discovers a fantasy world in the kitchen. "I'd forgotten that."

"Another time she got on the table cuz Uncle Dixon wouldn't let us play Toxic Swamp before bed."

"Really?" Aubrey stopped running and stared at Sienna, figuring out the pattern she'd described. Ginger had sleepwalked based on vivid pre-bedtime thoughts. "What book did we read tonight? *Aladdin,* right?"

"Because Ginger was mad about no treasure hunt."

"That's right. Cecily was going to take you to the caves to hunt treasure like in *Aladdin.*"

Small caves lined a side trail. Maybe Ginger had gone there. It was worth a try. She ran toward Dixon, calling his name. When she was close enough to be heard, she yelled to him her plan and took off at a full gallop, pressing Sienna to her body to reduce the jouncing. *Please be safe, Ginger. Please be safe. I'll never let you out of my sight again.*

They reached the narrow trail, loaded with jutting rocks that could trip a dazed little girl, and Aubrey flashed her light here and there. Nothing, until they took a dogleg and found a pale shape on a boulder. Was it Ginger or just an odd rock formation? Her ears ringing, her lungs burning, Aubrey ran closer.

"It's her!" Sienna cried. Aubrey set her down, and they both hurried closer. Ginger was looking vacantly across the trail toward a shallow cave.

Aubrey squatted in front of her. "I'm going to carry you back to the tent, Ginger. Okay?" The experts advised gently guiding the sleepwalker to bed.

Aubrey placed Ginger's arms around her neck and pushed to her feet. Ginger released a sigh, but rested peacefully in Aubrey's arms.

Dixon arrived at a run. "How did you know where she'd be?" he asked, breathing hard.

"Sienna and I puzzled it out. Before bed, Ginger had been thinking about the cave treasure hunt with Cecily, so we guessed she might come here."

"You're kidding." Dixon sounded amazed.

"We guessed right," she said.

"Let's go back now," Sienna said, putting her hand in Aubrey's.

"Not barefoot," Dixon said. "I'll carry you."

"I want Aunt Aubrey." Sienna looked at Aubrey.

Aubrey handed the sleeping Ginger to Dixon, who caught her gaze. "I would never have figured that out," he said. "Good work."

Aubrey swung Sienna into her arms again, pride filling her. When she'd first come, she didn't even know what ice cream flavors the girls preferred. Now she'd been able to figure out Ginger's sleepwalking destination.

Dixon was no longer ahead of her at every turn.

She *knew* the girls. She knew that of all Belinda Wilder's casseroles, they liked the Chinese noodle one best. She knew to cut the tags out of Ginger's clothes because they irritated her neck. She knew Sienna liked hotter baths than Ginger, but if Sienna controlled the faucets, she would choose a cooler temperature.

Aubrey was part of their lives now. They loved her and trusted her.

"Not so tight," Sienna said and Aubrey realized she'd been squeezing her niece with both arms.

"Sorry."

When they returned to the tents, Dixon put Ginger in her sleeping bag and Aubrey zipped Sienna into hers. "I'm sorry I let Ginger out," Sienna said.

Aubrey looked at Dixon before she spoke. "It wasn't your fault. I should have been here with you instead of…" She paused. "…where I was."

Dixon nodded. "We're supposed to watch out for you. We're sorry we let you down."

"Just do better next time," Sienna said sleepily, turning onto her side. Ginger wouldn't remember what had happened. Would Sienna be troubled by it? Would it set her back? God, she hoped not.

"I'm going to be just outside saying good-night to Dixon, then I'll be right back, and I won't leave the tent the rest of the night."

Sienna only sighed.

Outside, Aubrey faced Dixon.

"We forgot about the girls," he said grimly. "We can't do that. Ever."

"You're right. The girls matter most." Her heart froze in her chest. Was this a warning? Was being together too much of a risk?

She couldn't read Dixon's face.

"Do you think we should stop?" she asked him, feeling like a hole was about to open beneath her feet and swallow her.

He met her gaze, his eyes flaring golden again. "I don't

want to stop, but if we don't have any more control than that…" He shook his head.

Don't give up. Not yet. It's too soon.

She wasn't giving up without a fight, so she rose onto her tiptoes and kissed him…hard.

Breaking off the kiss a few seconds later, Dixon clutched her against him. "I don't know what to do," he said, his breath hot near her ear.

She leaned back to see his face. "We deserve a chance," she said. "We'll be careful. We'll make sure the girls are safe. We'll keep this between us for a while, so the girls don't know."

He studied her. She could feel his mind racing, considering, wondering, judging. "We'll decide when we get back to Phoenix," he said. "At the moment, you have a race to win." His smile was tired, but hopeful. He wanted this as much as she did. They would work it out. Her heart soared.

"WE'RE JUST TWO teams down, Aubrey," Rafe said, looking out over the racing river from the cliff where they'd stopped for a Power Bar.

The full moon shone over the odd spikes and mounds below, and Aubrey felt like they were in a science fiction movie exploring a strange planet. Funny, but she longed to share this with Dixon. He'd appreciate the silence, the space, the eerie beauty.

Dixon had been a worthy partner, a decent substitute for Neil, but Rafe was a machine—fast, smart, efficient and insanely strong—almost superhuman on the climbs and hikes. They'd kayaked past the third-place team like they were paddling in place.

It was night and she was dying to crawl into her sleeping bag. Every muscle in her body ached and her lungs felt raw. Her bad ankle was swollen and throbbed nonstop.

If Dixon were here, he'd rub it for her while they found constellations in the sky. She'd missed him all day long.

Dixon would have snapped a photo of the coyotes trotting through the trees, pointed out the eagle circling overhead, noticed the way the trees arched over the river, dappling the water with shadows.

Of course, she'd been impatient with Dixon when he'd paused to admire the view, so this was a wistful fantasy. What she needed now was what she had, a relentless competitor who wanted to win as much as she did—maybe more.

Rafe was still staring into the distance, hands on his hips.

Was he missing Shari? Fighting tears?

She started to say something to him, though he'd waved off her sympathy from the beginning, grimly determined to lose himself in the race.

When he turned to her, he said, "The moon's bright. I say we haul ass all night. The bike stretch is coming up and we've got helmet lights."

"Really? I could use a catnap."

He looked her over. "Your ankle acting up?"

"Some, yeah."

He reached into his pocket and brought out a pill, which he held out along with a water bottle. "Tylenol 3 will ease the pain and I'll bandage your ankle tight. Once we hit the bikes, you'll be off it for hours."

"I don't know, Rafe."

"How bad do you want this?"

"Pretty bad." She'd sacrificed a lot to get here, lost two teammates, but she'd hung in.

"If you win, ALT will *have* to sponsor you. Let's make all this misery count for something," he said.

How could she argue with that? She swallowed the pill with a slug of water. "Get the wrap."

"Good girl."

Near dawn, they passed the second-place team sacked out near the trail, which gave them enough confidence to risk an hour nap.

Aubrey woke up stiff, her ankle aching. By noon, the first-place team was in sight. All that remained was a steep hike, a short climb, a swim across a swift-moving section of river, then a final run into camp.

They pushed hard on the hike and just as they neared the last rock climb, they passed the top team, taking the lead. *You're winning. You're number one. First place.* Aubrey could hardly contain herself. The sponsorship was practically in the bag. The race was theirs to lose and she was determined to stay on top.

At the summit, though, rushing to ditch her gear, Aubrey lost her balance. Too exhausted to catch herself, she landed badly. Something snapped in her heel. She shrieked.

Rafe rushed to her. "What happened?"

She knew if she kept going, she could cause serious damage to her foot, but they were *so close.* If she could limp the few hundred yards to the river, she'd rest it on the swim, which might give her the strength to manage the final footrace. Gritting her teeth against the pain, she said, "Let's go."

Adrenaline helped her, but she favored the foot and that slowed her down. They were still ahead when they reached the river. Scout opted out of the swim, choosing to pick her way over tree limbs and rocks to the other side. The cold seemed to numb Aubrey's foot, and it was a relief to take her weight off of it. With her pack under her stomach, she managed a halfway decent breast stroke, aiming for a beeline to shore. The last climb had taken too much of her arm strength, however, and she found herself slipping farther downstream. Damn it.

Just as she saw Rafe hit shore, a cramp locked her calf like a vise. Gasping against the pain, she reached back to squeeze it and her pack got away from her, drifting along the current.

Damn. She went under, taking in a mouthful of water. She came up coughing, rubbing desperately at her locked muscle. As she struggled, she followed the path of her backpack, speeding away from the spot on shore she'd aimed to reach.

The cramp finally eased, so she swam with all her might. The pack had kept her afloat, making it easier to move. Without it, she seemed weighed with lead. She was so *tired.* For a few seconds, she considered giving up, letting the current carry her downstream until she washed ashore. This was so hard. She'd pushed and pushed. The fun was long gone, leaving only strain and striving and agonizing pain.

Think this through. Focus on what counts. She rolled onto her back to float, taking big breaths to gather the dregs of will. *You're stronger than you know. Conquer yourself and you can conquer anything.*

She thought about the girls and Dixon, who would be waiting for her at the finish line. She'd come so far, worked so hard. She couldn't give up now. It was a matter of drive and determination. She had plenty of both. She'd proved it with adventure after adventure. And all for this, to achieve this.

She would not give up. No way.

She took a breath, rolled over, but her arms gave out and she dropped underwater. Damn. She pushed to the surface, forcing her arms to move. A few yards ahead, a branch extended from the shore, not too high above the surface. If she could grab it, resist the current and hang on long enough to overhand herself to shore, she'd be golden.

Fueled by her mission, by her love for the girls and for Dixon, she gathered everything she had, all she'd built up in herself, and lunged out of the water to grab the limb. *Hold...hold...hold,* she told herself as her muscles screamed for relief. She steadied her body beneath the branch, slid one hand across the rough bark, then the next. Again and again, slowly at first, then faster as momentum took over, until her feet touched the muddy bottom. She let go and crawled onto the riverbank.

Rafe burst through the brush, looking frantic, his face red. "I couldn't get to you. I watched you go under." He pulled her to her feet and hugged her. "Thank God. I thought I'd lost you." She'd never seen him look terrified.

They didn't have time for this. "Are we still ahead?"

"Huh?" He took a second, then clicked into competitive mode. "Not by much. Can you run?"

"I can try." She managed a dozen steps before the pain was too much.

Rafe pulled her onto his back and moved on. Her weight slowed him down, but he kept going. "Almost there.... Last stretch.... Camp's close."

Then she heard running feet coming from behind. They'd never make it with Rafe carrying her. "Let me down. I can run."

He nodded and crouched so she could get on her feet. The pain was so sharp, she nearly fainted, but she took deep breaths, blanked out her mind and let the drive to win take over. It was a living force, a powerful wind pushing her on. *Don't stop. Push through the pain. Pain is weakness leaving your body. People are counting on you. Show them what you can do if you believe in yourself. Do it for your fans, for your career, for yourself. Do it for the girls and for Dixon.*

They would be so proud of her. She pictured them waiting for her, cheering. Dixon loved her. She loved him. They would be together for the girls. Love conquered all. The thoughts were crazed in her head, her senses blurred.

There was a roar in her ears and a roar from the crowd, and she didn't realize the race was over until Rafe got in her face. "Stop. We won."

She nodded, slowed, stopped. Her gaze flew over the crowd seeking her family, eager to see their pride and excitement. *There.* Dixon and the girls running toward her, the girls yelling her name.

Adrenaline had faded and the pain screamed through her. Before she could find a place to lie down, her legs folded and she crashed to the ground, scraping her palms and biting her tongue. Totally undignified.

Dixon crouched. "Aubrey, are you okay?"

"Just lost my balance," she lied, not wanting him to worry. The pain wouldn't back off. She tried to hold it in, but couldn't, and cried out.

"What is it?" Dixon asked, then looked down at her body, spotting her swollen ankle. Her shoe was so tight she'd have to cut it off. It looked bad, she had to admit. "Your foot. Damn!" He stood and shouted, "We need medical help! Now!"

Seconds later, hands lifted her onto a cot, bumping her foot so she screamed. Then they were asking questions, poking her body, making the pain worse. Her eyes kept closing and she slid in and out of awareness. In the background, she heard familiar voices: Dixon, the girls, Tabitha, Rafe, who was loudest. "She's a fighter...." Then muttered words. "Yeah, she went under." Mumble, mumble. "I thought she'd drowned, that I'd lost her..."

She opened her mouth to correct him, explain she'd never come close to death, only ducked under the surface for strength, but she couldn't make herself speak. If she could just close her eyes for a minute, she'd pull herself together…

"MR. HANSON?"

It took Dixon a few seconds to realize the doctor in scrubs standing in the hospital waiting area meant him. *Hanson* was Aubrey's last name.

He stood. "Is she all right?"

"Your wife is fine," he said, offering a businesslike smile.

"My wi—?" They weren't married, but he saw no point in correcting the man. Privacy laws the way they were, Dixon probably had to be related to Aubrey to be told about her condition. Not that many hours ago, he'd hoped one day they would be married. That was over. For good.

"The surgery went well," the doctor continued. "We removed several bone chips. Running on it as she did could have caused permanent nerve damage. The indicators are good, but only time will tell. She's in recovery now. They'll call you when she's awake."

"Thank you, doctor. Very much." Relief shook through him, easing the knot his body had become. He dropped to the chair, loose as the Chinese noodles in the girls' favorite casserole.

She was safe. She would heal. Thank God.

Now he could get angry at her for taking stupid chances, for scaring the girls the way she had. He looked at the twins, pale and frightened, sitting rigidly upright as they had since they'd arrived at the hospital, having followed the ambulance. To the end of his days, he'd remember their faces at the finish line—their thrill at seeing Aubrey win, their horror when she fell to the ground, shrieking in agony.

"Let's get some ice cream," he said. "Come on."

The girls trooped to the cafeteria with him, but barely touched the soft-serve sundaes he'd piled with goodies—cherries, nuts, chocolate sauce and coconut.

When they returned to the surgical area, the nurse told him Aubrey was awake and he could see her.

"Stay here, girls," Dixon said. "I'll come get you."

He entered the curtained-off area around her bed, startled by how small and pale she looked, lying there with her eyes closed. His gut churned. *What if she had died?*

She'd almost drowned in that icy river. What would that have done to the girls? To him?

Fury swelled, overriding the heartbreak of seeing her so damaged.

The only good that had come of this was he'd been slapped out of his fantasy that they could be together.

They lived in different worlds, despite the love they shared for the girls and, maybe, each other. His chest ached as if the truth had been a punch.

"Aubrey?" he said softly.

Her eyelids fluttered, then opened. Her eyes were a foggy blue until she recognized him, when they snapped to crystal, sparkling with gladness. God, he loved when she looked at him like that. Idiot that he was, he probably always would.

"I got it," she said, her voice croaky from the anesthesia. "Tabitha said so."

"Got what?" Then it came to him. "The sponsorship?"

She nodded groggily, her smile lopsided, but as big as she could manage. Jesus. She'd nearly drowned, scared them all to death, been rushed to the hospital for emergency surgery, and her first thought was about the damned endorsement.

Even allowing for her medicated state, that was too much. Before he could formulate a response, he heard quick footsteps and turned as the twins rushed in. "You didn't die," Sienna cried, throwing herself against Aubrey's chest.

Ginger burst into tears and joined her sister, resting her cheek against the back of Aubrey's hand.

"It was only an operation," Aubrey said.

He was confused by the girls' outburst, until the reason dawned on him. "You thought Aubrey would die here because your parents were in a hospital?"

Still staring at Aubrey, the girls nodded.

That was why they'd been so quiet, so pale, so rigid in the chairs.

"Hospitals make you well," Aubrey said. "Didn't you explain that, Dixon?"

"I didn't think to. I didn't realize." He'd been too preoccupied, too angry, too worried to think about their reactions. Shame on him.

"Never mind. It's okay now," Aubrey said, cheerful again, too out of it to absorb the depth of the suffering they'd all been through. "I won the race, girls, and you saw me do it, huh?"

They nodded, their eyes big, still upset.

"Don't be sad. I'm sorry I made you miss the rest of the festival. We'll have a party when we get home. We'll go to Bucky's. How's that?"

"Good," the girls said faintly.

If the EMTs hadn't insisted she needed surgery, Aubrey would have settled for pain pills and an ice pack so she could be at the closing party.

How could you do this to them? How could you be so selfish?

"You helped me win," she said. "All of you." Aubrey shot him a look of fierce love. One more punch to the heart. "I knew you were cheering for me. I knew you'd be proud of me, so I kept going, even when it got so hard I didn't think I could stand it."

Are you insane? Don't tell them that.

Already, they'd heard Rafe, that idiot, bragging about how Aubrey had almost drowned, but saved herself because *she was a fighter, a true competitor.* The girls' eyes had been big as saucers. If Dixon could have gotten past Tabitha and her cameraman, he would have clocked the guy.

Now the girls nodded like bobblehead dolls, swept up in Aubrey's crazy enthusiasm. He realized this dynamic would occur over and over again. Aubrey would swoop into town with some outrageous scheme to drag the girls into. They would go along because they adored her, and he'd have to be the voice of reason, calming them down, soothing their hurt feelings or, worse, treating their real injuries.

On top of that, it would be hell seeing her all the time. He already missed her, for God's sake. All these *feelings* were flying through him, making his gut burn and his head spin. Love and sorrow and grief and worry and anger.

"Thank you so much, Dixon," Aubrey murmured. "You made this all possible. If it hadn't been for you…none of this would have…" Her eyes drooped. "I know we have a lot to talk about…the future and all…but I'm kind of… sleepy…"

"You should rest. We'll talk later."

And it would not be easy or happy.

The hospital released Aubrey four hours later. Hearing she'd be in a cast for six to eight weeks had taken her good cheer down a few notches. The drive back to Phoenix was quiet. The girls slept and Aubrey dozed. They reached home at 2:00 a.m. He carried the girls to bed, helped Aubrey get under the covers and fell onto his bed fully clothed.

Aubrey was still sleeping when he left for Bootstrap eight hours later with the girls—Aubrey was in no condition to watch them. He left her a note to that effect, told her to rest.

WHEN DIXON AND the girls entered the house at six, they found Aubrey sitting at the table, leg on a chair, frosting a cake.

"You're supposed to rest," he said.

"I am. I'm resting and making a cake so we can celebrate."

"Yay!" Ginger said. "Can I help?"

"Me, too!" Sienna said. "I get to help, too."

"You can both help." She gave them knives and placed the frosting bowl between them. He could see she was nervous, so there was more to the cake than a celebration. "What's this about, Aubrey?"

"I have some news. Exciting news." She bit her lip, her eyes darting here and there on his face. "Tabitha called to tell me I might be on a reality TV show based on my blog. Also, she set up a big magazine story about me. I'll be on the cover of *Ever Outdoors*." She paused, waiting for him to speak.

He had no idea what to say.

"That's a big deal, Dixon."

"You'll be on TV?" Sienna asked, the frosting knife in midair.

"The producers have to like me." Now she took a deep breath, rushing to get to the end of her speech. "That's why I have to go to L.A. tomorrow. I have to sign papers at ALT, then meet with the TV people."

"Can we come?" Ginger asked. "We're 'venture girls now."

"Not this time, sweetie. This is an adventure only for me."

The girls' expressions drooped. He hated seeing that and knew it would happen a lot with Aubrey in their lives. He noticed he'd clenched his fists and his jaw ached from being locked.

"I'll be back as soon as I can," Aubrey said, clearly upset about disappointing the girls. "When I know my schedule, we'll mark the calendar for when I'll be gone and when I'll be here, okay?"

And when will that be? When you're not shooting a TV show or running some damn race or a podcast in a hot-air balloon? A derisive sound slipped out.

The girls stared at him. He didn't want to upset them. "How about you two have a piece of cake out back so Aubrey and I can talk?"

"Are you going to fight?" Sienna asked.

"We're going to talk," Dixon said. "There will be no yelling, I promise." He set out paper plates, napkins and forks, while Aubrey cut hunks of cake for the girls. She was smiling, but her hands shook, and her false cheer was gone. Now he could see how exhausted she was. She'd pushed herself to make this cake to soften the blow of her abandonment, just as she'd pushed herself to win the race.

He pitied her and was pissed at her at the same time. The girls needed *her,* not cake…or ice cream, for that matter, which was his cure of choice.

Once the girls were outside, Aubrey said, "I'm sorry I have to leave so soon. The reality show is only a possibility and if it's too much time, then I'll turn it down or—"

"Stop." He held up a hand. "Let's be honest here. This is what you want, Aubrey. The sponsorship, the TV show, the magazine articles, all of it. Don't pretend it's not the most important thing to you."

"It's important, but so are the girls. And you."

"Not important enough."

"That's not fair. You're angry about the girls being scared by the operation. I'm sorry they didn't understand. You could have explained it to them."

"They shouldn't have had to go through any of it."

"You mean the trip? But you said it was good for them. You were glad you'd come, too."

"You nearly died! You risked your *life*. How could you do that to them? To me?" He'd yelled, breaking his promise to the girls, but he was angry. He took hard breaths to calm down. He could see that he'd scared Aubrey. Hell, he'd scared himself.

CHAPTER SIXTEEN

AUBREY STARED AT Dixon, her heart in her throat. She'd never seen him so angry. She'd known he was upset—they'd barely spoken since the hospital—but she'd assumed he was concerned about her, not furious at her.

She had to correct his mistake, fix this before it was too late.

"I was never in danger, Dixon. I got a cramp and lost my pack, so it was hard to swim for a bit."

"Your *teammate,* that ass, bragged that you nearly drowned. The girls heard every word."

"I'm sorry. I didn't realize…"

"No, you didn't. You were consumed with winning the race. You ran on a serious injury, Aubrey. You could have ended up with permanent nerve damage. You didn't see their faces when you screamed and collapsed." He swallowed, clearly struggling with emotion.

Her head spun, as if the chair had shifted beneath her. She hadn't thought this through clearly. "I was out of it or I would have corrected Rafe. Yes, I pushed on with an injury, but you know how much was at stake, how much pressure I was under."

"And you think that's over? The pressure? It's only begun. Tabitha will push you from one stunt to the next, and you know it."

"I won't do anything dangerous. I promise you."

"You can't keep that promise. I know you. You won't."

There was disdain in his voice, the crackle of outrage in his eyes.

"That's not fair," she said, barely able to force out the words.

"When you have children, you have to think of them first. You have to be careful. You don't seek out danger."

"I seek out *challenges,* not danger. And I don't take unnecessary risks." He was overreacting. Why? She could feel something beneath this, as if he'd been looking for an excuse to attack her.

"Besides, there are no guarantees," she said, strengthened by that realization. "You told me that yourself. *Life is risk,* remember? We all die. We don't know when. You could be hit by a car tomorrow. I could get cancer next week." The possibility fell through her, threatening to sink her altogether.

Dixon's face was a stubborn mask. He'd decided against her. It didn't matter that she loved him or he loved her. He was done. She felt suddenly alone, the way she'd felt after Brianna died. She didn't want to cry in front of him. She swallowed hard, blinked.

The buzzer signaled that the wash load was finished. "I have to change the laundry." She grabbed her crutches, grateful for a moment alone.

The sound of someone banging on the glass of the arcadia door made them turn as one. The girls, faces streaked with chocolate, wanted in.

Dixon opened the door.

"We're thirsty," Ginger said.

"We need milk," Sienna said. "It's an emergency."

"Chocolate milk...to go with the cake."

Dixon looked at Aubrey.

"Fix the milk. I'll change the laundry." She needed time

to figure out how to fight back, to defend herself—and them. Surely, they deserved a chance to try.

She hobbled to the laundry room, her palms and underarms burning from being on crutches too long. Her ankle throbbed like crazy. She'd killed herself doing the laundry and making that stupid cake to make up for having to leave. It had been dumb, but she'd had to do *something*.

Now she was sick at heart, certain that no matter how convincing her argument, how brilliant her compromise, Dixon was done.

In the laundry room, fighting despair, she shifted the clean clothes to the dryer and began loading another batch. Emptying the pockets of Dixon's jeans she found a folded page of legal paper. A grease spot had made it transparent enough that she was able to read her name. Brianna's note to her had been on legal paper. So this must be Howard's to Dixon's.

She shouldn't read it, she knew, but she was upset and it obviously concerned her, so she opened it up.

As her eyes raced over the words, a burning path of hurt and outrage raced through her head and heart. She'd been right about Howard's opinion of her. Dixon had been carrying it around with him, which likely meant he agreed with his brother.

Shaking, she refolded the letter, laid it on the crutch grip before she wrapped her palm around it and went to the kitchen to have it out with Dixon.

He was shutting the door behind the girls, who not only had glasses of chocolate milk, but also their Rollerblades.

"They wanted to practice on the patio," Dixon said.

She'd have preferred to stand for this confrontation, but she was in too much pain, so she dropped into a chair and propped her foot on the seat of another. "You think

I'm bad for the girls, don't you?" she demanded. "Just like your brother."

He opened his mouth to object, but she cut him off. "Before you deny it, I found this in your pocket." She peeled the letter from her palm. It was crinkled and curved like a scroll.

Recognizing it, he reached for it. "You shouldn't have read that."

She pressed it against her chest, not ready to relinquish it. "Probably not, but what can you expect from someone so *impulsive* and *irresponsible*." He'd called her both at one time or another.

"Aubrey, I—"

"Let me hit the highlights," she said bitterly, unfolding the page. She found the lines she wanted: "I know and you know that Aubrey's not the mother type…" She skipped down to another line. *"…we can't take that chance. Not with our girls."* She slapped the letter onto the table and glared at him. "You agree with him, don't you?"

"Not the way he meant it."

Though they were delivered softly, the words were a slap, sharp and stinging. She'd expected him to deny it, to apologize for Howard's nasty words, to say he was wrong. "Then how do you mean it?" she snapped, braced for more hurt. *Rip the bandage. Get it over with.*

His face softened…with *pity.* That made her furious. "I know you worked hard to get here," he said. "You should enjoy it, push as hard as you want, go as far as possible. But I can't let you upset the girls again. I won't."

His words sent ice water coursing through her. "What are you saying? You can't keep me from my nieces. You have no right." *He has every right. He's their guardian.* Her skin prickled. "I love those girls with all my heart."

"I know you do," he said. "They love you, too. Of course

you can see them." But he wanted to keep her away. She could see it in his eyes, in the grim set of his jaw. He wanted her gone. It hurt to breathe, as if she'd fallen from a boulder climb and gotten the wind knocked out of her. The man she loved wanted her to disappear. "You said you loved me. You wanted us to be together." Her throat was so dry it hurt to swallow.

"It's not realistic. I see that. Surely, you do, too."

She couldn't form a word, the loss rolling through her, knocking down every happy hope she'd built in her head. The breakup with Rafe had been a tickle of sea foam compared to this crushing wave.

"There's a reason they tell you not to make major changes for a year after a death," he continued. "You shouldn't sell a house or move or…"

"Fall in love? You read that on the internet, did you? More expert advice?" She welcomed her anger. At least she wouldn't cry. "Why don't you trust your own heart?"

"Because it's been wrong before. Our lives don't fit, Aubrey. What we've been through has made us close, but that doesn't mean we can be together. We knew that from the start."

Before Aubrey could react, Ginger was pounding on the arcadia door, crying and holding her skates.

Dixon opened the door.

"Sienna got stuck on the fence. She can't get down."

"On the fence? What fence?" Dixon asked.

"At the school. We wanted to try our skates on the playground, to show Auntie Aubba we were 'venture girls, so she would take us with her, but it's too high. She might fall."

"Let's go." Dixon picked up Ginger and took off. In her hurry, Aubrey knocked her crutches down. Hopping on her good foot, she grabbed them and headed out the door, leaving it wide-open. The school was a few blocks away and by the time she got there, Dixon had gotten Sienna down from the five-foot chain-link fence and was crouched at eye level with both girls. Sienna was taking shuddering breaths.

Aubrey threw down her crutches and sat on the grass, her injured leg extended. She saw scratches on Sienna's legs and arms. The girls had been trying to be brave *for her.* "You're not supposed to leave the yard without permission," Aubrey said, the knot in her throat making it hard to speak. Her eyes burned.

"I told them that," Dixon threw in.

"We had to do a 'venture. Cuz we're brave." Sienna jutted her jaw. "See?"

"I know you are," Aubrey said, taking each girl's hand. "You're adventure girls now and forever, okay? You don't have to prove it to me."

They nodded.

Say the right thing. Make this right. "But adventure girls don't take chances like you did, climbing a fence without someone to spot you." She glanced at Dixon, who nodded his agreement, encouraging her to go on. She could tell he was relieved she was taking over this discussion.

"I took too many chances on my race," she said. "I scared you and Uncle Dixon. That was wrong of me. I promise I'll be very careful from now on."

"Pinkie swear?" Sienna asked.

Don't break down. Keep it together. She clenched against the flood of emotion. "I will if you will."

"Pinkie swear," both girls said solemnly, holding up their little fingers.

Aubrey gripped them with hers.

"You, too, Uncle Dixon," Ginger said.

Dixon wrapped his finger around theirs.

"Okay," Aubrey said. "Repeat after me.... We hereby pinkie swear to always, always be careful."

The girls repeated the vow, Dixon's voice a soft baritone backing them up.

Aubrey pulled both girls close, even though Sienna didn't like smothering hugs, and breathed in sweat, bubblegum and chocolate cake.

The four of them walked back slowly enough for Aubrey to keep up on her crutches. Anyone passing by would mistake them for a happy family returning from a walk. But they were a family in name only, and Aubrey was as far from happy as she could imagine.

As she walked, armpits aching, bad foot throbbing, she realized that she'd put the girls in danger just by being who she was. They'd risked serious injury to prove themselves to Aubrey so they could keep her from going to L.A. or convince her to take them with her.

She had to make this right, but she had no idea how.

"I'LL DO THAT for you," Dixon said, taking the clothes from Aubrey's hands. "Sit on the bed and put your leg up."

Aubrey sat without objection. That meant she was really suffering.

He carried items to her suitcase, which lay open on the bed. The girls were asleep, and she was packing to leave in the morning.

The clothes smelled of her perfume, and he wanted to bury his face in them. *You're such a fool.*

"It's too soon to be driving," he said, sounding like Howard. *Dammit.* He'd meant only to show concern.

"I'll elevate it, don't worry. I have to have a car in L.A." She didn't even bristle. Clearly, she was too torn up to argue. She'd struggled all evening to keep it together for the girls' sake. He admired her strength of will, watched her fight tears during supper and bathtime. When she choked up reading the bedtime story, she'd pretended her throat was sore and handed the book to him.

For his part, he wanted to dump the suitcase on the bed, take back every sensible word he'd said and beg her to stay. Shortsighted and selfish, he knew. Her leaving was the best thing for all of them.

He finished with her suitcase, leaving out what she'd need in the morning, then went to the kitchen to arrange his farewell gesture.

By the time she clumped her way to the living room, he was ready. He held two glasses of champagne, bubbles still ascending in tiny streams along the sides of the flutes.

She took one, looking puzzled. "What's this for?"

"I wanted to toast your success." He touched his glass to hers, the ting sharp in the silence. "I should have congratulated you by now."

She colored, and a smile trembled on her lips. "You don't need to—"

"Yes, I do. You worked hard for this and I'm happy for you." *God, he loved her.* He wanted to touch her cheek, but he resisted, not wanting to make either of them more emotional.

"So we're friends?" she asked.

"We're more than friends, Aubrey. I meant it when I said I love you. I still do." And then he did touch her cheek. He couldn't help it.

She backed away. "But love's not enough, is it?"

"Not for us, no."

When their eyes locked, they both set down their glasses and fell into each other's arms. He welcomed her soft warmth, the way she fit perfectly against him. "I'm going to miss you," he said near her ear.

"Me, too." She buried her face in his chest, and they

held on tight, both breathing hard, struggling against sorrow, and, a few seconds later, the inevitable punch of desire. He wished he could justify one more carnival ride, but he knew that would only make this so much more difficult to do.

Aubrey released him and they both picked up their glasses for another drink.

The champagne tasted sour, as it had the night Howard and Brianna died, a different sadness spoiling the celebratory flavor.

Aubrey's blue eyes pierced him now, and her voice was urgent. "I want you to know I meant it when I said I'd be careful. I won't take risks, no matter what ALT wants."

"I believe you." He did. She'd been sobered by what he'd told her about the girls seeing her collapse and by the fence-climbing incident.

"And one more thing." She took a shaky breath. "I can't pop in and out of their lives. I know that now."

He started to object, to tell her he'd been too harsh, but she kept talking. "I'll stay away until I have my schedule locked down. You need to get settled as a family and I need to be…" Her voice wobbled, so she stopped to swallow before finishing. "…less a part of their lives…" She glanced away, then back, her eyes gleaming with tears. "It's the only way to minimize their misery."

"No. You're family, Aubrey. The girls need you. Come whenever you want. Stay as long as you can. They'll get used to saying goodbye. We all will."

She studied him, her tear-wet eyes flickering with that old hope, a spark in the crackling blue. "Do you mean that?"

"With all my heart."

"Your heart? That untrustworthy organ?" There was no sarcasm in her tone or her smile.

"Sometimes it's all you've got." The deeper truth was he was clutching at her next return like a drowning man flailing for a line. He hoped he was right that they'd all get used to this.

"I've been thinking ahead," she said. "When I've saved enough money, I'd like to rent a house in a suburb, so they can stay with me on school vacations. When they're older, of course." It broke his heart how hopeful she sounded. Tears trapped in her eyelashes glistened like diamonds.

"Aubrey…" he whispered, aching for her. "I wish…" What? That they could be together? That she would give up her career and stay here? That he would suddenly want to zip line the globe with her? That they were different people entirely? "I wish this wasn't so hard."

"But there's no easy way, is there?" she asked and he knew she was right. There hadn't been from the beginning.

FIVE DAYS LATER, Dixon's phone rang as he followed the girls into the house after work. When he saw it was Aubrey, he dropped onto the sofa, an insane rush of pleasure making him grin. Her scheduled calls were at breakfast and bedtime, so the early call meant something was up.

Except there had been early calls and late calls all along. Calls just to check in, to tell him about her day, to ask about his, sometimes just to breathe at each other for a few seconds.

"Hey," he said, hoping not to sound moony. He pressed the phone tighter against his ear, as if that would bring her closer.

"Hey," she repeated, sounding as lovesick as he. They breathed at each other, and he settled into the relief of connecting to her. All day, he felt like he held his breath until he heard her voice or saw her on Skype, despite the bright, fake smile she wore.

"Something up?" he finally asked.

"Actually, yes. I have news. On the spur of the moment I called my grandfather."

"You're kidding!"

"No. I was lonely and I just picked up the phone and dialed. I'm impulsive, remember?"

"That can be good," he said softly.

"Anyway, a woman answered. She's his wife, but not my grandmother, who passed away five years ago. Anyway, this woman, Evelyn, was very friendly. She told me that my grandfather had always regretted the estrangement with his son—my father—and that he would welcome meeting us."

"That's great, Aubrey."

"It is. She said I should write a letter first and send photos. He doesn't do well with surprises, she says, but with the letter, he'll have time to get used to the idea. So I'm sending it tomorrow."

"I'm glad for you. And for the girls."

"So it turns out I have an uncle, an aunt and three cousins, all in Seattle. And there's one more thing you won't believe."

"Hit me," he said, grinning in advance.

"One of my cousins has two little girls. Twins. Age seven. Can you believe that?"

"That's amazing."

"Yep. The girls have cousins—second cousins, I guess. I can't believe it. And I can't wait for us to all get together. I have family." She got choked up.

"You do. And so do the girls."

"Anyway, she says the Metzgers rent a big house every summer on a lake and everybody comes for a week in August. She says she's almost positive we'll be invited."

"That's wonderful, Aubrey."

"I want you to come, too, Dixon. I know it's too soon to be counting chickens, but it will be fun and I want you to be part of it."

"I'd be honored," he said, choking up himself.

"I just wish that Brianna was here, that she could be part of it."

"She did the next best thing. She passed the task on to her sister."

There was silence and he knew her shoulders were shaking as she silently cried. "Thank you," she finally said, then cleared her throat.

"So, you've got that reality show meeting coming up, right?" he said to give her a chance to gather herself. If she got the show, she'd be locked down in L.A. for months at a time, he knew.

"I do. The magazine interview, too. If I'd known they'd push back the meetings I would have delayed the ALT paperwork and stayed longer in Phoenix."

"It was probably for—"

"Don't say it was for the best, Dixon. Please."

"You sound tired," he said.

"I am, I guess." She paused. "It's more that I'm lonely. I miss the girls. And you. I miss you a lot." She said the last very softly.

Whoosh. Love blew through him like a hot wind. Love and yearning. "I miss you, too." Like a vital organ had been torn out—his untrustworthy heart.

"This is so hard," she whispered.

"I know." He gripped the phone hard, his body tightening against the ache of all he missed—her laugh, her smile, her smell. He missed the piercing blue of her gaze and the *surprise* of her, the way he never knew what she might say or do next and couldn't wait to find out. "Whatever doesn't kill us makes us stronger, they say."

"I'm strong enough, okay?"

"It will get better. We'll get numb."

"I don't want to get numb. Do you?"

"If it's better than this, absolutely."

She gave a rueful laugh. "Any word on the grant?"

"Actually, yes. They called with a few technical questions, which means they're seriously looking at feasibility. I think we've got it. That'll keep us going another year at least."

"I'm so glad, Dixon."

"Me, too." The new hires seemed solid. The job bank was back in shape and they'd added more workshops. They were doing okay.

The girls barreled into the room. "Is it Aunt Aubrey?" Sienna demanded. Not waiting for an answer, she went to grab his laptop.

"Looks like we're going to Skype early tonight," he said, reluctant to let go of their private moment.

"That's cool. Laptop's right here," Aubrey said.

The girls argued half-heartedly about who got to click the call button. They weren't fighting as much anymore, which was a relief.

The instant Aubrey answered, Sienna said, "We're getting a cat."

"Uncle Dixon said so," Ginger added. "Because we miss Scout too much."

"Oh." Aubrey looked stricken.

Dixon's gut twisted. "I said we'll see." He should have talked it over with Aubrey first instead of giving in to the urge to ease the girls' gloom.

"Then Scout will have a friend," Ginger said.

Aubrey's smile wavered. "Cats fight over who's the boss of the house," she said. "I'll read what the experts say about how to help them make friends." She was talking herself into it. He remembered that she'd worried that he'd replace her with a girlfriend. Now he'd be replacing her cat. Damn.

"I should have talked to you first," he said.

"It's all right. They should have a pet." There was that fake bright smile.

"See, Uncle Dixon. We should have a pet," Sienna said.

"I need a snack," Ginger said. "Bye, Auntie Aubba."

"Do good in gymnastics Saturday," Aubrey said.

"I get to pick the snack," Sienna said, running off.

"Say goodbye to your aunt," Dixon called to her.

"Bye," she yelled.

"I'm sorry," he said to Aubrey.

"It's okay. They're busy girls." She was trying to hide her disappointment, he could tell. "Send me the video, okay? Of gymnastics?"

"Of course," he said.

"I wish I could be there."

"Me, too." With everything in him. "I'm sorry about the cat idea. I'll try to talk them out of it."

"Too late. The cat's out of the bag...so to speak." She bit her lip, which trembled. "It's what I expected. They're moving on. You all are. It's for the best." But she was about to crumble. "I need to run. Talk later." She disappeared and he was sure she was crying, and probably not silently.

Were they moving on? He didn't feel like he was. He missed Aubrey more than ever. The girls missed her, too. Toxic Swamp was dull without her and the last time they'd tried "French Cuisine," the girls got bored and just ate the first samples he set out. He wasn't sure he wanted to move on. He was waiting for something. He wasn't sure what.

"DID WE CHEER you up yet, Uncle Dixon?" Ginger said, "Cuz we're tired."

Aubrey jumped at the sound of Ginger's voice coming

from the laptop, and switched from her calendar to Skype. It had frozen midconversation a half hour ago. Evidently, it had kicked in again.

She saw Dixon's knees, so he must be sitting on the sofa with the laptop on the cocktail table.

"Why do you think you have to cheer me up?" Dixon asked.

Aubrey was about to let them know she was online, then decided to hear what Ginger said first.

"You get sad when Auntie Aubba calls," she said.

"Do I?" Dixon again.

"You do," Sienna affirmed.

Aubrey sucked in a breath. She felt the same way. The calls were almost worse than missing him.

"You're supposed to feel her in your heart," Ginger said. "Like with Mommy and Daddy."

"Oh." There was a long pause as he absorbed that.

This feeling between them *was* like grief. She hadn't thought of it that way.

"I'll try to be more cheerful for you," Dixon finally said, his voice rough.

Scout landed on the sofa and curled up on Aubrey's lap like she did whenever she heard the girls' voices.

"Do you love her?" Sienna asked.

Aubrey's attention was riveted to the screen, though all she could see was Dixon's legs. One knee was bouncing. He was nervous. Would he tell the girls the truth?

"I, um, have feelings for her. She's in our family and—"

"Then why don't you marry her?" Sienna said.

How the hell would he handle that? Aubrey was glad Sienna hadn't asked her. She had no clue how to explain so the girls could understand why, if they loved each other, they weren't together.

"Why would you ask that?" Dixon asked, clearly buying time.

"Because when grown-ups love each other they get married." Sienna's impatient tone suggested she thought her uncle was being dumb.

"Not…always," he said. Poor Dixon. This was not his kind of conversation.

"I'll marry you, Uncle Dixon," Ginger said. "When I'm a grown-up."

That made Aubrey smile.

"That's nice of you, but I'm sure you'll find a boy your age." Aubrey could hear the amusement in his voice, as well as the relief that they'd changed topics.

"Will you marry another lady?" Ginger asked.

"Not for a long, long while." He sounded resigned to the idea, as if what had happened had cured him of ever wanting to try. She knew how he felt.

"Will Aunt Aubrey get married?" Sienna asked, not letting up, jabbing at one sore spot after the next.

"Someday, I'm sure she will." He cleared his throat.

"Then she'll have a baby, huh?" Ginger added.

Dixon didn't answer right away. Aubrey saw him rub his palms on his thighs. "I imagine she will."

"But then she won't love us anymore." The anguish in Ginger's voice made Aubrey gulp back a cry. Aubrey had had the same fear that Dixon's girlfriend might replace Aubrey in the girls' hearts. She wanted to reach through the screen and pull them close, promise them she would never stop loving them ever, no matter what.

"Of course she'll love you," Dixon said. "She adores you and always will. Nothing could ever change that. I promise you." *Thank you, Dixon.*

"But she left us." Ginger sighed.

The pain was so sharp Aubrey pressed a hand to her chest.

"She has to have her 'ventures," Sienna said sadly.

"But she'll visit once she pins down her schedule. Maybe we'll drive out and visit her some weekend. Would you like that?"

The picture of his knees froze and the sound cut off, so she didn't hear the girls' replies, but she'd heard enough to break her heart all over again.

THE SKYPE CHAT was still running through Aubrey's mind the next morning when Tabitha arrived with the reporter doing the cover story for *Ever Outdoors*. Aubrey didn't even have time to get nervous.

The woman had done her research, so her questions were good. Aubrey laid out her mission, the rewards of what she did, the impact she'd had on her readers. She talked about her nieces, saying that she would take them on adventures, grow the new generation of Extreme Girls, just as she'd been inspired by her own mother's adventures.

"So your mother gave up her dream for you and your sister. That must have made you feel a little guilty..."

"Guilty? No. Our mother loved us with all her heart. She still traveled, but she brought us along."

"That makes sense." But the reporter didn't buy it. She figured their mother had regretted the sacrifice. That wasn't true.

Aubrey opened her mouth to say so, then stopped.

Wasn't that what you believed, Aubrey? That when she told you to carry on for her, she meant because she'd had to quit?

She realized that wasn't true. Her mother had been happy with her life. She hadn't regretted any of it.

"It wasn't that she gave up her dream," Aubrey said

slowly. "It was that she expanded it. She opened her arms wider to include us."

The reporter nodded politely.

Aubrey didn't care whether the woman believed that or not, because it was the truth, and it lit a sparkler in her chest. Maybe she needed to widen her dream, open her arms to bigger possibilities.

Near the end of the interview, the reporter said, "It sounds like you're adding family adventures to your blog, what with your nieces more part of your life."

Tabitha, standing behind the woman, shook her head violently no. *Kids aren't our demographic.*

But Aubrey wasn't willing to quote the party line. "It's a possibility," she said. *Sometimes sponsors are a good fit, sometimes not,* Rafe had told her. What if ALT didn't fit her anymore?

Are you nuts? After what you did to get here? You miss the girls and Dixon. That's all this is. Give yourself time. A million people would kill for an opportunity like this. Don't throw this away.

But Aubrey's doubts stayed with her, even during the meeting with the reality show producers. The program would be amazing, but as she listened, Aubrey felt distant from the idea. The concept was right up her alley, but she couldn't stop thinking about how many months she'd be tied to the studio, to L.A. Three months ago, she would have welcomed the grueling schedule the producers outlined. Not anymore. Now all she could think about was the girls and Dixon, when she would see them again, how long she could stay.

CHAPTER SEVENTEEN

DIXON READ THE card his mother had included with the box of prepackaged gourmet meals she'd sent. They would get one a month for a year. *Of course I had to take out a loan to pay for this, but spending money is one thing I can't screw up.*

Her P.S. had said she wanted to take the girls to see the Rockettes when they came to Phoenix at Christmas and wondered if he'd like a ticket, too.

He shook his head, as the subtext of her note reached him. Assuming Dixon disapproved of her, his mother had sought a way to help that she thought her son would accept. She'd never visited at Christmas before, so he knew she was concerned and thinking about them. He'd been oblivious, assumed the worst of her, as if he'd been hanging on to that invisible list of her failings, expecting her to fail every time.

The truth hit like a gut punch. He'd all but cut her out of his life. Why?

The answer was obvious—from fear that she'd disappoint him again, break his heart as she had when he was a kid. But he wasn't a kid. He was a grown man. By cutting her out, he'd hurt her and himself.

Had he done the same thing with Aubrey? Cut her out for fear she'd hurt him?

Sure, the dangers of her career worried him, and her

crazy schedule made a relationship difficult, but that wasn't the real problem.

She'll leave and you'll get hurt. Deep down, that's what he expected. She'd leave the way his father had physically and his mother emotionally.

How had he missed that?

When grown-ups love each other they get married. The clarity of the twins' child logic rang in his head and echoed in his heart.

If you loved someone, you at least *tried* to be together. What example was he setting for the girls by giving up on love at the first sign of trouble?

He couldn't ask Aubrey to let go of her dream. She had promised to stay safe, to set limits, to visit more. Maybe it would be good for him and the girls to add some Aubrey-style chaos to their settled lives.

L.A. wasn't that far. Highways and airplanes went both ways. Maybe it wouldn't work. Maybe he'd get hurt. Maybe the girls would be upset when that happened. Relationships had ups and downs, but love endured. The girls would see that, too. Aubrey and Dixon would always put the girls' welfare first. But that didn't mean they had to sacrifice their own.

He remembered what Howard had said at the wedding. *What Brianna and I have is big. It's forever. It's so good to have someone to count on, thick and thin, someone to take care of, who'll take care of you.*

That was how he felt about Aubrey. When he pictured the future, she was in every frame. He saw her making face pancakes, drawing French moustaches on cheeks. He saw her teaching the girls to ride bikes, sitting beside him on little chairs, knees up to their ears, on parent-teacher night. He saw her helping the girls put on makeup, listening to them cry over boys, waving them off to the prom.

They already looked like a family. They might as well live like one. The girls deserved the whole package. So did Dixon and Aubrey.

Electricity burned through him. He had to talk to Aubrey. He had to show her that he was willing to shift his expectations, that sometimes compromise was better for both sides. They weren't that different where it counted. They loved the girls and wanted to make the best life for them possible. And they loved each other. Needed each other.

That was what his heart told him. And this time he trusted it.

He strode into the girls' room. "How about we surprise Aunt Aubrey and Scout this weekend? We'll leave early in the morning."

"Yay!" Ginger said, jumping up, grinning.

"But tomorrow night is gymnastics," Sienna said.

"Gymnastics can wait. Surprises can't."

LATE THAT NIGHT, Aubrey found herself on a website she'd avoided all her life, terrified of what she might learn. The site was about breast cancer.

It was stupid to hide from the facts. The threat of breast cancer had altered her life, after all. It had made her push hard on every challenge, squeeze every thrill from life, cheating death again and again. It had been a big reason to never have children.

She never went on a challenge without doing research. It was about time she checked this out. She wiped the sweat from her fingers, then clicked the hyperlink for *Frequently Asked Questions.*

When the screen opened, she ran down the list until she found the one that stopped her heart: *My mother died of breast cancer. Will I?*

Scared as hell, shaking to her bones, she clicked it and began to read.

An hour later, she fell back on her bed, blowing out the most relieved breath ever.

She'd learned a lot. Breast cancer, while scary, wasn't quite the relentless, death-dealing horror she'd believed it to be. First off, 90 percent of breast tumors were benign. Further, nearly that percentage of cancerous ones were successfully removed, with high survival rates that improved all the time. Best of all, her mother's death from breast cancer didn't increase her likelihood of getting it by that much. It was far from a death sentence. It was barely a blip on a chart.

So maybe her breasts weren't time bombs waiting to kill her, after all. Maybe she would live a long, healthy life.

She sat up straight. Maybe it was time to stop *cheating death* and start *enjoying life.* She'd been pushing so hard, grabbing every thrill before it was too late, that she'd missed a lot along the way—quiet moments that didn't require a leap into the unknown to be worthwhile, like love and family.

Like Dixon and the girls.

Her brain blasted with white light. She jumped up, flew to her desk and pulled open the drawer that held Brianna's letter.

If I thought for one *minute that you were ready to settle down and have a family, I would have written your name in that open space for guardian in a heartbeat…. My dearest hope for you is to one day experience the joy and wonder of being a mother. You'll be a great one. I don't care what you say. Maternal is as maternal does.*

Maybe her sister wasn't wrong.

Abruptly, she heard Brianna's voice in her head, as clear as day, repeating what she'd said in that last phone call:

if you wanted to quit, have a family, go to school, whatever, you can. You've done more than Mom ever dreamed.

That was likely true. And besides that, her mother wanted her to be happy in whatever life she chose.

And Aubrey wanted something new.

You'll give up your dream? All you've worked for?

No. She would grow her dream, broaden it as her mother had done.

She didn't want to be the cool aunt who took the girls on trips and bought them extravagant gifts. She wanted to be there for every skinned knee and broken heart, every A+ paper, every pimple.

And she wanted Dixon, who'd been her partner through those desperate weeks of grief. He thought real life would kill their love. He was wrong.

She'd been afraid, she realized. She hadn't let fear stop her from walking into a lion's cage, how could she let it keep her from the man she loved and the family she wanted?

Her heart raced, her head pounded, but her confidence swelled as it did when she faced a challenge.

She would shift the focus of her blog to reflect the life she wanted now—with kids and a man she loved. She would talk to ALT, of course, explain the marketing advantages of this shift, but if they didn't agree, if they dropped the sponsorship, then she'd find another sponsor, a family-friendly one.

She'd rename the blog *Adventures with Kids*. Hell, *Adventures in Parenthood*. Once she opened her arms, there were countless possibilities.

She would still travel, still challenge herself, but family would come first. She'd lost her mother and her sister, but she had the girls and she had Dixon. Soon, she'd have an extended family, as well.

Jobs change. Families are forever.

She heard a thump and looked over as Scout dragged her carrier bag into the room. "Absolutely," Aubrey said. "If we leave early we'll make that gymnastics meet."

"NUH-UH. WE DIDN'T PASS it already, Uncle Dixon," Sienna said indignantly. "I can read the sign. Date...Ranch... Candy Store."

Damn. That wasn't what the billboard said, but she'd gotten the gist. The girl was too smart for her own good— or at least for his. Dixon wanted to skip the Date Ranch Market so they'd reach Aubrey's apartment about the time she usually called to tell the girls good-night.

Dixon could warn Aubrey, but he wanted to see the surprise on her face, the delight, hear the burst of her laughter, sweet and fluid as music. *Damn,* she'd turned him into an emotional fool.

Not a bad thing, he had to admit. Controlling his emotions hadn't gotten him very far. There were no guarantees, like Aubrey had said. Life was risk. Love was, too. But worth it. So worth it.

She would be thrilled to see them. At least the girls. Him? There was a chance she'd doubt him, be afraid to trust him.

He would spend the rest of his life proving she could count on him the way she'd counted on her sister, the way he'd counted on Howard. He would be her rock.

"Don't you want to see Aunt Aubrey sooner?"

"But we have to bring her the special red licorice. And Ginger has to pee."

"No, I don't. You're the one. You have accidents."

"Not anymore. And stop hurting my feelings." Sienna slugged her sister. "Ginger's hurting my feelings, Uncle Dixon."

"Ow." Ginger started crying. "She's hurting my arm. That's worser."

"Okay, we'll stop," he said, swerving for the exit. Howard wouldn't have folded, but Dixon didn't feel like putting his foot down at the moment.

He pulled into the market parking lot. The place was crowded as hell. The girls ran for the door. He smiled, watching them.

They were doing better. Their fights were less hysterical. They cried less. Sienna was less angry, Ginger less clingy. She'd quit sucking her thumb and stopped sleepwalking. Sienna hadn't wet the bed in a while.

How about you, Dix? How are you doing?

His brother's voice, clear as a bell, stopped Dixon in his tracks. He leaned against the car, overcome by bittersweet feelings—relief that his brother's voice had returned to him and sadness that it was only as a memory, not the man himself. *Not bad, Howard. Not bad.*

He still missed his brother like a hacked-off limb, but as Aubrey had predicted, the good memories had been slowly returning. When the waves of grief hit, they didn't knock him to his knees as they had at first. His heart would ache, his spirits sink for a while until he could shake himself back to normal. He would survive the loss. They all would.

So much had changed in the past six weeks. His life had been turned upside down. He'd lost his brother, nearly lost the agency, taken on the girls...and fallen in love. It was a lot for anyone to handle.

Was he only doing this out of crazed grief? Racing to L.A. to escape the sadness of missing Aubrey, his brother...hell, his old life?

It was possible, sure, but he knew his love for Aubrey

was real and strong—a beacon of light that lit the path ahead. Grief had pulled them close but love would keep them there.

AUBREY STOPPED DEAD just inside the market door. She could have sworn she heard Sienna's voice. *You're imagining it again.* Over and over in the days since she'd left Phoenix, she'd heard their voices, seen them in cars, on sidewalks or restaurants. Every time, her heart would skip a beat. *They'd come to get her, to bring her home.* So irrational. So disappointing when the kids turned out to be too old, the man too short, not handsome enough, with ordinary eyes, not intense ones filled with love.

Meow. Meow. MeOW. Scout sounded frantic.

"Okay, okay. We'll go to the bathroom first," she said. It wasn't like Scout to get overwrought about bodily functions.

"I heard Scout! I know I did!"

What? No. It can't be? Aubrey turned at the dear voice, her heart leaping in her chest, scared it was just another hallucination. If it was, then Scout was having it, too, because she yowled even louder.

It was them. Sienna, Ginger and Dixon. They stood together in the wide aisle between baskets of peaches and berries and a mountain of yellow corn.

Scout yowled again. Aubrey unzipped the carrier and the cat ran and jumped into Sienna's waiting arms. "What are you doing here?" Aubrey asked. "How did you know...?"

"We came to surprise you," Ginger said, running to hug her. Aubrey bent and picked her up, squeezing her so hard Ginger yelped.

"I came to surprise you, too," she said, grinning at Dixon, who was looking at her with those shining eyes that warmed her like the sun. "I wanted to make it for gymnastics tonight."

"Gymnastics can wait," Sienna said. "Surprises can't."

"You're right," Aubrey said, her throat tight, her heart so full it might burst. "I stopped to get you red licorice," she said, tears making it hard to see, "and so Scout could pee."

"So did we!" Ginger said. "To pee and for licorice. Uncle Dixon didn't want to stop, but we made him, didn't we, Uncle Dixon?"

"They did. And it's a damn good thing." Dixon held her gaze.

"You said *damn,* Uncle Dixon," Sienna chided.

"I did. And I'm not sorry."

The girls gasped.

Aubrey burst out laughing. She was dying to touch him, to be in his arms. "Why don't you girls take Scout to the bathroom? We'll get sandwiches and eat them outside under the trees."

"Can we have date shakes, too?" Ginger asked.

"Sure. Date shakes," Dixon said.

As soon as the girls were out of sight, Aubrey stepped into his arms, welcoming the thud of his heart against hers.

"I can't live without you, Aubrey," he said near her ear. "Neither can the girls. We're a family. We belong together."

She leaned back to look at his dear face, the steady love in his eyes, the determination in the set of his jaw. "I agree." Her smile seemed to pull happiness from all the corners of her soul where it had hidden for these weeks of sadness and strain.

"I know it will be complicated." His brow knitted. "You'll be tied up with that show and all your travels, but I'll fly you home whenever you have a break. And we'll visit. I'll take off some Fridays and make it a long weekend. We'll muddle through somehow."

"It won't be that much of a muddle. I'm not doing the show and I'm moving to Phoenix. I'm telling ALT that my family comes first. If that doesn't work for them, I'll get another sponsor, find another way."

"But you worked so hard. It's what you wanted."

"I want more now. I want you and the girls."

"I don't know...." He looked hopeful and worried at the same time. "That's a big shift for you. I told you what the experts say about major changes a year after a death."

"You're listening to the wrong experts."

"I am?"

"You should listen to the girls. They told you that when grown-ups love each other they get married."

"What?" He frowned, totally puzzled.

"Skype kicked on when you were talking to them the other night. I kind of listened in."

"To make sure I didn't blow it?"

"Kind of."

"How'd I do?"

"Not bad. It sounded like you were speaking from your heart."

"Yeah. Somebody told me experts don't know everything."

"She was right. You told the girls that I would be a good mother. That meant a lot to hear."

"It's true. Howard was wrong. You'll make a terrific mother. You already are to the girls."

I'm glad you feel that way because..." She flushed. "I think I'd like to maybe..." She couldn't quite say it.

"Start from scratch?" he guessed. "Have a baby?"

"Yeah. If you're interested."

"Oh, yeah. I say we start trying tonight."

She laughed, so happy she felt like she was floating between the bushels of peanuts and the pyramid of watermelon. "We should wait, I think. Make sure the girls are secure and happy. It won't be easy. We have different ideas about how to raise them. For example, no more ice cream every time the girls get upset. People are comfort, not food. And you'll have to fight your inner Howard."

"Swear to God." He held up his hand.

"He was right about you, though, when he wrote that you're a strong, solid guy, with more heart than you know. It's true."

Now Dixon's eyes shone with tears.

"I'm not giving up adventure trips though," she said to lighten the moment. "Remember the gift I bought for Howard and Brianna—that New Zealand vacation? You and I will be taking it, so prepare yourself."

He gave an exaggerated moan. "Are there alligators in New Zealand?"

"If there are, I'll show you how to wrestle them."

"Fair enough. Sounds like a perfect honeymoon."

Their lips met in a kiss full of hope and love.

"Kissing! Gross." Sienna scrunched her nose.

Arm in arm, Aubrey and Dixon turned to the girls. "You won't think it's gross when you're older," Dixon said.

"Daddy always said that," Ginger said, smiling, not saddened by the memory.

"Mommy and Daddy were gross, too," Sienna added, hands on her hips.

Aubrey's eyes met Dixon's and they smiled. Ahead of them lay date shakes and the long drive home to a future they would share with the girls. Somewhere, somehow, she knew her sister was smiling, her secret dream for Aubrey coming true.

* * * * *

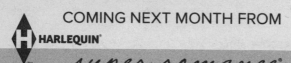

COMING NEXT MONTH FROM

HARLEQUIN®

super romance®

Available December 3, 2013

#1890 CAUGHT UP IN YOU • *In Shady Grove*
by Beth Andrews

Eddie Montesano does what's best for his son. No way does he want his kid in special classes, regardless of what the teacher says. So Eddie will stand up to her...even if the teacher is one very sexy Harper Kavanagh!

#1891 A TEXAS CHILD • *Willow Creek, Texas*
by Linda Warren

Years ago, Assistant D.A. Myra Delgado betrayed Levi Coyote—but now she desperately needs his help. Will working together just make them relive past heartaches? Or will their commitment to finding a missing child bring them together?

#1892 THE RANCH SHE LEFT BEHIND
The Sisters of Bell River Ranch • by Kathleen O'Brien

Penny Wright has always lived up to other people's labels. But no more. She won't live on the family ranch, even if she's come home to help. Her little house in town is perfect for her...and so is the gorgeous man next door, Max Thorpe!

#1893 SLEEPLESS IN LAS VEGAS by Colleen Collins

Private investigator Drake Morgan would rather work with anyone than Val LeRoy. She's nothing but trouble. Still, he's learning to appreciate her *unusual* approach to investigating. Now all he has to do is control his attraction to her.

#1894 A VALLEY RIDGE CHRISTMAS by Holly Jacobs

Aaron Holder doesn't mean to sound like old man Scrooge. But Maeve Buchanan's bubbly holiday cheer brings it out in him. It's a sudden act of Christmas kindness that finally draws them together, though will they admit their true feelings even when they meet under the mistletoe?

#1895 THE SWEETEST HOURS by Cathryn Parry

Kristin Hart has romantic notions of Scotland, but she doesn't expect to find a real-life Scotsman in her Vermont hometown. Turns out Malcolm MacDowell isn't exactly Prince Charming when he closes the factory. To save her town she must go confront him...and maybe find a little magic along the way.

HSRCNM1113

This might be the best Robbie Burns' Day ever
for Kristin Hart. Why? Because the gorgeous
consultant, George, who her company hired
joined her at her family's celebrations. And now,
the night is coming to a close.... Read on for an
exciting excerpt of the upcoming book

The Sweetest Hours
By **Cathryn Parry**

"I hope that you got all you need from us today," Kristin said,
as she walked George out.

He turned and smiled at her, descending two steps lower
than her on the stairs. His eyes now level to hers. "I did."

His hand touched hers, warm from the dinner table inside.
His fingers brushed her knuckles. Kristin was glad she hadn't
put on mittens.

"Kristin," he said in a low voice.

She waited, barely daring to breathe. Involuntarily, she shivered and he opened his coat, enveloping her in his warmth. It
was a chivalrous response, protective and special.

"Is it bad that I don't want this day to end?" she whispered.

"No." His voice was throaty. The gruff...Scottishness of it
seeped into her.

His eyes held hers. And as she swallowed, he angled his head and…and then he kissed her. He was tender. His lips molded gently over hers, moving with sweetness, as if to remember her fully, once he was gone.

The car at the end of the drive flashed its lights at them.

He straightened and drew back. Taking the warmth of his coat with him.

"I have to go." He looked toward the car. "Maybe some day I can tempt you away. To Scotland."

Maybe if she were a different person, in a braver place, she would dare to follow him and kiss him again…. But she wasn't that fearless.

"Goodbye, George," she whispered, touching his hand one last time.

"Kristin?" His voice caught. "I hope you find your castle."

And then he was off, into the winter night, the snow swirling quietly in the lamplight.

After this magical night, will George tempt her to Scotland? And if he does, what will Kristin find there? Find out in THE SWEETEST HOURS by Cathryn Parry, available December 2013 from Harlequin® Superromance®.